PK

THIS BOOK
DATE SHO'

'EST
.OWED

AUTHOR SCOTT, M.	**CLASS** A FSC
TITLE The hallows	

D1353675

**THE WORST DESTRUCTION HAD
BEEN WROUGHT IN THE BEDROOM.
THE BED ITSELF HAD BEEN SLASHED
TO RIBBONS BY A RAZOR-SHARP
BLADE . . .**

Whoever had done this hadn't got what they were looking for. They would be back.

Nestling at the bottom of her bag, still wrapped in its newspapers, was the prize her assailants had been after: The Sword of the Dyrnwyn. The old woman smiled bitterly. If only they knew how close they'd been to getting it. Her gnarled fingers closed around the rusted hilt, and she felt a ghost of its power tremble through her arms. She had never harmed anyone in her life, but if she could get her hands on the animal who had done this . . . The metal grew warm and she jerked her hand back; she had forgotten how dangerous such thoughts were in the presence of the artefact . . .

ABOUT THE AUTHOR

Dublin-born Michael Scott began his career as a bookseller and dealer in antiquarian books. An omnivorous reader, he was soon drawn to the related areas of Irish history and Celtic mythology, and is now considered one of the leading experts in the folklore and mythology of the Celtic lands.

He began writing fifteen years ago and has published such diverse works as a critically acclaimed fantasy trilogy entitled *Tales of the Bard*, the bestselling historical novel *Seasons*, the non-fiction *An Irish Herbal*, the definitive *Irish Folk and Fairy Tales* series, and a number of highly successful books for children. His horror novels are considered classics of the genre and draw heavily upon his knowledge of folklore and the occult.

To quote the *Irish Times*, 'Scott's forte is his gift for storytelling, his unusual yet believable characters, and his elaborate plots with their unexpected twists and cliff-hanging turns. I have no qualms about hailing him the King of Fantasy in these isles.'

MICHAEL SCOTT

THE
HALLOWS

A SIGNET BOOK

SIGNET

Published by the Penguin Group
Penguin Books Ltd, 27 Wrights Lane, London w8 5tz, England
Penguin Books USA Inc., 375 Hudson Street, New York, New York 10014, USA
Penguin Books Australia Ltd, Ringwood, Victoria, Australia
Penguin Books Canada Ltd, 10 Alcorn Avenue, Toronto, Ontario, Canada m4v 3b2
Penguin Books (NZ) Ltd, 182–190 Wairau Road, Auckland 10, New Zealand

Penguin Books Ltd, Registered Offices: Harmondsworth, Middlesex, England

First published 1995
1 3 5 7 9 10 8 6 4 2

Copyright © Michael Scott, 1995
All rights reserved

The moral right of the author has been asserted

Filmset by Datix International Limited, Bungay, Suffolk
Printed in England by Clays Ltd, St Ives plc

065177770

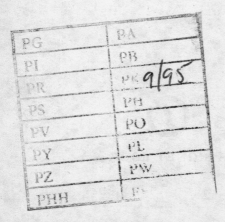

This is for Octavia

Behind a door of glass and wood and stone, the legion waits
Patiently.

Anon.
16th century Grimoire

CHAPTER ONE

Saturday 24 July

When the Horned Man finally caught her, red eyes burning, jaws gaping, Evelyn Saville came suddenly fully awake, heart pounding, breathing in great heaving gasps. The single sheet that covered her naked body was stuck to her flesh and the thin material was torn where she'd pulled it apart in her sleep. Lying still, willing her heart and breathing into a regular rhythm, she stared at the distorted shadows on the ceiling and tried to recall the nightmare, forcing herself to face it in the belief that if she did so, it would not return.

Initially, the dream hadn't been unpleasant: it had been vividly exciting and erotic, but at some point it had turned dark, brooding. Evelyn tried to concentrate on the details, but already the dream was fading, fragments spinning away like leaves . . .

Leaves.

Leaves.

She had been walking in a wood. It was late in the day, late in the year too, the golden sunlight slanting in low through the trees had brought the leaf-strewn floor to blazing life. Autumn, but with the touch of winter in the breeze, the air sharp and crisp. There were leaves stuck to her naked thighs and buttocks, twisted into her long blonde hair. The cool breeze that blew across her body sent ripples of pleasure into her stomach and through her heavy breasts, bringing her nipples to painful hardness, until she was acutely aware of her arousal.

She was ready for him. The man in the forest. The Horned Man.

Evelyn realized then that she had been following the flickering image deeper and deeper into the ancient wood. The shape had lurked at the very edges of her vision, melting away into the greenery every time she had turned to look at him. She knew it was a man; she had caught a glimpse of deeply tanned flesh, but she also knew that the creature she sought was more than a man.

The chase had been endless, across a rolling, unchanging dreamscape of trees and whirling leaves, and when the end had come, when she had finally caught up with the figure, deep in the heart of the forest, it had happened with shocking suddenness. The figure was standing in the centre of a clearing before a slab of flat grey stone. Tall, his flesh the colour of seasoned wood, he was naked except for a horned head-dress of a stag and a cloak fashioned from the skin of the creature. His head was thrown back, arms raised to the trees.

Evelyn had come up behind the man and wrapped her arms around his chest, pressing her breasts against his back. On a vaguely conscious level, she had known she was dreaming, but she had dreamt vividly and lucidly all her life. And this dream was so vivid. She could actually feel the ridges of muscles in the coarse flesh beneath her hands, the indentation of his spine against her cheek, smell his sour-sweet musk. And then he had turned, his hairy arms wrapping themselves tightly around her body, pulling her close. She

2

frowned, attempting to make out the man's face, but it remained in shadow ... until he bent his head, mouth opening, tongue moist against his lips. She caught a glimpse of hard, cruel features, a jagged line of a mouth, and black pitiless deep-sunk eyes ... and she realized then that he wasn't wearing a helmet: the curling horns were ...

Evelyn had awoken then.

Now, lying in the sweat-damp bed, she smiled, relieved that she knew what had awoken her. A dream. Nothing more than the particularly vivid dream of a frustrated and disappointed newly-wed. And she didn't need her recently earned fancy degree in psychology to begin analysing it.

Sitting up in the bed, she pulled the sheet up to her chin and folded her arms across her breasts. She hadn't had a dream like that for a long time. During her troubled teenage years she'd dreamt every night: fantastic, erotic, frightening, occasionally terrifying dreams. And only some of them could be put down to the dope she'd smoked or the acid she'd dropped. When she'd entered college, there hadn't been time for dreams. When she wasn't cramming for exams, she was partying, and either too stoned, or exhausted to dream. Drawing her knees up to her chest, she wrapped her arms around them. Maybe it was an acid flashback; she'd read somewhere that it could happen for years. But she didn't do drugs anymore: no dope, not even cigarettes, and alcohol only in moderation – God, if only her friends could see her now. She was twenty-six and she'd become what she'd most despised during her youth: respectable.

Smiling wryly, she slid down in the bed ... and

3

distinctly heard a muffled thump. Evelyn sat up, suddenly recognizing the sound that had brought her awake in the first place.

She heard it again, the low muffled thud of something falling over, bouncing on carpet. It was coming from the flat downstairs.

Reaching out she squeezed Andrew's shoulder and shook him awake. He rolled over, tugging the sheet away from her.

'Wake up, Andrew. I think something's wrong downstairs.' She squeezed his arm for emphasis.

Lifting the alarm clock, Andrew Saville squinted at the faintly glowing hands. 'It's ten past three, for Christ's sake.'

'I heard a noise from downstairs. Mrs Clay's flat.'

'The old bitch is probably drunk again.'

'She could have fallen and hurt herself. Go and see, Andrew – please.'

'No. I've got an eight-thirty meeting in the morning with the Japanese. I need to be fresh.' Andrew Saville rolled over and pulled the sheet over his head. 'Whatever's going on down there, you don't want to get involved.'

Evelyn heard another thump, followed by the distinct sound of glass breaking. Throwing back the sheet she swung her legs out of bed and pulled on a white towelling dressing-gown. 'I'll go and see for myself.'

'You do that,' Andrew mumbled.

Shoving her feet into fluffy slippers Evelyn moved silently through the flat. As she passed through the small sitting-room she could hear the sounds clearly: someone was blundering around the flat downstairs, knocking into furniture. Maybe Mrs Clay was trying to attract attention, Evelyn wondered, turning the key in the lock and stepping out on to the landing. The noises were distinct and now she could hear what sounded like voices, but they were muffled, the words indistinct. Radio? Television?

Moving silently down the carpeted stairs, Evelyn stopped outside the old woman's door and raised her hand to knock, then she stopped and pressed her face against the wood, realizing that the room had fallen silent. Concentrating, she thought she heard a faint rasping, like the sound of laboured breathing.

Maybe the old woman had had a heart attack?

Evelyn turned and dashed back upstairs. Mrs Clay had given her a key to the flat, in case of an emergency, months ago. Where had she put it?

The key was on the hook behind the door, a single Yale key on a knotted piece of twine. The thin cord snapped as she grabbed it and ran back downstairs.

The smell hit her as soon as she stepped into the flat: a sharp metallic odour, harsh and unpleasant, mingling with the noisome stench of faeces completely blanketing the usual dusty smells of must and decay.

Evelyn recoiled, gorge rising, pressing her hand to her mouth, and reached for the light switch. She flicked it up, but nothing happened. Leaving the door open to shed light into the tiny hallway, she walked forwards . . . and realized that the carpet beneath her feet was squelching, sodden and sticky with liquid. What was she standing in? She decided she didn't want to know; whatever it was, it would wash off.

'Mrs Clay . . . Mrs Clay?' she said softly. 'Elizabeth? It's Evelyn Saville. Is everything all right? I heard some noises,' she added, raising her voice.

There was no reply.

Evelyn pushed open the door into the sitting-room. And stopped. The stench was stronger here, acrid urine stinging her eyes. By the reflected light, she could see that the room was a mess. Every item of furniture lay overturned, the arms of the fireside chairs had been snapped off, the back of the sofa was broken in two, stuffing hanging in long ribbons from the slashed cushions, drawers pulled from the cabinet, the contents emptied on the floor, pictures torn from the walls, frames warped as if they had been twisted. The Victorian mirror lay on the floor, radiating spider cracks from a deep indentation in the middle of the glass where it had been trodden on. The glass ornaments that had sat on the shelf below it were now ground into the carpet.

A burglary. Evelyn breathed deeply, trying to remain calm. The flat had been burgled. But where was Mrs Clay? Picking her way through the devastation, glass crunching underfoot, she prayed that the old woman hadn't been here when it happened – and knew that she had. Elizabeth Clay rarely left her flat.

Books scraped as she pushed against the bedroom door, opening it wide enough to slap at the light switch, but again, no lights came on. In the faint glow of the light from the hall, she could see that this room had also been torn apart, and that the bed was piled high with dark clothes and blankets.

'Elizabeth? It's Evelyn.'

The bundle of clothes on the bed shifted and moved and she heard snuffling breathing. Evelyn darted across the room and saw the top of the old woman's head. Catching the first blanket she yanked it back, but it came away in her hand, warm and wet and dripping. The woman in the bed convulsed. The bastards had probably tied her up! She was reaching for another blanket when the bedroom door creaked and swung inwards, throwing light on to the bed . . .

Evelyn Saville realized then that Elizabeth Clay wasn't covered in blankets The old woman had been tied down to the bed, and then the flesh had been systematically flayed from her body in long narrow strips to reveal the bloody weeping muscle beneath. What Evelyn had taken for blankets had been slivers of the woman's own flesh. Only her face remained untouched, mouth and eyes wide in soundless agony, breathing a harsh rattle.

A shadow fell across the bed.

Speechless, sick with terror, Evelyn turned to face the shape that filled the doorway. Light ran off damp naked flesh. She could see that it was a man, but with the light coming from behind him, his features were in shadow. He lifted his left arm and light ran liquid down the length of the spear he was holding. The man stepped into the room, and she could smell his odour now: the rich meaty muskiness of sex and sweat and copper blood.

'Please . . .' she whispered.

'Behold the Spear of the Dolorous Blow.' His shoulders shifted and rolled and the light from the weapon darted towards her.

Evelyn felt the sudden coldness beneath her breast, then the warmth. Liquid trickled across her stomach. She tried to speak, but she couldn't find the breath to shape the words. She was aware of light in the room now, cold blue and green flames sparking, writhing up the leaf-shaped blade of the spear.

She had been stabbed – dearest Jesus she had been stabbed.

The lines of fire coiling around the haft of the spear rose to illuminate the flesh of the hand holding the weapon. In the emerald light, the skin looked dead, decayed. As Evelyn fell to her knees, both hands pressed against the gaping wound in her chest, she noticed that the nails were very long and black. It would be important to remember that . . . for the police . . . when she made her report.

The spear rose, serpents of cold fire splashing on to the head of her attacker, illuminating the face. When she saw the eyes, the woman realized she would not be making a report . . .

CHAPTER TWO

Sunday 25 July

'Another one,' Judith Walker said aloud, voice echoing flatly in the empty room. She was carefully folding away the newspaper when she suddenly crumpled it into a ball and flung it across the room. She squeezed her eyes shut as the tears curled down her cheeks to splash on to the faded tablecloth.

Another death, and this was the one she had been dreading. Bea Clay, Judith Walker's closest friend, though she hadn't seen Bea Clay in the flesh for . . . what, it must be nearly fifty years. They had kept up a regular correspondence, writing two or three times a month, letters that had brought them closer together than if they had lived next door. Judith stood and lifted her friend's last letter off the mantelpiece, running her finger over the writing; Bea had beautiful rounded handwriting. Whenever Judith thought of her, she remembered a beautiful young woman, with jet-black hair so thick it would sparkle and crackle with electricity every time she combed it.

Poor Bea. There had been so much pain, so much loss in her life. She had lost both parents in the Blitz, buried two husbands and had outlived her only child. She had lived through hungry years and recession, and then, when property values had spiralled and she'd finally had a chance to make some real money, she'd waited just too long to sell her home, gambling that prices would continue to rise. When the next recession hit hard and prices had tumbled, she'd been forced to watch her once-fashionable street turn into little better than a slum. In her last letter she had been talking about leaving Edinburgh, cashing in her meagre savings and seeing out her days in a nursing home on the south coast.

'Too late now,' Judith Walker said, her voice the only sound in the silent house. She realized she had spoken aloud again and smiled grimly. A sure sign of senility. She straightened slowly, pressing her hand to her arthritic hip and crossed the worn carpet to pick up the newspaper. Carrying it back to the table, she smoothed out the page and read through the story again. It rated half a paragraph on the third page.

PENSIONER AND GOOD SAMARITAN SLAIN

Police in Edinburgh are investigating the brutal slaying of Elizabeth Clay (64), and the neighbour Evelyn Saville (26), who went to her assistance. Investigators believe that Mrs Clay, a widow, disturbed burglars in her flat, who tied her to the bed and gagged her with a pillowcase. Mrs Clay died of asphyxiation. Police suspect that Mrs Saville, who lived in the flat upstairs, heard a noise and came to investigate. In a struggle with one of the burglars, Mrs Saville was fatally stabbed.

Judith pulled off her glasses and dropped them on to the newspaper. She squeezed the bridge of her nose. What did the report *not* say? What facts had been suppressed?

Reaching into her knitting bag, she pulled out scissors and carefully cut out the story. Later she would add it to the others in the scrap-books.

Bea Clay's was the fourth death in the past four months. Or at least the fourth that she knew about. If the murder of two women rated less than eight lines, then the death – accidental or otherwise – of a pensioner would probably pass unnoticed.

She had known all the victims.

Thomas Sexton had been first. She had never liked Tommy; he had been a bully as a child and he had grown up to be a bigger bully, earning his living as hired muscle in the fifties and sixties and then making a living running a high-profile bodyguard agency in the seventies. But four months ago, he had been slain in what the police called a gangland killing. The manner of his killing had excited some press interest: his body had been opened from throat to crotch and his heart and lungs removed.

Judith hadn't been surprised by the killing. She had always known that Tommy was going to come to a bad end. She remembered that time during the war when they had all been evacuated to the country. One night, he had been caught shining his torch up into the heavens when the bombers flew over, trying to attract their attention. He'd managed to lie his way out of it, but later, he boasted to the others that he'd been hoping they would bomb the town: he'd wanted to see a dead body.

When she had learned of Georgina Rifkin's death, Judith had felt the first icy trickle of fear. The deaths of two people each of whom knew the secret were too much of a coincidence. Officially, Georgie had fallen into the path of the Intercity express. Later, Judith had discovered that the old woman had been tied spread-eagled to the line.

Nina Byrne had died next. She had been nailed into her wooden rocking chair and doused in petrol.

And now Bea.

How many more were going to die? And when would it be her turn?

Judith stood and lifted a picture off the mantelpiece. Carrying it to the window, she tilted it to the light and looked at the irregular row of thirteen smiling faces. The black and white photograph had long faded to a uniform grey and it was difficult to make out any detail in the faces. Tommy and Georgina were standing at the back, and she thought the girl kneeling in the front was Nina. Bea was standing beside her; the two girls were wearing identical dresses, with their black hair loose around their shoulders, looking alike enough to be taken for sisters. Now Judith's hair was steel-grey. She wondered if Bea had kept her beautiful hair until ... until the end.

She brushed a patina of dust off the glass. 'Fifty-one years ago,' she said aloud. And now four of those children were dead, and Judith knew it was no coincidence.

Walking slowly, leaning heavily on the stick she'd sworn she'd never use, she moved around the small terraced house, checking that all the windows were locked and the doors bolted. She wasn't sure how effective a barrier they would prove when *they* came for her, but maybe it would delay them long enough for her to swallow the sleeping tablets she carried with her.

She could go to the police, but who was going to believe the ramblings of a mad old woman? What was she going to tell them: that four of the children she had been evacuated with during the war had been killed and that she knew that she would be one of the next victims.

'Tell us why someone would want to kill you, Mrs Walker?'

Because I am one of the Keepers of the Hallows of Britain.

Judith paused at the bottom of the stairs, smiling at the thought. It sounded ridiculous even to her. Fifty-one years ago, she had been equally sceptical.

She climbed slowly, making sure she had a firm grip on the banister, planting the stick firmly before moving on to the next step. She had broken her right hip two years ago falling downstairs.

Fifty-one years ago; a glorious war-time summer. Thirteen children had been billeted in the village in the shadow of the Welsh mountains; for most of them it was the first time they had ever been away from home, the first time they had been on a farm. It was a grand adventure.

When the old man had come to the farm, he had been just another curiosity, until he had started telling them his wild and wonderful tales of magic and folklore.

Judith turned the key in the spare bedroom and pushed open the door. Dust motes spiralled in the late afternoon sunshine and she sneezed uncontrollably in the dry, stale air.

For weeks the old man had teased them with secrets and fragments of tales, hinting, always hinting, that the children were special and that it was no accident that they had come to this place.

Judith opened the wardrobe, wrinkling her nose at the bitter-sweet smell of mothballs.

Fifty-one years ago, but it might have been one hundred and fifty-one years ago. It was a different age, an innocent age. Adults thought nothing of allowing the children to be in the company of the old tramp, and the children had gone with him in all innocence. The children of today wouldn't do it, modern parents wouldn't allow them to get close to the old man in the first place.

For weeks he had called them special, his warriors, his young knights, his Keepers. But as the summer drew on and August approached, a new urgency had entered the old man's stories. He had begun speaking to them individually, telling them special stories, disturbing, frightening stories that were almost familiar to each of them. She thought of it every July as August, and the ancient Celtic festival of Lughnasadh or Lammas, approached.

Judith shivered. She could still remember the story he had told her. It had created echoes and stirred resonances that had never been stilled. Those fragments of vivid dreams and startling nightmares she had used to forge a career as a children's writer; putting the fantastic images down on paper seemed to rob them of a little of their power.

Reaching into the wardrobe, Judith Walker pulled out a heavy overcoat that had gone out of fashion in the sixties. Hanging the coat on the back of the door, Judith lifted a paper-wrapped bundle from one of the enormous pockets and carried it to the bed where she slowly, and with great reluctance, unwrapped the parcel.

It took a great deal of imagination to realize that the chunk of rusted metal nestling in the yellowed newspaper was the hilt and portion of the blade of a sword. But she had never doubted it. When the old tramp had first pressed it into her hands, fifty-one years ago, he had whispered its true name into her ear. She could still feel his breath, spicy and foul against her face. All she had to do was to call the sword by its true name, but she hadn't spoken its name in years . . .

'Dyrnwyn.'

Judith Walker looked at the lump of metal in her hands. She repeated the name. 'Dyrnwyn, Sword of Rhydderch.'

Once, it would have come to trembling life, cold green flames shooting from its hilt, forming the remainder of the broken sword.

'Dyrnwyn,' Judith called a third time.

Nothing happened. There was no magic in the Hallow. Perhaps nothing had ever happened and it had only been in her imagination. The dreams of a pubescent girl . . . She dropped the rusted metal on to the bed and brushed flakes of rust from her lined flesh. The rust had stained her skin the colour of blood.

Thomas and Georgina, Nina and Bea had also possessed one of the ancient Hallows. Judith was convinced that they had been tortured and brutally killed for those artefacts. But fifty-one years ago the old man's last words to each child had been a warning: 'Never bring the Hallows together.'

No one had ever asked him why.

CHAPTER THREE

They had practised the ritual until it was perfect.

They would arouse one another, using lips and tongues and hands to bring each other to the point of orgasm ... and stop. Then the woman known as Vyvienne would lie atop an ancient stained altar stolen from a desecrated church, and the Dark Man would enter her, male and female becoming one, their power flowing together, joining, melding in a parody of the act of creation.

Four times they had enacted the ancient ritual, generating the most powerful of the magical elements to aid them in their quest. Four times they had sought the spirits of the Keepers and when they had discovered them, gone forth to do battle with them. Once it would have been inconceivable to challenge the Keepers, but times had changed, and now the Keepers were nothing more than tired old men and women, untrained and unskilled in the Art, most of them unaware of the treasures they possessed. It took much of the sport from the hunt, although there was still the kill to be relished, though recently they had hired others to do the butchery for them.

Vyvienne watched the man carefully, gauging the tension of muscles, the rhythm of his breathing, her legs locked around his buttocks, keeping him deep inside her, but making no move that would bring on his orgasm. That had happened too often, and in that instant the moment of power would have passed. It would then take three days of fasting – no red meat, no alcohol, no sex – to reach this point again.

'The Chessboard.' She whispered the words into his open mouth.

He swallowed her words. 'The Chessboard,' he repeated, sweat gathering in his hairline, curling down his stubbled cheeks.

They were close now, so close. Vyvienne's every sense was heightened; she could smell them both in the room, the musky odour of his maleness and her sex, the incredible pleasure of his touch, the sensations in her groin, the weight of her breasts, the faintest trickle of old power in the room, tasting metallic and tart in her mouth. 'The Chessboard of Gwenddolau,' she reminded him, forcing him to concentrate, to visualize the Hallow.

The Dark Man squeezed his eyes tightly shut, moisture gathering in the corners like tears to roll down his face and splash on to her belly. She felt their liquid touch and gasped, the sudden involuntary ripple of stomach muscles bringing him to a shuddering climax. He fell across her, head pillowed on her heavy breasts.

She stroked his hair. 'I'm sorry, I'm so sorry.'

When he raised his head, his smile was savage . . . and triumphant. 'No need. I saw it. I saw the crystal pieces, the gold and silver board. I know where they are.'

The woman drew the man deep into her body and pressed her lips against his, mouth opening wide. 'Then let us do this for pleasure.'

CHAPTER FOUR

Monday 26 July

Skinner rose to his feet as the old woman came down the steps of the British Museum, moving slowly and carefully. Pushing his mirrored shades up on to his shaven head, squinting in the blinding sunlight, he was comparing her with the small black and white photograph he had taped to the palm of his hand.

He was almost certain . . .

He nudged Larry with his foot. The hollow-eyed youth glanced up quickly, peering over the top of his dark glasses and nodded. 'That's her.'

'How can you be so sure?' Skinner snapped. He hated working with junkies; you couldn't depend on them, and they didn't give a shit.

'She's limping,' Larry mumbled, pushing his scratched Ray Bans up on to his nose. He jerked his chin in the direction of the woman who was now heading down Great Russell Street. 'The report said she'd broken her hip.'

Skinner nodded. He remembered now. She'd fallen and broken her hip two years ago.

'The right hip,' Larry added. 'She's favouring that leg.'

Skinner took a deep breath and nodded quickly. 'OK. Let's do it then. Get the car, I'll follow her.'

Larry came slowly to his feet, turned and ambled away. Skinner ground his teeth at his lack of urgency, and swore he was going to give the bastard a good kicking real soon. He fell into step behind the old woman, matching his pace to hers. She was moving slowly, balancing a heavy bag on her shoulder, papers and notebooks poking through the top. He glanced back once, looking at the solid edifice of the British Library and wondered what she had been doing in there for the past three hours. The last library he'd stood in had been the school library, working on some stupid project or other: Flora and Fauna of the Andes. Much bloody good it had done him; he still didn't know where the Andes were.

He was turning to look for the car when the Volvo cruised by him. It picked up speed as it moved past the old woman and pulled into the nearest available space, a hundred yards ahead of her.

Perfect. Skinner grinned, showing yellow, uneven teeth. Just perfect. This was going to be the easiest thousand pounds he'd ever earned.

Judith Walker shifted the heavy bag on to her left shoulder, trying to take some of the weight off her hip. She hadn't been conscious of time slipping by as she sat in the hushed stillness of the library, and now her hip ached abominably, and the muscles in her shoulders had locked into a solid bar of pain. The fact that the morning had also been a complete waste of time only added to her frustration.

Researching the Hallows of Britain was like chasing smoke. She had come away with pages of notes, scraps of legend and folktales, but no hard evidence. Later she'd organize the notes, add them to the hundreds of jigsaw pieces she had collected down through the years. Maybe when she looked over the material again, she would find some hint to the true nature of the artefacts.

Somehow she doubted it.

If the Hallows had remained hidden down through the centuries then there was little chance of her turning up anything. The very fact that there was so little solid information made her suspect that their existence had been systematically removed from the history books.

A spasm of pain made her stop. She felt as if there was ground glass in her hip joint. Leaning against a lamp-post, Judith turned to look back down the street, suddenly deciding that she would take a taxi. From bitter experience she knew that if she pushed on, she'd spend the rest of the day and most of the night in agony with her hip.

Naturally, there wasn't a taxi in sight.

Debating whether to turn back and head down into New Oxford Street, she was abruptly aware of the shaven-headed youth bearing down on her. His eyes were hidden behind mirrored sunglasses, but she could tell by his fixed expression that he was coming for her.

The old woman was swinging the bag even before the youth reached for her. Laden with notes and books, it caught him on the side of the head, catching him off balance, driving him to his knees, sending his broken sunglasses spinning into the gutter.

Judith screamed. A dozen heads turned in her direction, and she saw drivers passing by, heads swivelling to look, but no one made any attempt to come to her aid. She turned to run, but there was another youth behind her, blocking her path, long greasy blond hair framing a gaunt hollow-eyed face.

Junkie, she realized. Her bag. They just wanted to

snatch her bag. And she'd made the mistake of resisting them. Stupid mistake. She turned back as the shaven-headed youth climbed to his feet, his face fixed in a rigid mask of hate.

Skinner felt his cheeks burn with embarrassment. He'd torn the knee of his 501s, skinned his hands and lost his sunglasses. The bitch had caught him off guard. His hand dipped into his pocket and pulled out a flat metal bar. His wrist moved sharply back and forth and the butterfly knife clicked open, the blade appearing from between the handles. 'Stupid fucking mistake,' he hissed. Iron-hard fingers bit into the old woman's shoulder, making her cry out in pain. Her bag was pulled away and she suddenly found she was being forced towards the car, the point of the blade jabbing at her stomach, pricking her skin.

'Get in,' Skinner hissed.

Judith struck out at him again, clawed blunt-nailed fingers reaching for his eyes. She knew if she got in the car, she was dead. She opened her mouth to scream, but the bald youth punched her in the pit of the stomach, doubling her over. The junkie giggled behind her, the sound almost child-like.

A hand wrapped tightly in her hair, close to her scalp, hauling her upright. 'Get in the fucking car!'

'Just what the hell do you think you're doing!'

Through sparkling tears, Judith caught a glimpse of a dark-suited young man moving towards them. She tried to call out to him, to warn him about the knife, but she was having difficulty drawing breath.

Skinner spun around, bringing the knife up. 'Why don't you mind your own f . . .'

Without breaking stride, the young man lashed out

with the flat of his foot, catching the skinhead just below the kneecap. There was a distinct popping sound and Skinner crashed to the ground on to his injured knee. Judith spun around and caught the edge of the car door, slamming it shut. It closed on the junkie's fingers, tearing skin and snapping bones. She scooped up her fallen bag and hobbled towards the young man, who reached for her hand and pulled her away without a word.

They had taken a dozen steps when the injured youths started screaming.

CHAPTER FIVE

'No police,' Judith Walker said firmly. 'No police.' Her fingers tightened on the young man's arm, squeezing painfully. 'No police.'

'But . . .'

Taking a deep breath, attempting to calm her thundering heart, Judith continued calmly. 'It was just a bag snatch . . . or a mugging.'

'*Just* a mugging!'

'My name is Judith Walker,' the woman said suddenly, stopping and extending her hand, forcing the young man to turn back, breaking his train of thought.

'I . . . I'm Gregory Matthews. Greg.' He shook her hand. Turning to look back down the street, he was suddenly at a loss for words.

'Thanks to you, there's no harm done,' Judith continued forcefully, allowing a little authority to seep into her voice. She continued to hold his hand, using the physical contact to strengthen the link between them, swamping his consciousness with hers. It was a skill she hadn't used in a decade, but she knew she needed to take control of the situation or the boy would go to the police, and she didn't want that. 'Now, I don't know about you, Greg, but I'd love a cup of coffee.'

The young man nodded absently. 'Yes.'

Judith manoeuvred Greg Matthews towards a small Italian café. The three tables outside the shop were all occupied by couples deep in conversation. As they approached, Judith concentrated on a couple sitting a little apart from the others, their table partially hidden by the striped umbrella, willing them to leave. Moments later, the couple stood up and walked away without glancing back. When Judith and Greg sat down, they discovered that the couple had left their pastries and coffee unfinished. The young man was still too bemused to notice. Somewhere at the back of his mind, he felt as if he had lost something, or had missed something – like watching a badly edited movie. Events of the last ten minutes were confused. He had been returning from lunch, heading back to the office, when he had spotted the skinhead. The youth was wearing those mirrored shades Greg detested. The skinhead had brushed past him, eyes fixed on someone directly ahead. Glancing over his shoulder, Greg had spotted the silver-haired old woman and known immediately that she was the target. Even before the youth had grabbed for her, and the woman had screamed and swung her bag, knocking him to the ground, Greg had been moving towards them, drawn by a sudden and almost uncontrollable spasm of anger.

The bitter tang of coffee brought him back to the present. Greg blinked, blue eyes watering, wondering what he was doing here . . . wondering where here was.

'That was a very brave thing you did.' Judith wrapped both hands around the thick cup to prevent them from trembling and breathed in the rich aroma before sipping delicately. Although her head was bent, she could feel his eyes on her. 'Why did you do it?'

'I just . . . just . . .' He shrugged. 'I'm not sure why I did it. I've never done anything like it before,' he admitted. 'I couldn't just walk away and allow them to mug you.'

'Others walked away,' the old woman said quietly, 'but not my knight in shining armour,' she added with a smile.

The young man blushed, colour touching his cheeks, and in that instant he reminded her of James, dear James, standing proud and tall in his green uniform, his cheeks flushed with pride and colour. He had been her eldest brother, and although she'd only been a child when she'd last seen him, on the night before he went off to fight in the war, the vivid image of the blushing eighteen year old had remained with her. She had never seen him again; James Walker had been one of the first British casualties of the war.

'Are you sure you won't let me make a report to the police?' Greg asked.

'Positive,' she said firmly. 'It would waste a lot of time – yours, mine and the police, and in the end none of us would get any further. I assure you such assaults are not unusual. These people target the elderly, thinking us easy targets.'

'They picked on the wrong one this time, though,' he grinned.

Judith lifted her bulging bag. 'I think this is what they were after. I'm afraid they would have been sadly disappointed; there's nothing in it but notes.'

'You're a teacher,' Greg nodded decisively. 'I thought so. You look like a teacher.'

'I was – once a long, long time ago. I've been retired twelve years this year. Now, I write.'

'What sort of books?'

'Children's books usually.' Judith finished her coffee

in one quick swallow, grimacing as she tasted bitter dregs. 'Now, I really must go.' She stood up quickly, then groaned aloud as a slender needle of agony lanced through her hip and she sank back on to the metal chair.

'What's wrong? Are you hurt? Where?' Greg came around the table to kneel by her side. 'Did they hurt you?'

Blinking away tears of pain, Judith Walker shook her head. 'It's nothing. Honestly. My replacement hip is aching, nothing more than that. I've been sitting for too long, that's all.'

Greg spotted a maroon taxi turn into the street and automatically raised his arm. 'Come on, I'll take you home.' He hooked an arm beneath her shoulders and eased her to her feet.

'I'll be fine,' Judith hissed.

'I can see that.'

She wanted to be left alone, wanted nothing more than to go home and climb into a scalding bath, wash away the skinhead's touch. She could still feel his blunt fingers in her hair, on her shoulder, her arm. She dabbed absently at her cheek, where his spittle had stung her flesh. She knew why they'd come for her. She knew what they wanted. Knew also that they would be back.

Suddenly she didn't want to be left alone, not just now. She wanted company, any company, someone to talk to, someone living and vibrant, with mundane interests and mundane worries. The young man's dramatic appearance was an interesting coincidence . . . but Judith Walker didn't believe in coincidence. She reached out, resting her fingers lightly on the back of his hand, her touch startling him. 'Would you take me home please?'

Greg Matthews was confused, the events of the last thirty minutes were already sliding and fading in his consciousness, the details blurring like an old dream.

He wasn't entirely sure how he had ended up sitting in the back of a cab beside someone he'd met only moments before. Greg glanced sidelong at the woman. She was . . . fifty? Sixty? It was hard to tell. With her silver hair brushed straight back off her forehead, tied in a tight bun, wisps of stray hair curling around her ears and on to her cheeks, she reminded him of his grandmother. Maybe that was why he had come to her assistance. He glanced quickly at her again, confirming his suspicions: she did look like Granny Matthews, even down to the indentations on the side of her nose, where her glasses pinched. That would account for it. He'd never done anything like this before; two weeks ago, he'd crossed the street to avoid having to walk past five shaven-headed youths kicking a Pakistani boy outside a fish 'n chipper.

'Penny for them,' the woman said suddenly.

Greg blinked. 'Sorry?'

'You were staring at me, but you seemed to be miles away . . .'

'I'm sorry. You reminded me of someone . . .'

The woman continued to look at him, saying nothing.

'My grandmother,' he continued, filling the silence. 'You look a lot like her.'

'She would be very proud of what you did today. You should be very proud.'

Greg shrugged. 'It was nothing.'

'Don't denigrate what you did. Few would have had the courage to do what you did.' The taxi pulled into a small side street of identical post-war houses and Judith leaned forward. 'Second house from the end.' She was about to tell the young man to keep the taxi and return to his office when she noticed that her hall door was open. She felt the coffee sour in her stomach, knowing instinctively what she was going to find inside. Reaching out she touched Greg's hand, establishing contact again, meeting and holding his eyes. She knew people found it very difficult to refuse something when there was actual physical contact.

'You will come in . . . ?'

Greg started to shake his head. 'Really, I can't. I must be getting back to the office. Don't want to get fired for being late back from lunch,' he said with a smile, but even as he was speaking, he was gathering up the woman's bag as the cab pulled in to the kerb.

'You must give me your address and work address,' Judith said softly. 'I will write to your employer, commending your actions.'

'That really won't be necessary . . .'

'I insist,' the old woman said firmly.

Greg climbed out, held the door open and helped Judith down. He waited by the gate while she paid the cab. A letter of recommendation to old man Hodgson would not do him any harm.

Judith waited until the cab had driven off before turning to Greg. 'Now, some tea, and then I'll send you back to work.' She had her key in her hand as she approached the hall door, but concentrated on fumbling with her purse giving the young man the opportunity to see the open door before her.

'Do you live alone?' Greg asked suddenly.

'Yes.'

'Your hall door is open.'

Judith stopped so suddenly that Greg crashed into her.

'Did you lock it this morning?'

'I always lock it,' she whispered. 'Oh no.'

'Wait here.' Greg placed the bag of books on the ground and approached the open door carefully. Using his elbow, he pushed the door inwards.

CHAPTER SIX

'She's home.'

Static crackled on the car-phone.

'No, she's not alone. There's a young man with her. I don't know. I've never seen him before in my life.'

Robert Elliott listened carefully to the voice on the other end of the phone, abruptly glad of the distance separating him from the man.

'I think that would be unwise at present,' he advised cautiously. 'I don't know the youth, I don't know how long he's likely to be there. He could be police for all we know.'

Static howled and spat.

'I can't hear you,' Elliott said gratefully. He dropped the phone back into its cradle, turned on the engine and pulled away from the kerb. As he cruised slowly past the woman's home, he was unable to resist a smile as he remembered what she was going to find.

CHAPTER SEVEN

The house had been thrashed.

Judith had an inkling of how bad the damage was going to be when she stepped into the hall and realized that the carpet had been torn up and there were now gaping holes in the floor, where the floorboards had been levered up. Anger welled up inside her, burning in the pit of her stomach, flooding her throat with bile, stinging her eyes. She heard the young man swear softly. Reaching over, not looking at him, she squeezed his arm. 'Go next door. Phone the police.'

Greg took a look around the ruined hallway and nodded quickly.

Judith walked to the end of the hall, stepping over the shredded carpet and tried to open the door to the sitting-room. It would only open half way. Peering around the corner of the door, she realized that the carpet here had also been torn up, holes in the floor where random floorboards had been ripped up. The hideous horse-hair sofa she'd always detested had been gutted, the back slashed open in a big X, wiry hair spilling across the floor, mingling with the feathers from the eight ornate cushions she had embroidered herself. The cabinet was lying at an angle against the upturned easy chair, drawers and doors hanging open, tiny ornaments she'd spent a lifetime collecting scattered on the floor. None of them were whole. All of the pictures had been pulled off the wall, the frames twisted and shattered.

'Mrs Walker . . . Mrs Walker? Judith?'

Judith stepped out into the hall, pulling the door closed behind her. Greg was standing in the doorway, Mrs Patel, Judith's neighbour, hovering behind him.

'The police are on the way.' Greg reached out and caught her arm, but Judith pulled away. 'Is there anything I can do?' he asked lamely.

'There's nothing you can do,' Judith said tiredly. 'Nothing anyone can do.' She put her hand on the banisters. 'Let me just have a look upstairs.'

'Do you want me to come with you?' Greg asked.

'No. No, thank you all the same. Wait for the police.'

Her hip started aching as she neared the top of the stairs, the pain throbbing in time to the pounding at the base of her skull. The muscles across her shoulders were taut with tension and her chest felt tight, making breathing difficult.

Although it was a shock, it was no surprise that the house had been burgled, it merely confirmed what she'd suspected: someone was collecting the Hallows. She was only thankful that she'd been out when it happened. The attempted kidnapping today was no coincidence. She wondered if the house had been burgled before the kidnapping attempt or if that had come later. From the condition of the house – from the *stillness* of it – she guessed that the house had been turned over hours ago.

The worst destruction had been wrought in the bedroom. The bed itself had been slashed to ribbons by a razor-sharp blade. The down-filled bolster lay in shreds on the floor – even the sheets had been sliced apart. Every item of clothing had been pulled out of the wardrobe and systematically slashed and torn. The remains of a hat she had worn to a wedding nearly eight years ago dangled from the light fitting. The bulb had been shattered. Judith closed the door, and leaned her forehead against the cool wood, while the tears burned at the back of her eyes. But she was determined not to cry.

The bedroom she had converted to a library and study was also ruined. The floor was awash with paper, decades of carefully collected and collated notes tossed over it, yellow filing cards scattered everywhere. Not one book remained on the shelf. Paperbacks had been torn in half, hardbacks had had their covers pulled off, and some of the older volumes were now lacking their leather spines and covers. The framed covers of her children's books were all on the floor, the glass shattered, wooden frames broken. The twenty-five-year-old Smith Corona typewriter she'd worked on all these years lay crushed as if someone had jumped on it, alongside the crumpled remains of the plastic phone. Stooping, she lifted an A4 page from the floor at her feet. Page twenty-two of the manuscript of her latest children's book: it was smeared with excrement. Judith allowed the page to flutter to the floor and the tears came then, hot and salt and bitter. It would take her years to sort out the mess. Wiping the heel of her hand across her eyes, Judith Walker knew she simply didn't have that time. Whoever had done this hadn't got what they were looking for. They would be back.

Placing her shoulder bag on the scarred wooden desk, she removed the books and papers she'd been carrying around with her all day. Nestling at the bottom of the bag, still wrapped in its newspapers, was the prize her assailants had been after: The Sword of Dyrnwyn. The old woman smiled bitterly. If only they knew how close they'd been to getting it. Her gnarled fingers closed around the rusted hilt, and she felt a ghost of its power tremble through her arms. She had never harmed anyone in her life, but if she could get her hands on the animals who had done this . . . The metal grew warm and she jerked her hand back; she had forgotten how dangerous such thoughts were in the presence of the artefact.

CHAPTER EIGHT

Richard Fenton pulled off the towel and slid naked into the water, hissing with pleasure. A perfect eighty-five degrees. A bit too hot for some, but when you reached his age, the blood grew thin and old bones felt the cold. With long even strokes he swam a length of the swimming pool, turned and swam back to the deep end again. On a good day he could swim twenty lengths, but he'd had a late night last night, and it had been dawn before he got to bed. He hadn't woken until one-thirty in the afternoon, and was feeling stiff and tired . . . and *old*.

Today, he felt like an old man.

He *was* an old man, he reminded himself grimly, seventy-three next month, and although he looked at least twenty years younger and had a body to match, there were days when he felt every one of his years. Today was one of them. He would try and do ten lengths of the pool and then he'd have Max give him a massage. He had planned to have dinner in the club tonight, but perhaps he'd give it a miss, stay in and relax.

Pressing his feet against the tiled wall he pushed off again, his over-long fine white hair streaming out behind him, plastering itself to his skull when he raised his head above the water. Sunlight lanced through the high windows, speckling the water, dappling the tiled floor of the pool, sunlight bringing the ornate design on the floor to shimmering life. He'd had the architect who'd designed this wing of the house copy the pattern from a Greek vase: stylized human figures copulating in a dozen unusual and improbable positions.

Somewhere deep in the house a phone thrilled.

Richard ignored it; Max or Susan would handle it. He ducked under the water, opening his eyes wide. The water was clean; he would not allow chlorine or any of the other detergents into his pool. The water was completely recycled twice a day, usually just before he took his morning swim and then again, late in the evening. Looking down, he watched the design on the bottom tremble and shiver, the figures looking as if they were moving.

The phone was still ringing when he raised his head above the water.

Richard ran his hands through his hair, brushing it back off his face and turned to the double doors at the opposite end of the room. Where was Max ... or Susan for that matter? They should have answered the phone ... unless they were otherwise engaged. He suddenly grinned, showing a perfect set of teeth that were too natural looking to be real. He'd suspected for a while that those two were becoming more than colleagues. The old man's smile faded: they could do what they liked in their own time, but he employed them to work.

The phone stopped

Richard Fenton flipped over and floated on his back, raising his left arm to look at the watch that never left his wrist. Two-thirty. It had been his father's watch and his father's before him. It had cost Richard a fortune to have it rendered waterproof, but the money had meant nothing. The watch was a symbol. Every time he looked at it, he was reminded of his father who'd finished his days coughing up his lungs, the blood black and speckled with coal dust. His grandfather had died down the pits; 'exhaustion' the death certificate said, but everyone knew there had been gas leaking down the mines. Richard barely remembered his grandfather, though he had vague memories of the funeral. However, he remembered his father's funeral vividly, remembered standing at the edge of the grave, a clump of earth in his hands, cold and damp and heavy, and swearing that he would never go down the mines. It was an oath he'd only broken once in his lifetime, and that was when he'd been photographed with a band he discovered in the sixties: the Miners. They'd done a publicity shoot in the cages and tunnels, the five lads posing wearing miners' helmets, holding the picks and shovels like the musical instruments they never learned to play.

Richard grinned. He hadn't thought about the band for years; a sure sign he was going senile. They'd had two top-twenty hits and seemed destined for great things. The next Beatles, the future Stones, the music press called them. Fenton had sold their contract to one of the big American companies – was it Decca? – and walked away with a fortune in his pocket. The boys had complained of course and looked for their share, but they had signed a contract, a cast-iron contract which allowed him to be reimbursed for his expenses. And his expenses had been high, very high. They'd threatened to sue, until he pointed out how expensive that would be, adding that they would lose. Eventually, they'd given up; they were convinced that in the States they were going to make ten times what he'd stolen from them. They'd never made another record.

The phone started ringing again, and Richard surged up in the water. Where was Max? What the hell was going on? He struck out for the shallow end of the pool, anger making his strokes ragged and choppy.

Richard Fenton caught the barest glimpse of the object in the air – dark, round – before it hit the pool in an explosion of pink-tinged water behind him.

'Jesus!' Fenton looked up; one of the ornamental hanging plants had fallen from the rafters. He could have been killed. He turned, treading water, looking for the plant. If he didn't get it out of the pool right now, the soil would bung up the filters.

'Max? Max!'

Where the fuck was the bastard? Controlling his temper, Richard ducked beneath the surface, looking for the plant. He spotted it in the deep end, surrounded by a growing cloud of dark earth and struck out for it. He was going to make someone pay for the clean-up of the pool, and new filters, and for the fright it had given him; he could have had a heart attack. He'd sue the gardeners who'd installed the flowers, or the archi-tect, or both. Breaking the surface, he took a deep breath, then ducked back down again. It was only when he swam into the cloud billowing around the plant that he realized that it was pink, shot through with black thin ropy tendrils. As he reached for the thick ball of earth, it rolled over . . . and Richard Fenton found himself looking at the severed head of his manservant, eyes wide and staring, face blank with surprise. The mouth opened and blood, pale and pink, bubbled upwards.

Fenton surged out of the pool, coughing and hacking, heart hammering so hard in his chest he could actually feel the skin tremble. He coughed up the water he'd ingested, felt his gorge rise and swallowed hard. He was trembling so hard he could barely hold on to the metal ladder and pull himself on to the slick cold tiles. He tried to marshal his thoughts, but his head was spinning, and the constriction in his chest was tightening, black spots dancing before his eyes. Bending double, he breathed deeply and straightened. He swayed as blood rushed to his head, but he could think clearly now.

There was a loaded gun in the safe behind his desk, shotguns in the cabinet on the wall, ammunition in the drawer underneath. All he had to do . . .

The water gurgled, bubbles bursting. Fenton turned. Max's head had floated to the surface, bobbing like an obscene buoy.

Richard Fenton had no doubts that whoever had done this to Max had come for him. He'd made too many enemies in his long life, cut too many sharp deals and on more than one occasion he'd been forced to 'take care' of people who got in his way. But that had been a long time ago. He hadn't really been active in many years . . .

People had long memories.

Richard Fenton padded barefoot to the double doors and peered out into the circular conservatory that connected the main body of the house with the swimming pool. The Spanish tiles were speckled with dark blood. Whoever had killed Max had carried his head out here to throw it into the water . . . which meant that they had watched him . . . which meant that they were still in the house . . . which meant . . .

Maybe he'd forget about the gun. If anyone was waiting for him, they'd be in his study. He could cut across the hall, through the kitchen and into the garage. The keys were always kept in the cars.

Crouching low, he darted across the tiles and stepped up into the hallway. After the chill of the tiles, the carpet was warm beneath his feet. And moist. He lifted his foot. It came away sticky with gore.

Fenton turned. He clapped both hands to his mouth, trying to prevent himself from crying out, but too late. His shriek echoed through the empty house. Susan dangled upside-down by one leg from the curtain rail. Her throat had been cut so deeply that her head dangled too far back, exposing tubes and the hint of bone. Her face was a red mask, her blonde hair dark and stiff. She was still wearing her glasses.

'Why don't you come into the study, Mr Fenton?'

Richard whirled around. The study door was open. He glanced towards the hall door. Thirty, maybe forty steps away. He was in good condition. He'd make it.

'It was not a request, Mr Fenton.'

Through the door, down the drive and out on to the main road. The nearest house was a hundred yards away, but he'd make it. A naked old man running down the road would attract attention.

The hall door creaked, then slowly opened, shafting early afternoon light along the length of the highly-polished floor, picking out the dust motes spiralling in the still air. A figure stood in the doorway, a long elongated shadow growing along the floor. Richard frowned, squinting short-sightedly. There was some-thing about the figure . . . something wrong.

The figure swayed, then toppled forward. Richard realized then that it had no head. He was looking at the decapitated body of Max.

'Come into the study, Mr Fenton.'

Richard Fenton crossed the hall and pushed open the door of his study. He stood in the doorway, arms wrapped around his thin chest, shivering, blinking in the gloom. The curtains had been pulled, and the ornate desk lamp turned to face the door, blinding him, leaving the figure sitting behind the desk in shadow. The harsh light made his eyes water and he rubbed angrily at the tears on his cheeks. The old man felt the pain in the pit of his chest and, for once, welcomed it. Knowing that it might save him the other pain he knew was coming.

'You have something I want, Mr Fenton.'

The voice was soft, accentless, controlled.

'There's money in the safe,' Richard Fenton said quickly. 'It's yours.' Maybe this was nothing more than extortion; a young turk out to make his reputation by ripping him off. He'd give him what he wanted . . . then hunt him down like a dog.

'I don't want your money,' the shadowy figure said mildly.

There was movement beside the curtain and Richard realized there was a second person in the room. Al-though the air was rich with meaty blood and the odour of leather from the chair and ornate leather bindings, he thought he detected the odour of flowers, but there were no flowering plants in this room – a perfume? A woman?

'I want the Chessboard of Gwenddolau.'

Richard started forward, arms falling to his side.

'I know you have it. I want it.'

The old man started to shake his head. He hadn't thought about the chessboard in decades. Crystal pieces, gold and silver board, it was one of the most beautiful things he possessed and yet he never displayed it with his other treasures for reasons he could never fully explain.

'I want it.'

Richard Fenton started to shake his head.

A knife clicked wetly open.

'You will tell me, sooner or later.'

Richard turned – and felt the hot-white pain in his thigh. Looking down, he saw the metal hilt of a knife protruding from his flesh.

'You're going nowhere, Mr Fenton.'

CHAPTER NINE

'I insist,' Greg said firmly.

Judith Walker shook her head slowly, but said nothing. She needed this boy to think that he was making the decisions.

Sitting on the back-seat of the police car, Greg nodded emphatically, convincing himself that this was a good idea. 'It makes sense. You can't stay there – not until the place is cleaned up, and you've told me yourself you've no place to go. I know my mother won't mind and we've got the space. Stay the night, and in the morning, I'll contact your niece, and together we'll help you get the place back together.'

'I really couldn't. It would be such an imposition . . .'

'No, it wouldn't,' Greg insisted, but without the certainty now. What was he doing? He'd met this woman less than an hour ago, and now he was offering her a bed for the night . . . ?

Judith heard the sudden indecision in the young man's voice and touched the hilt of the newspaper-wrapped sword, drawing power from it, then she reached out and squeezed his hand. 'It's a generous offer.'

Suddenly Greg felt sure again. He patted Judith's hand. 'I'll have the police drop us back home . . . then I'd better phone the office and tell them I'm taking the rest of the afternoon off,' he added.

'Thank you. You're such a kind young man. It's so

'rare these days.' The old woman's smile was porcelain, fragile and brittle, and it never extended to her eyes. She felt no qualms of conscience about using the power to manipulate Greg in this way. She had to protect the sword – at all costs, until she decided what she was going to do.

Lying in the strange bed, watching the reflection of the street lights on the ceiling, Judith Walker listened to the vague sounds of voices drifting up from the kitchen below. She recognized Nora Matthews' strident clipped delivery drowning out Greg's softer protestations, and knew she was the subject of conversation. Judith reached beneath the pillow and touched the paper-wrapped sword, then concentrated on Greg's face, trying to pour a little strength into him. She knew he must be regretting his decision to bring her home.

Judith's reception by the Matthews family had been a mixture of disbelief and dismay. They lived quiet suburban lives in a quiet suburban street and obviously resented this bizarre intrusion. However, they had been solicitous, cool, distant but polite, and tea had been a formal, frigid affair. Nora Matthews had engaged her in brittle, inconsequential conversation, while James, Greg's father, had barely spoken. Greg's younger brother and two little sisters, obviously warned by their mother to be on their best behaviour, had spoken in whispers throughout the meal. Much to everyone's relief, Judith claimed exhaustion following the events of the day and retired immediately after tea. She had been given the older girl's room, a tiny box-room decorated with posters of pouting half-naked teenagers who belonged to pop groups Judith Walker had never heard of. One end of the bed was piled high with stuffed toys and teddy-bears. She found the contrast between the burgeoning sexuality of the posters and the toys vaguely disturbing; the girl was no more than twelve. Another sign of the times; innocence was one of the first sacrifices to the modern age.

Climbing into bed, Judith unwrapped the sword and ran her fingers down the rusted metal. Holding it by the hilt, she brought the broken blade to her lips and kissed it . . .

Old magic, ancient power.

Judith felt the warmth flood through her body. Aches and pains from stiffened joints vanished, tired, worn muscles relaxed, her sight grew sharp, her hearing distinct as her senses expanded. She was young again. Young and vital and . . .

Old magic, ancient power, fading.

Her sight went first, sharp crystal-clear images of her surroundings, dissolving to an unfocused blur. Her hearing – sounds of the argument from the kitchen below – faded, noises becoming dull, muted. And the aches and pains returned.

Sighing, she tucked the metal beneath her pillow, then lay back on it, feeling the hardness of the old iron against her skull. As a child, she'd slept with it beneath her pillow every night, and the dreams . . . the dreams then had been wondrous. But it had been a long time since she'd dreamt; when she'd started writing, putting the images she'd seen in her sleep down on paper, the dreams had immediately faded. Maybe it had been a mistake to make her dreams public, maybe that robbed them of a little of their magic. Or maybe the sword was fading, losing a little of its ancient power.

Someone still believed that the Hallows were powerful, someone prepared to kill to acquire the artefacts.

And the boy, where did he fit into the overall scheme? Was his appearance, his intervention, more than coincidence? Almost unconsciously, she shook her head; even dormant the Hallows were attracted to people of power and the boy was obviously one of those people.

In the kitchen below, the argument ended with a slammed door, then stairs creaked. There was a gentle tap on the door.

'Come in, Greg,' Judith Walker said softly, sitting up in the bed.

Greg Matthews stepped into the room, smiling sheepishly. His cheeks were red and flushed and his hands were trembling slightly. 'I just came to see how you were,' he said quietly.

'I'm fine, Greg, thanks to you.' She patted the bed. 'Sit for a moment.'

The young man perched on the edge of the bed, his eyes moving about the familiar room, looking anywhere but at Judith's face.

'Your family don't really understand, do they?' she asked.

Greg shrugged. 'They're fine. They were just a bit surprised, that's all.'

'I'll be gone in the morning, you know that. I imagine your mother suspects I'm here for the rest of my life.'

Greg shook his head quickly, though his mother had

suggested that very idea. Once these people move in, they never leave. 'No. Nothing of the sort.'

Judith reached out and touched the boy's hands. In that instant she regretted what she had done – using him to provide her with secure shelter for the night, a place that couldn't be traced. 'What you did today was something you should be proud of,' she said, her voice low and insistent. 'You acted in the finest tradition of old; you came to the aid of a damsel in distress.' She squeezed his fingers and smiled.

Greg nodded, suddenly feeling confident and sure about his actions today. He had been sure – they had seemed *right* until his mother had explained the hundred different reasons why he should have left well enough alone. Nora Matthews simply could not comprehend why he hadn't looked away and crossed the street.

'Do you believe in God?' Judith asked suddenly.

Greg shrugged. 'We're C of E, but . . .' he shrugged again.

'No, I'm not talking about a church; I'm talking about a god or gods. Do you believe in a Being, a Spirit?'

Uncomfortable with the direction the conversation was taking – maybe his mother was right, maybe the old woman was mad – he shrugged again. 'I suppose I do. Why?'

'Because what you did today was *right*. It was *good*, and your god or gods would have been very proud of you. Do not allow people to belittle what you did.'

'I'm not sure why I did it,' Greg admitted. 'I've never done anything like that before. But when I saw them attacking you, I just got so angry. I couldn't walk away . . .'

Judith smiled, wrinkles spiderwebbing alongside her eyes and mouth. 'Once – not so long ago either – what you did would have been the norm, although what happened today would never have occurred. In my youth, the elderly could walk the streets in safety,' she added. She closed her eyes and slid down in the bed, indicating that the conversation was at an end.

Greg sat with the old woman until her breathing deepened and slowed. He was acutely aware of the house around him and the people moving about. He could actually feel his mother's radiated anger from the kitchen below, his father's dull annoyance, his brother and sisters' irritation, especially Jonie who'd had to give up her room.

Greg smiled grimly. He'd managed to do it again; he'd managed to upset them all in one go. It was a gift. Christ! He was twenty-four, in a good job, with a great future, earning a good salary . . .

The young man's smile turned bitter. He was twenty-four, in a lousy, dead-end job he hated, and he handed over most of his good salary to his mother. He should have got a flat years ago, when he'd had the chance. But he hadn't taken it, and in the last couple of years he'd begun to think that maybe he never would. He'd watched his friends move away from home, get flats or share houses, find girlfriends and boyfriends, and *live*. Some of them were even married now.

Greg gently disengaged the old woman's fingers from his hand and stood looking down at her, so frail and tiny in the bed. Today, he'd done something positive, something good . . . and his mother had scolded him like a naughty boy. Well, maybe he shouldn't have brought her home, but he couldn't leave her, and somehow, bringing her here had seemed like the only decision to make.

Well, she'd be gone in the morning, and everything could return to normal, though he knew it would be a long time before his mother let him forget it. He turned away, shaking his head and quietly opened the door. He had to get out of this house before it choked him.

Judith's cold grey eyes snapped open when she heard the door click shut. She listened to Greg step into the room next to hers, heard the bed springs creak, the tinny crackle of a radio abruptly silenced. Even without the sword to enhance her senses, she could feel his unease and discomfort. He was obviously dominated by his mother, which explained how she had been able to take control of him so easily, but that still didn't explain why he had come to her aid in the first place. His type always walked away . . . but not this time.

Judith fell asleep dreaming of the boy.

In her dreams, his face was older, lined, the eyes deep sunk, shadowed, hair grey and sparse, skin coloured to old walnut by the weather.

Greg dreamt of the woman.

But she was younger, much younger, barely into her teens, eyes bright and sparkling, hair black and shining, cropped short in a boyish cut.

CHAPTER TEN

The white king was magnificent. Three inches of solid crystal, incised and carved in marvellously intricate detail, down to the delicate tracery on the sword blade he held aloft. The queen was a masterpiece, the expression on the face perfect and made all the more human by the mole high on the left cheekbone.

'How old are they?' Vyvienne ran her index finger down the length of the white queen. Richard Fenton's blood stained the white crystal darkly crimson. The old man had died hard, guarding his secret until close to the end. Only in the depths of his absolute agony, when she had stripped the flesh from his chest and back with the tiny flensing knives and then started on his inner thighs, did he reveal the secret of the location of the chessboard he had guarded most of his life.

The Dark Man stepped across the blood that gathered in the tiles at the edge of the pool, picking his way through gossamer strips of flesh that coiled with the consistency of old paper. He carefully lifted the crystal queen from the woman's long-nailed fingers and dipped it in the pool, cleansing it. 'Two thousand years certainly,' he said eventually. 'And possibly another thousand beyond that.' Holding the piece up to the light, he tilted it, admiring the ancient craftsmanship. 'The Chessboard of Gwenddolau,' he whispered, 'each piece based upon a living figure. Each piece imbued with a fragment of the soul of that person.' He smiled thinly. 'Or so the legend has it.'

'And do you believe in legends?' the woman asked, looking at the chess pieces in the velvet padded box.

Slowly, sensuously, he rubbed the queen across her pale face, pressing it between her moist lips. '*These* are legend.'

Noxious bubbles burst in the waters of the polluted pool, and the remains of Richard Fenton floated to the surface. The corpse was barely recognizable as human.

CHAPTER ELEVEN

Tuesday 27 July

Greg Matthews stood in the bedroom door with the cup of tea in his hand, eyes and mouth wide in surprise. The room was empty, the bed neatly made, the covers folded down and smoothed flat. There was no sign of Judith Walker, the only clue that she'd ever been there in the first place the faintest trace of floral perfume on the air. Puzzled and confused, Greg returned to the kitchen, sipping the tepid tea he had made for her. The Capital DJ was reading the seven o'clock news.

What time had she left? He'd been up at six-thirty, so she must have gone before then. But why?

He heard creaking upstairs, his father's heavy footsteps on the floorboards. The floors and walls were so thin, he could trace his father making his way from the bedroom to bathroom. He wondered if Judith had overheard the argument last night. Probably, he decided. And she had almost certainly sensed the icy atmosphere. No wonder she'd left at the crack of dawn. He finished the tea quickly and spent ten minutes looking for his briefcase, before he remembered he'd left it in the office. So even though Judith had left, and solved that problem, there still remained Mr Hodgson, his boss. His mother had taken an almost malicious pleasure in reminding him that he might very well lose his job. Last night he hadn't cared . . . but this morning . . .

He was pulling the door closed behind him as his father hurried down the stairs. Occasionally – very occasionally – they managed to catch the train together. Greg hated that: a journey into the city with his father was always vaguely embarrassing. He never knew quite what to say to him, and he knew his father wanted nothing more than to be left alone to read the newspaper. As he hurried down the street, he couldn't help but feel relieved that Judith had gone. He still couldn't quite fathom what had come over him yesterday. He could understand coming to her aid, but after that . . . things had become a little hazy.

Well, it was over now.

'As laudable as I find your motives, I must remind you that I am running a business here, and if you cannot accommodate us, then perhaps it might be better if you were to look for other employment.' Ian Hodgson kept his eyes fixed in the centre of Greg's chest. Since calling him into the office he hadn't invited him to sit down, nor had he looked him in the face. 'In normal circumstances, I would reprimand you, possibly even dismiss you . . .'

Greg bit the inside of his cheek to prevent himself from saying anything.

'However,' Hodgson continued slowly, 'Sir Rupert Eales phoned this office not ten minutes ago. Sir Rupert is one of the senior partners of our parent company. It seems Sir Rupert was contacted this morning by a Miss Judith Walker, the lady you assisted yesterday. She was *complimentary* . . .' The words were coming more slowly now, and Greg bit harder on the soft flesh of his inner cheek, though this time it was to prevent himself from smiling. 'Sir Rupert was delighted with your actions yesterday. He feels that it projects the correct image for the company, and asked that I personally convey to you his compliments and good wishes.'

'Thank you, Mr Hogdson.'

Hodgson glanced up sharply. 'This woman you *saved* yesterday, had you ever met her before?'

'No sir.'

'Did you, by any chance, know that she was associated with Sir Rupert?

'No sir.'

Ian Hodgson straightened a pencil on his desk. 'So you came to the assistance of an old woman you had never met before, escorted her to her home, and when you discovered it had been burgled, you brought her home to your house where she spent the night?'

'Yes sir.'

'Are you in the habit of picking up strangers?'

'No sir.'

'Well, what made this woman so different?'

'I don't know sir.'

Hodgson laced his fingers together and fixed his gaze on a space above Greg's head. 'Do you want to know what I think, Mr Matthews? I think this whole business stinks to high heaven. You are fully aware that your position here is tenuous; your work has been lacklustre to say the least. You have ignored the recommendations of senior staff. I believe you know that in the upcoming restructuring of this department, there may be no position for you.' The older man took a deep breath and ran his hand across his flaking skull. Hodgson was a bully, and it was common knowledge in the department that he liked nothing better than dressing-down a staff member, particularly female staff members, but recent sexual discrimination cases had forced him to vent his ire on the men. 'I think you knew this woman was connected to Sir Rupert and you set it up with her to ingratiate yourself with him. I simply don't buy the good Samaritan story.'

Greg was about to protest, but decided against it.

'You can go. But I'll be keeping my eye on you.'

Greg bobbed his head and turned away quickly, before the older man could see the broad grin across his face. He kept his face impassive as he strolled through the outer office, under the imperious stare of Miss Timms, Hodgson's niece and secretary. He was smiling as he strolled down the long echoing corridor. Hodgson had looked as if he'd swallowed a lemon as he'd passed on Sir Rupert's commendation. The first thing he'd do would be to source Sir Rupert's address and write him a personal letter of thanks . . . No, the first thing he'd do would be to contact Judith Walker and thank her for bringing him to the notice of one of the senior partners. She had said something yesterday about contacting his boss, but he'd forgotten all about it; obviously she hadn't.

The tiny office Greg shared with two other junior accountants was deserted, computers humming softly in the silence. Perched on the edge of his desk, he flipped through the phone directory looking for Walker, J. There were dozens, but none of them matched the address he'd gone to with the woman.

Clutching the phonebook to his chest, he rested his chin on the spine of the book and stared into space. He was sure he could find the address again, although the trip there was vague and confused in his memory. He knew she used the British Library for research . . . and that she was a writer, a writer of children's books. He could always contact her publisher, but they wouldn't be likely to give out her address, nor would the Library . . . but the public library would have a copy of the register of electors. He could pop in during his lunch . . .

The insistent buzzing of the outside line disturbed him.

'Hello?'

'I would like to speak with Gregory Matthews.' The voice was male, cultured, the faintest trace of an unidentifiable accent.

Greg frowned. Only clients had this number, and none of them knew him as Gregory. 'This is Greg Matthews.'

'Gregory Matthews of 66, Pine Grove, Sevenoaks?'

'Yes. Who is this please?'

'You came to the assistance of a woman yesterday. A Miss Judith Walker. You should have minded your own business . . .'

'Just who is this . . . ?'

'She gave you something. Something that belongs to me. I would like you to return home now and get it, Gregory Matthews.'

'I don't know what you're talking about. Judith Walker gave me nothing.'

The line popped and crackled, the voice echoing slightly. 'My representatives will call at your address within the hour. I would suggest you be there, with the artefact Miss Walker gave you.'

'I told you, Judith Walker . . .'

The line clicked and went dead.

CHAPTER TWELVE

The suburban street was quiet, the drone of the nearby motorway diminished to a dull buzz, metallic petrol fumes disguised beneath the odours of well-tended gardens.

Greg Matthews was sweating heavily as he hurried down the street, squinting against the harsh noonday sun, dark rings chill beneath his armpits, an icy stain along his spine. Traffic in the city had been at a standstill and he'd sat in a taxi in Oxford Street for ten minutes, before abruptly paying the surprised cabby with a handful of loose change, then leaping out and darting into the Tottenham Court Road tube.

The journey home had been interminable, and all the time he hadn't quite been able to shake off the feeling that this was nothing more than a joke, a bad practical joke. On the tube, he'd almost convinced himself that this was a scheme dreamed up by Ian Hodgson just to get him fired. And when his boss discovered that he'd simply walked out of the office without telling anyone, then he probably would get the sack. But the voice on the phone had been so calm, so insistent, so chilling ... deep in his heart, Greg knew that this was no joke.

He slowed as he approached the gate, then stopped in the shadow of the neighbour's neatly-trimmed box hedge and looked at the house. Everything *seemed* in order. All the windows were closed, the gate shut, his younger brother's mountain bike resting on its stand,

Jonie's racer lying on the perfectly-manicured lawn.

Greg glanced up and down the street, but there was nothing out of the ordinary. No strange cars, no characters loitering. He glanced at his watch; the caller had said that his *representatives* would call within the hour, but that had been nearly ninety minutes ago. Had they come and gone? Were they waiting inside, even now watching him through the opaque net curtains? What did they want? Something Judith Walker was supposed to have given him.

Greg stepped out of the shadows and walked up to the gate. And stopped. Something was wrong.

Something . . .

He looked at the neighbours' houses on either side, comparing them to his own. They were identical in style, shape and size; solid red-brick houses of the 1960s, large, generous rooms, high ceilings, tiny squares of windows . . .

The windows were closed.

In the neighbouring houses on either side, all the tiny windows were pushed wide in an attempt to circulate air through the rooms. But the windows in his own home were firmly closed.

Maybe his mother, brother and sisters had gone out. But they wouldn't have left the bikes in the garden . . .

The gate squeaked quietly as he pushed it open and suddenly all the sounds were magnified: the distant thrum of the traffic, the crackle of scores of radios, his own thundering heartbeat. Children's voices sounded high and excited in the distance.

He was going to put the key in the lock and push the door open and his brother Martin would come running down the hall, and then the kitchen door would open and his mother would appear, all grim and disapproving, surprised to find him home so early, and . . .

And he would be relieved.

He wasn't sure what he was going to tell her, but he'd be relieved, and then he'd think up some excuse for Hodgson.

The key turned easily in the lock, the heavily lacquered door opening silently on well-oiled hinges. He stood blinking on the doorstep, squinting into the dim hall, and he had opened his mouth to call out when the smell hit him. A mixture of odours, foul and noxious, completely alien to the flower-scented interior of his home. Some he recognized: the bitter stench of urine and faeces, the sharper tang of vomit, but there were others – dark, meaty, metallic – that he couldn't identify. Greg stepped into the hall. Liquid bubbled and squelched underfoot and he jerked his leg back, rubbing it on the white step, smearing thick dark crimson across the stone.

CHAPTER THIRTEEN

Wednesday 28 July

He was wallpapering. Fifteen years old and he was helping his father hang wallpaper in the sitting-room. The wallpaper was hideous, fat, bulbous, bruise-coloured roses against a bone-white background. He dipped his brush in a bucket of paste and slapped it on to the back of the wallpaper, but the thick white paste was turning pink, and the brush wasn't flowing easily. He splashed more on, but this paste was darker, thicker, a glutinous gel that pulled the hairs from the brush, left them sticking to the paper. The paste had turned bright crimson, and when his father lifted the paper from his hand and pressed it against the wall, the red paste spurted out on either side, writing arcane hieroglyphs up along the walls.

He turned to look around the room. Paper was curling from the walls, peeling back like ragged strips of skin, revealing pale weeping flesh underneath, blood dribbling from the slashed wounds.

'Mr Matthews? Mr Matthews? Gregory?'

Only his mother called him Gregory.

'Gregory?' The voice was female. Bright, chirpy. More mature than Jonie's voice – *bright hair black with blood* – but younger than his mother, *blue eyes wide and blank and staring.*

Greg Matthews came upright with a scream that tore the lining of his throat. He screamed again and again, breathing in great heaving gasps, blood pounding in his temples, heart hammering in his chest, tasting metal in his mouth, the same meaty metallic odour that had permeated the house.

There were voices all around, people, faces, lights, but he saw none of them, was aware only of the images, the terrible image of his mother in the kitchen, little Jonie and baby Sara on the stairs, Martin huddled behind the sofa in the sitting-room . . . and his father, dear God, what had they done to his father? And so much blood. So much blood.

He fell into the sea of blood and drowned in it.

'How do you feel?'

The face swam into focus. A young woman's face, eyes professionally concerned, white nurse's uniform.

His eyes followed her as she moved around the bed, gradually becoming aware of his surroundings. He was in hospital, in a private room. There must have been an accident, but he couldn't recall anything. He didn't seem to be in any pain, and there were no tubes in him, no plaster casts.

Greg licked dry, swollen lips. 'What happened?' he attempted to say, but it came out in a ghostly whisper.

'You're going to be fine,' the nurse said, not answering his question. She lifted his left arm, pressing two fingers to his wrist, then jotted his pulse on the chart. When she had finished taking his temperature and blood pressure, she tilted the back of the bed upwards, raising him into a sitting position.

'What happened?'

'There are some people who want to talk to you. Do you feel like talking to them now?'

Greg struggled to sit up, but the nurse pushed him back on to the pillows. 'How long have I been here?'

'Twenty-four hours.'

'What happened?'

The nurse wouldn't meet his eyes. 'There was an accident in your home,' she said eventually, 'some sort of gas leak. That's all I know,' she added quickly, turning away before he could ask any more questions. Greg stared at the door. A gas leak? He didn't remember a gas leak . . . but then he couldn't remember how he got here. He lifted his hands and touched his face, the skin soft and damp, the faintest trace of stubble on his chin. No cuts, no bruises, no marks. Squeezing his eyes shut, he tried to remember . . . but the images that flickered at the edges of his consciousness darted and twisted away, leaving the impression of shadows, dark, shadows.

'Mr Matthews?'

Greg opened his eyes and knew instinctively that the young woman with the close-cropped blonde hair standing at the end of the bed was a police officer. A hard-faced older man perched on the window-ledge watching him intently.

The woman indicated the older man. 'This is Detective Fowler and I am Sergeant Heath, London Metropolitan Police.'

'What happened?' Greg interrupted. His voice cracked with the effort and he started coughing.

Sergeant Heath came around the bed to pour him a glass of water. She pressed a hand to the back of his head and held the glass to his lips while he sipped and swallowed, then sank back on to the pillow.

'What happened?' Greg asked again.

'We were hoping you would be able to tell us that,' Inspector Fowler said abruptly, pushing himself off the window-ledge to stand at the end of the bed, big, hard-knuckled hands clutching the metal bed rail. His lips were so thin they were almost invisible.

'The nurse said there was a gas leak . . .'

'There was no gas leak,' Fowler said firmly.

The sergeant pressed the glass to Greg's lips again. 'What do you remember?' she asked quietly, catching and holding his attention. He noticed that her eyes were two different colours, brown and green. 'We know you received a phone call at 11.10, on Tuesday morning. You left your office immediately, caught a cab, then ditched it in Oxford Street approximately fifteen minutes later. You caught the 11.40 tube out of Tottenham Court Road station, so you arrived home some time around 12.15 . . .'

'And then,' Detective Fowler interrupted sharply, 'what happened then?'

Greg looked at him blankly. It was the same question he had been asking himself.

'Why did you leave the office so quickly?' the sergeant asked. 'Was it the phone call?'

The phone call. He'd completely forgotten about the phone call. The vaguely threatening phone call.

Images danced, dark and bloody.

'The phone call?' Sergeant Heath said gently.

'The man said that I had something belonging to him, and that his representative would call for it . . .'

Heath glanced quickly at Fowler, but the older man was staring fixedly at Greg Matthews' face. She turned back to Greg, anxious to keep him talking. 'Does this caller have a name?'

'He didn't give a name,' Greg said quickly. He needed to talk and keep talking, because when he stopped the images, the shadows, drew closer. 'But he knew my name, my address.'

'Have you ever spoken to this man before?'

'Never.'

'What have you got belonging to this man?' Fowler asked quickly.

'Nothing.'

'So he just picked you at random?'

'He said the old woman had given me something.'

'What old woman?' Heath asked patiently, keeping her face expressionless.

'The woman who stayed the night. The man on the phone said she had given me something that belonged to him and that his representatives would call for it.'

'For what?'

'I don't know!'

'Who was the woman?'

'I don't know.' Greg shook his head. 'No. Walker. Judith Walker. She had been mugged the previous day, and I took her to her home, but when we got there we discovered that her house had been burgled, and I invited her to stay the night at my home, but when I woke up the following morning, she was gone. And then there was this phone call . . .'

The shadows were closer now.

The words were coming quickly and he was breathing in great heaving gasps. 'But I didn't know what the caller was talking about. Judith Walker gave me nothing. And then, when I got home, I found . . . I found . . .'

*

Fowler and Heath stood in the corridor and listened to Greg Matthews' screams fade as the sedatives took effect.

'What do you think?' Victoria Heath asked. She patted her pockets, looking for the cigarettes she'd given up six months ago.

Tony Fowler shook his head. 'No one is that good an actor,' he said regretfully. He'd had Greg Matthews pinned as the murderer. In the vast majority of cases of domestic murder, the crime was usually committed by a member of the family or a close friend. And from what he'd been able to put together from the reports of relatives and friends of the deceased family, Greg had always been very much under the thumb – some would have said heel – of his domineering mother who controlled every aspect of his life. So, one day he cracked, butchered the entire family, extracted twenty-four years of revenge in an orgy of blood-letting.

His screams had drawn the neighbours, who'd found him standing in the middle of the dining-room, in a pool of blood, surrounded by the dismembered and flayed bodies of his entire family. An open and shut case, Fowler had thought. But now, having listened to Matthews scream aloud his hurt, he wasn't so sure. And if Matthews wasn't guilty . . . Tony Fowler didn't even want to consider that. Right now however, Matthews was their only suspect and he was going to proceed along those lines.

The door opened and the exhausted-looking doctor appeared. 'I thought I told you not to upset him!' he snapped.

'We didn't,' Heath said easily.

'When can we talk to him again?' Fowler demanded.

'I've sedated him. He will remain unconscious for eight hours at least. And then I would prefer if you left him alone. He's been through a very traumatic experience. I want you to give him time to recover.'

'Well we can't have everything we want,' Tony Fowler said, turning away. 'We'll be back in eight hours.' As they walked down the corridor, he pulled out his radio. 'Let's see if we can get anything on this Judith Walker. Be interesting if she didn't exist, wouldn't it?'

'Be even more interesting if she did,' Victoria Heath smiled.

Chapter Fourteen

Robert Elliott pulled on a pair of black leather gloves before lifting the receiver in the stinking phone booth. Although the booth seemed to double as a public toilet and junkies' shooting gallery, the phone was untouched. Looking at the monosyllabic female names and phone numbers scratched, gouged and scrawled in black marker on the wall above the phone, alongside words that could either be names or brands, he thought he knew why. Working people needed a working phone.

Using a disinfected tissue he fastidiously wiped the mouth and ear-piece clean before bringing the instrument close to his face, but taking care that it didn't touch his skin. He would have preferred to use the phone in the car, but his employer had insisted that all calls should be made from public call boxes and never the same box twice.

Elliott dialled the number from memory, amused, but unsurprised to discover that his fingers were trembling slightly. There was no shame in fear, he reflected. Fear was mankind's most potent weapon, most valuable tool. It had kept him alive from the time he had first climbed down from the trees, had fuelled most of the finest inventions, and it was that same fear which would ultimately prevent mankind from destroying itself. In order to survive humans had learned to recognize and then fear that which was stronger and deadlier than themselves.

On the other side of the country, a phone started ringing.

Robert Elliott was an expert on fear. Small, unprepossessing and physically weak, he had discovered its value in the playgrounds of his childhood, and in the years that followed he had studied the nature of fear, learned how to inspire it, how to prosper from it. In doing so, he had explored the limits of his own fears, and discovered that little frightened him . . . until he had received that phone call at three o'clock on a bitterly cold winter's morning from a man who knew too much about him and his dealings. And who had backed up his vague threats by sending him the rotting remains of a troublesome youth Robert Elliott had buried six months earlier.

Across the country, the receiver lifted, and hollow static clicked on the line.

Knowing from experience that no one would talk, Elliott spoke first. 'I've found the young man. He's in hospital at the moment, suffering from shock. I will visit him shortly.'

'And the . . . item?'

Sometimes, when he concentrated, Elliott thought he could detect a trace of an accent. West country perhaps? Welsh? Irish? But, despite his best efforts, he had been unable to trace his mysterious employer. 'It wasn't in the house, and I searched his office last night. Nothing there. However, I'll ask him when I see him.'

'Do that. Having seen your handiwork, I'm sure he will realize that we are serious, I'm confident he will cooperate.' The connection was broken and Elliott carefully replaced the receiver. Although he'd made all the arrangements, Elliott hadn't been in the house on Tuesday morning. He didn't know what had happened in the house; he'd made sure he had a very public alibi for that time. However, he'd seen a copy of the police report; he'd kept copies of the ten by eight colour photographs for his private collection. As he stepped out of the phone booth, he couldn't help but wonder if the boy *would* cooperate. Killing *all* the family was a mistake; one or two were all that was needed to make a point. Now, the boy had nothing left to lose.

In Elliott's experience, people with nothing to lose made dangerous enemies.

CHAPTER FIFTEEN

Judith Walker sat on the park bench, arms wrapped tightly around the bag on her lap, the weight of the ancient metal heavy on her thighs. She'd been sitting on the bench since the park had opened, eyes fixed on the metallic sheet of dirty pond water. If she closed her eyes she could see herself reaching into the bag, pulling out the paper-wrapped bundle and tossing it into the centre of the pool; in her dreams no hand rose out of the water to grasp it, and it sank without trace.

But it would change nothing.

She'd heard about the *accident* to the Matthews family on the six o'clock news – 'gas leak wipes out entire family' – and she'd known immediately that it had been no accident. One of the reasons she had left the house so early yesterday morning was to try and minimize any risk to Greg and his family. But too late. A whole family destroyed . . . and for what? A rusted hunk of metal. And people would continue to die as long as this scrap of the sword remained in the world. Far simpler to cast it into the centre of the pool and allow it to rot.

Judith reached into the bag and touched the metal through the torn newspaper. Immediately, a warm tingling sensation spread up along her arthritic fingers into her wrist, flowing up her arm. This wasn't a rusted chunk of metal. This was Dyrnwyn, the Sword that is Broken.

An iron-age chunk of metal, a relic of another age.

And one of the Hallows of Britain.

Judith's fingers moved slowly, sensuously across the rusted metal, no longer feeling the flaking slivers of oxidized iron, the metal now polished smooth beneath her touch, gold wire bound around a leather-wrapped hilt, a cut chunk of quartz deep set into the pommel, the blade smooth, deeply grooved, the metal ragged and torn where it had been shattered a handspan above the hilt. She opened her eyes to look at the shapeless chunk of rusted metal.

Someone was prepared to kill to possess this.

At least five of the Hallow Keepers had been slain. Richard Fenton, arrogant, aggressive, double-dealing Richard who'd sown the seeds of his fortune on the black market after the war, had been the most recent killing. It had taken place on the same day she'd been attacked; maybe they'd taken him because she'd escaped. The brief radio report said that he'd been found dead in his pool and mentioned his heart condition.

Five dead – five that she knew about – though no doubt some of the others had been slain also, their deaths disguised to look like accidents, and so remain unreported. Someone was collecting the Hallows – but why? And why kill the Keepers in such brutal fashion unless it was part of some ancient ritual. In their own time the Hallows – individually and collectively – had been incredibly powerful, invested with a fragment of ancient power that linked it to Britain's primeval past. Her researches into the Hallows had revealed that many of the artefacts had been blessed in blood and flesh, skin and fluid heightening their powers . . .

Judith stopped, heart suddenly racing as realization dawned. The Hallows were being *fired*.

Legend had it that there were rituals that could fire Hallows, reviving their ancient power, bringing them to life. The Once Kings knew the rituals, the Land Wed Rulers had practised the old dark magics, and had ruled through and by right of the Hallows. With the passage of time, and the dispersal of the Hallows, the rituals had been forgotten, though there was evidence that Henry and his daughter Elizabeth had utilized some of the rituals. Henry had played on the Chessboard of Gwenddolau, and Elizabeth had worn the Red Coat and her magician, John Dee had possessed both the Bowl and Plate of Rhygenydd, though both items had disappeared following his death. There was a rumour that Henry had sacrificed at least two of his wives to the Hallowed chessmen, bathing the crystal pieces in their blood, rumours too that Elizabeth had ordered Essex's death – and possibly Mary's – to appease the ancient rituals and consolidate her rule.

The Hallows could only be fired by the blood of sacrifice: and not just any sacrifice would do; they would have to be people of power. Once, only the blood of kings would have been sufficient to bring the objects to life, now, it was the blood and skin of the hereditary Keepers.

The old woman stood up, stiff hip protesting, and began the long walk around the pond, heading back towards the park gate. She needed to warn the surviving Hallow Keepers that they had been marked for sacrifice.

The power of the white coat, Robert Elliott mused as

he walked unhurriedly down the hospital corridor, head bent, hands dug deep into his bulging pockets. It was a uniform that carried more power, more authority than almost any other he could think of.

Elliott stopped at the nurses' station, leaned over and thumbed through the patients' files. The young nurse writing up her patients' reports didn't even glance at him.

The small, blank-faced man worked his way through the charts, pulling out files at random, glancing down along them, slowly making his way towards the Ms.

'Gregory Matthews.'

Without blinking, Elliott continued past the Ms and into the next section. He was aware of the big, hard-faced man standing in front of the nurses' station, a younger blonde woman behind him and knew instinctively that they were both police. He shifted his body slightly, turning away from them, ducking his head down.

'Where is he?' the man snapped.

Elliott pulled out a chart at random.

The nurse looked up and was about to protest when the woman produced identification, confirming Elliott's suspicions. 'Mr Matthews signed himself out two hours ago,' the nurse said quickly. 'Doctor Segarra tried to stop him . . .' she began, but the two police officers had turned and walked away.

Tucking a chart under his arm, Elliott strode away in the opposite direction. Where was the boy going to go? As far as Elliott knew there were no relatives living in England, and few friends. Robert Elliott smiled grimly; he knew this though: if he'd been in the boy's shoes, he'd want answers. And only Judith Walker could give him those answers. The small man glanced at his watch; it should be finished by now . . . and Greg Matthews would never find his answers.

CHAPTER SIXTEEN

It had taken him the best part of the afternoon to find Judith Walker's address, tearing all the Walker, Js from the phonebook, then cross-referencing them against the register of electors, until he'd finally come up with it.

Greg Matthews wandered the streets in a daze, hands dug deep into the pockets of his rumpled suit. The events of the past few days had condensed and flowed together, whirling into a confused jigsaw of images; and most of those images were dark and terrifying, stained with blood.

A young doctor had tried to prevent him leaving the hospital, but Greg had ignored him as he dressed and, just once, when the doctor had touched him, urging him back into bed, Greg had looked at the man and all the pain, the anguish, the rage that bubbled inside, had blazed through his eyes and the doctor had backed off.

The young man's last clear memories were of the day he had first encountered Judith Walker; two days ago, and yet it seemed like an entire lifetime. It was another time, another world, in which he had a life, a future, a family. That world was gone now, lost for ever.

And the link was Judith Walker.

A tiny, frail silver-haired old woman . . . who had brought death and destruction into his home.

A tiny, frail silver-haired old woman whom *he* had brought into his home.

The jigsaw images returned. They were mostly faces: his mother's, bruised and bleeding, his father's, terribly mutilated, his sisters, their faces surprisingly unmarked, which made the wounds to their bodies all the more terrible, his brother . . . the mutilations were terrible.

His fault.

Greg shook his head savagely. No, not his fault: Judith Walker's fault.

Although all the streets in this part of London looked identical, rows of postwar houses, bay windows, pocket gardens, metal railings, multicoloured 'FOR SALE' signs sprouting in every third garden, Greg recognized the street the moment he stepped into it. Abruptly the jigsaw images vanished and he found he was calm, thinking clearly again.

Second house from the end. That's what she'd told the taxi driver.

The voice on the phone said that Judith Walker had given him something, only he knew that she hadn't, but his family had been butchered because of it. Judith Walker was the catalyst; she had destroyed his world.

And now he wanted answers.

The gate squealed as he pushed it open, one end dragging across the path in a short arc. Greg slowed as he reached the hall door, and stopped, hand on the brass knocker suddenly wondering what he was going to say, wondering how he would approach her. Then the jigsaw images returned and he lifted the lion's head and allowed it to fall. The sound echoed hollowly inside the house. He heard the faintest of scuffling sounds and knocked again, harder this time, the report echoing in the silent street. Movement rasped and slithered within again.

Greg pushed open the letter-box. 'Judith Walker, it's Greg Matthews. I know you're in there.'

The smell wafted through the open letter-box, a mixture of excrement and stale sweat and the bitter metallic odour of blood. The jigsaw images locked together, and suddenly he was home again, standing in his darkened hallway, smelling the same odours, so alien . . . so terrifying.

'Judith . . . ?' Pressing his hand against the hall door he pushed. It swung silently inwards.

After a while the pain had gone away.

The faces of the mocking, grinning youths had faded into indistinct, almost abstract masks, the room had dissolved, melted, walls and floors flowing together into swirling patterns of colour. She watched the colours for a long time, concentrating on them, knowing that if her attention was to falter, even for a second, then she would be back in the cellar room of the violated house, tied to a chair while the cold-eyed youths hurt her, again and again and again . . .

They were looking for the sword, the broken sword.

The sword.

The broken sword.

The image of the sword grew in her mind, flowing out of the colours, solidifying into a solid bar of golden light. Judith Walker concentrated on the light, allowed it to pull her in, to draw her back to another time, a more innocent age, when thirteen children were drawn together from all across Britain to a village in the shadow of the mountains to fulfil an ancient destiny.

The tiny portion of her consciousness locked into the present was aware that the pain was intense now, a searing point of agony threatening to break through the images, the stink of burning flesh strong in her nostrils. Her burning flesh.

The image of the sword flickered, faded, then solidified.

In the dancing flames she saw the face of the tramp, the battered one-eyed tramp with the sour, bitter breath who had given the thirteen children the ancient objects and whispered arcane secrets to them. The tramp's face was just as she remembered it, skin so deeply creased with wrinkles that it seemed scarred, the left half in perpetual shadow from a drooping, broken-brimmed hat, half concealing the triangular patch that covered the left eye. There was a question she wanted to ask him, a question she had wanted to ask him more than fifty years ago. Then, she had wanted to know why she had been chosen to receive the sword . . . now she wanted to know why she was being tortured . . . why she was suffering so much pain . . . why . . .

'WHY!'

The scream stopped Greg at the foot of the stairs, raising the hackles at the back of his neck. The sound was human, but only barely so, a raw scream of absolute agony, high-pitched and terrible. It was coming from below stairs.

'Judith?'

There was a door under the stairs. He'd ignored it

as he'd searched through the downstairs rooms, thinking it nothing more than a cupboard.

'Judith?'

He stopped with his hand on the handle of the low door, then pressed his face against the wood. The smell was stronger here, a mixture of blood and faeces, and something else . . . the stale acrid odour of burnt meat.

'Judith?' Greg asked, pushing open the door.

'Judith?'

The one-eyed man had turned his head, only the merest sparkle in his single eye evidence that he was facing her. Had he called her name?

'Why, Mister Ambrose, why?' Fifty years and she'd never forgotten his name.

'Judith?'

'Because you are the Keepers of the Hallows. The blood of the blessed flows in your veins, diluted certainly, but there. You are the descendants of those chosen to bear the Hallows and keep the land. Only the descendants are worthy enough to keep the sacred Hallows.'

Had he spoken or had she imagined the answer, culled it from years of research into the artefacts.

'Judith?'

The voice broke through her consciousness, shattering the images, pulling her back, making her feel the pain.

'Dearest God!'

Greg clapped both hands to his mouth, feeling his stomach heave. The figure tied to the chair in the tiny cellar was barely recognizable as human; in the glow of the single bulb it looked like a side of meat from a butcher's window. Much of the skin was missing, lying in paper-thin curls on the floor, which was awash with blood. Raw muscles glistened with pale fluids and in places the flesh had been cut so deeply, especially across the chest and above the stomach, that the pale glint of bone showed through.

'Judith?' His voice was a rasp, barely audible in the noisome closeness of the cellar. He wondered how long she had survived the incredible agony.

But the woman raised her head, empty eye sockets turning to the sound, revealing a weeping mask of muscle and tendon.

'Judith.' Greg reached out to touch, then drew his hand back, realizing that every movement must be agony.

Incredibly the woman recognized his voice. She smiled, bloody gums in her mouth. 'Greg?' her voice was a gargled mumble.

'I'll get the police . . . and ambulance.'

'No.' She attempted to shake her head, then grimaced with the effort. 'Too late . . . much too late.'

'Who did this?' He knelt in the blood and fluids and worked at the thin wire bonds that secured the old woman to the chair. They had obviously been twisted shut with pliers and in places the wire had sunk deeply into her flesh.

'They came for the sword . . .' Her voice was a thread now, rasping, sobbing.

'The what?' He eased the wire out of her flesh, blood weeping from the torn skin.

'Dyrnwyn, the sword. Listen to me Greg, listen to me. There's a bag in the kitchen upstairs, on the table, a shopping bag. I don't think they found it. It's filled with notes and papers and what looks like a rusted piece of metal.' She coughed suddenly, fine blood misting the air. 'Take them to my niece, Elaine . . . you will find her address in the bag.' Suddenly her free hand shot out, flailing blindly until it touched his shoulder, bloody fingers biting deeply into his flesh. 'Promise me this. You will give it into her hands. Hers and no one else. Promise me this. Promise.'

'I promise.'

'Swear it.' Her body was trembling now, shivering wildly. 'Swear it.'

'I swear it,' Greg said.

'Bring her the bag . . . and tell her I'm sorry. So sorry.'

CHAPTER SEVENTEEN

Tony Fowler pounded on the wheel of the car. 'I don't believe it. She exists? There really is a Judith Walker?'

Victoria Heath grinned as she replaced the radio. 'There is. She was burgled on Monday. We've got the call logged in at 2:55. Officers arrived on the scene at 3:40. They took statements from Judith Walker *and* . . .' she paused for effect, 'Gregory Matthews.'

'Matthews! What was he doing there?'

Sergeant Heath shrugged. 'One of the officers did ask his relationship to her, and was told by Miss Walker that he was a friend. It seems they went off together in a taxi.'

'Find me that taxi.'

Victoria Heath grinned. 'I'll bet you money that it took them to Greg's home.'

Tony Fowler nodded glumly. 'Probably. Where does this Miss Judith Walker live? We'd better talk to her.'

'Five minutes away.'

CHAPTER EIGHTEEN

Greg touched the old woman's raw cheeks, then pressed his fingers against the side of her neck. There was no pulse.

He stepped away from the corpse, head pounding, stomach wracked with cramps, acrid bile in his throat.

'Police,' he said aloud, his voice flat and expressionless in the room. There was no point in calling an ambulance. He stopped on the stairs and looked around the tiny cellar again. So much blood; it speckled the walls, washed across the floor in viscous puddles, even the bare light bulb dangled a long thread of dark blood. In the last few days he had seen so much blood. He was twenty-four years of age and the only blood he had seen spilt before came from minor cuts and scrapes or the ersatz blood on television and movies.

As he climbed the stairs out of the cellar, he knew that whoever had butchered his family had also slain Judith. Why?

He found the bag in the kitchen on the table, where Judith had left it. The papers and the rusted metal were under a bag of fruit and a newspaper. He lifted the bag, the weight of the metal making it heavier than he expected. Was this what she had been killed for? And why had she allowed herself to be brutally tortured to death if the item her killers had wanted was just above her head?

The crunch of glass made him look up.

There was a face at the back door, the snarling mask of a skinhead – the same skinhead who had attacked Judith on Monday – wrap-around sunglasses giving his face an insectlike appearance. There were three others behind him.

Greg snatched up the bag, turned and ran. Behind him the youths kicked the kitchen door off its hinges.

Sergeant Victoria Heath tapped her colleague on the arm. 'This one here. Number twenty-six . . .' She was pointing towards the house when the hall door was flung open with enough force to shatter the glass panes and a wild, dishevelled figure raced out. He was looking over his shoulder as he vaulted the gate and slammed against the car.

For a single instant Tony Fowler and Victoria Heath stared at Greg Matthews . . . then he turned and ran off down the road.

Tony Fowler slammed the car into reverse, clipping the car behind him and took off after Matthews. Victoria snatched up the radio, and then stopped, jerking her head back, sharply; she had just realized that there was a perfect bloody handprint on the window directly in front of her.

'Leave him, Tony,' she whispered, 'we have to go back.'

It took him a long time before he realized that he wasn't being followed. He had raced through rows of identical streets, past women gossiping on doorsteps, through children playing on street corners, down alleys and lanes, across gardens, into side-streets, running until his breath was acid in his lungs and his stomach was cramped into a tight ball. Clutching the bag tightly to his chest, he staggered along, weaving unsteadily, until he discovered he was passing a tiny park. He pushed through rusted iron gates and slumped on the same warped and scarred wooden bench Judith Walker had used hours earlier. Holding his head in his hands, he attempted to make sense of the last couple of hours.

Judith was dead, brutally killed for . . . for what?

For the contents of the bag.

Reaching into the bag he touched the chunk of iron, and suddenly remembered the phone call to the office, the coolly insistent voice.

'*She gave you something. Something that belongs to me. My representatives will call at your address . . . I would suggest you be there, with the artefact Miss Walker gave you.*'

Was this what the caller had been looking for?

The mysterious caller's *representatives* had called on his family and killed them, and now they had called on Judith Walker, looking for the artefact, which she had died to protect. It had to be incredibly valuable, precious metals, jewels . . . Peeling back the newspaper, he discovered an unremarkable, rusted chunk of metal. The sword, Judith had called it. It didn't look like a sword.

And the police; what had they been doing there? Looking for him or Judith?

And why had he run? He should have stayed, spoken to the police, but the skinhead and the others had been waiting and he hadn't been thinking clearly. He should go back to them, talk to them, before they got the wrong impression. Greg bent his head, his forehead touching the cold metal in the bag on his lap. He should not have run . . .

'So that's why he ran,' Tony Fowler said, pinching his nose tight, breathing only through his mouth. He was standing on the stairs looking down into the cellar. The puddle of yellow light shed by the naked bulb highlighted the mutilated body like an obscene spotlight. Victoria Heath stood behind him, a hand-kerchief pressed tightly to her mouth, eyes swimming.

Tony moved back up the cellar stairs, forcing Victoria up before him, back into the hall. Closing the cellar door on the terrible scene, he took a deep breath, held it and exhaled sharply, trying to drive the stench of death from his nostrils. 'He must have come straight here from the hospital.'

'Why?' the woman mumbled, swallowing hard.

The detective shrugged. 'Who knows? We'll ask him when we catch him. But we were right first time; his reaction in the hospital was obviously nothing more than an act.'

'I believed it,' Victoria whispered. 'He fooled me.'

'He fooled me too. And now he's on a spree. First his family, and now this poor woman. God knows who's next.'

'We've got to stop him before he does this again,' Victoria said quickly.

'We will. I think we should wait in the car,' Tony added, pulling open the hall door, glad to be out of the house which stank of death. He knew from experience that it was an odour which would linger for years, until it eventually mellowed into a vaguely unpleasant sweetness that no amount of air freshener would be able to disguise.

'I honestly didn't think he'd done it,' Victoria said gently. 'He just didn't seem the type.' She was staring at the bloody handprint on the windscreen.

'They never do.'

CHAPTER NINETEEN

'There was nothing we could do. He ran out the front door, smack into a car that was pulling in.' Skinner leaned in the car window and Robert Elliott moved back, sure he could smell the metallic odour of blood from the skinhead's flesh and clothes. 'They were coppers,' Skinner grinned.

'How do you know?' the small man asked coldly. He looked away from the skinhead, across a desolate wasteland of brick and rubble that was in the process of conversion into a carpark. A two-tone Volkswagen van blended into the bleak landscape. Skinner's three accomplices were gathered around a burning barrel, passing a joint back and forth. They were all laughing in high-pitched excited squeals. 'How do you know they were police?' he repeated.

'They looked like coppers,' Skinner said defensively. 'Man and a woman. A blonde.'

Elliott sighed. The police from the hospital; they hadn't wasted any time. 'When Mr Matthews fled the building, was he carrying anything?'

'He was going through a bag on the kitchen table when we looked in.' Skinner stopped, realizing he'd said too much.

Elliott pulled off his sunglasses and dropped them on the seat beside him. He hit the power switch on the car window and the glass abruptly slid up, trapping Skinner's head in the opening, the edge of the glass biting deep into the pale flesh just below his protruding

89

Adam's apple. Robert Elliott put his two hands on the wheel and stared straight ahead. 'You spent the entire morning *questioning* the woman, and got nothing from her. And now you're going to tell me that the bag was on the table in plain sight the whole time.'

'It was a shopping bag . . . nothing more . . .' Skinner croaked. 'For Christ's sake, I can't breathe.'

'Why did Mr Matthews take it?' Elliott glanced sidelong at the sweating skinhead. 'The old woman was dead?'

'Yea.' Skinner attempted to swallow.

'You're sure. You made sure yourself, didn't you. Didn't you?' he insisted.

'No one could have survived what we did to her. When we heard movement upstairs, we scampered out the back. I had one of the lads check the front of the house, but there was no car. I thought it might have been a neighbour, so I was going back in to investigate when I saw the guy who kicked me on Monday. He was standing at the kitchen table, going through the shopping bag.'

'Mr Matthews?'

'Matthews. Yea. When he saw us, he grabbed the bag and ran. We were following him when we saw the police. They took off after him, then suddenly stopped and reversed back up the street. We got out then.'

Elliott sighed; his employer was going to be very upset. Elliott turned the key in the ignition, starting up the car.

'Hey!' Skinner squealed.

Elliott carefully engaged the clutch and let off the handbrake. The car rolled forward, and Skinner's shouts rose in intensity as he scrambled to keep up.

'No Mr Elliott, please. Mr Elliott, please.' His fingers scrabbled for purchase on the glass.

'What would happen if I drove off now?' Elliott mused.

'Mr Elliott please. I'm sorry. I'm . . .'

'I'm not sure if your neck would snap or you would suffocate,' Elliott said mildly. There was a slight sheen of sweat on his high forehead. He licked suddenly dry lips with a small pointed tongue. 'I suppose if I drove fast enough, and took a corner sharply, it might tear your head clear off your shoulders. Make a mess of the car though,' he added.

'Mr Elliott, I'll find this Matthews. I'll make him tell us what was in the bag . . .'

'If I drove slowly, you could cling on to the window, but your legs would drag on the ground.' He allowed the car to drift forward, and gunned the engine. 'I suppose you would be able to run for a while, but what would happen when you could no longer run; how long would it take to strip the flesh from your bones?'

'Mr Elliott, please.' Skinner was crying now, knowing the older man was perfectly capable of doing just that.

'I taught you about pain, Skinner, but I didn't teach you everything. There are some lessons still to be learnt.' He suddenly released the window, and Skinner fell back, hacking, both hands pressed to his neck. 'Don't make me teach them to you. Find Matthews.'

CHAPTER TWENTY

'Elliott believes the boy may have the sword.'

Vyvienne sat up on the bed, candlelight shimmering on her naked flesh, running molten on her raven hair. 'Elliott is a fool,' she hissed. 'And like all fools, he employs fools, weak, drug-controlled, pain-loving fools. A man is only as strong as the tools he uses,' she went on. 'And you are a fool for trusting him,' she added with unaccustomed boldness.

'Perhaps,' he shrugged. 'But he suits our needs . . .'

'For the moment.' The woman smiled, teeth sharp and white against dark lips. 'And when you're done with him – remember, he's mine, you promised him to me.'

'He's yours,' the Dark Man agreed.

The woman rose from the bed and crossed to the window, pushing back the heavy curtains, early evening sunlight washing the gloom from the wood-panelled bedroom. Against the light, her flesh was as waxen as the thick candles that dotted the room, her hair a deep shadow reaching to the back of her knees. She turned, arms folded across her heavy breasts. 'What are we going to do about the boy, Matthews?'

Marcus Saurin threw back the covers, and swung his legs from the bed. 'Look for him.'

'And then?' she asked. 'The boy is not part of the pattern. Not part of the Family.'

'I know that. But who knows what patterns are whirling and shifting now? We've lost Judith Walker without recovering the sword; this is our first setback. But we know – we *think* – the boy has it. So all is not lost.'

The woman padded across the room and pressed herself against Saurin, his chill flesh raising goose-bumps on her skin, hardening her dark nipples. 'Be careful. We know nothing about the boy. We don't know his family, his lineage, his relationship to the Walker woman. We don't know how much she's told him.'

'Nothing probably,' Saurin said quickly. 'Judith Walker was a manipulator, a user. Ultimately, all the Hallow Keepers become users; they are unable to resist the lure of the tiny fragment of power they control, the ability to make men do their bidding. Judith used the boy and by doing so brought destruction on his family. I wonder does he realize that?' he asked softly. 'Probably,' he nodded slowly. 'Maybe he went back to the woman for answers . . .'

'And she must have told him something,' Vyvienne said quickly, her warm breath ruffling the mat of coarse black hair on the man's naked chest. 'Why else would he take the bag?'

'You are right – as always.' The big man wrapped his arms around the woman, pulling her close, drawing the heat from her body, gathering it into himself, the tingle of energy arousing him. 'We will know soon,' he promised. 'We'll have him.'

'Don't be so certain. You've unleashed extraordinary forces by simply bringing the Hallows you possess into such close proximity. I've sensed the ripples through the astral, distortions in the fabric of the Otherworld. Only the Gods know what you have disturbed.'

Marcus Saurin laughed. 'He is but a boy, caught in a situation he could never comprehend. He is no danger to us. Elliott's people will have him soon. You can play with him then.'

CHAPTER TWENTY-ONE

Greg washed away the blood on his palms in the debris-clotted water of the tiny pool in the centre of the park. More blood had dried into the knees and legs of his trousers, but in the gathering gloom it was almost invisible against the dark cloth. He caught a glimpse of his reflection in the dark water, and was shocked by what he saw. His eyes were deep sunk in his head, black smudges etched beneath them, the whole effect startling against the pallor of his skin. His normally carefully combed hair now stuck out at all angles. When he ran his hand through it, flakes of dried blood – Judith's blood – spiralled away.

He needed to go to the police, to tell them what he knew about Judith Walker . . . but first he needed to fulfil his promise to the old woman. He would deliver the bag to her niece. Returning to the park bench, he lifted the bag on to his lap and began systematically sorting through it, looking for an address for Judith's niece.

He laid out the items on the bench beside him; the newspaper-wrapped iron sword, a cardboard folder stuffed with sheets of typed paper, a padded manila envelope filled with newspaper clippings, a bundle of letters tied in faded purple ribbon. Greg turned the letters over; they were all addressed to Judith Walker, but the stamps dated back to the fifties, sixties and seventies. Judith's purse was at the bottom of the bag. It contained twenty-two pounds in notes and change, and her British Library reading card.

He could find nothing with an address on it. Maybe Judith had been mistaken when she had told him that her niece's address was in the bag. The old woman had been in great pain; maybe she'd only imagined it was in the bag. Greg shook his head. She had been lucid, terrifyingly so. He couldn't even begin to imagine the pain she must have been going through as she'd given him the message.

He began returning the items to the bag, quickly riffling through the bundle of letters in case one was addressed to someone called Elaine. But they were all to Judith, and seemed to be in the same hand, from a person called Clay and covered a period of nearly forty years. The typed pages in the folder seemed to be notes for a novel – Judith had been a writer, he remembered suddenly – maybe these were research notes. The padded envelope – he turned it over: it was addressed to Elaine Powys, with an address at a flat in Scarsdale Villas, just off Earls Court Road.

Skinner drove in sullen silence, glad of the mirrored sunglasses that concealed his red eyes, aware that the other three in the van were watching him closely. They had all witnessed his humiliation, but he knew that was what Elliott intended ... the short, unassuming-looking man enjoyed causing pain: the ultimate passion, he called it. Skinner's knuckles tightened on the steering wheel of the battered Volkswagen van. He didn't blame Elliott; Mr Elliott was untouchable, and Skinner wasn't afraid to admit that he was terrified of the older man; Skinner blamed Greg Matthews. He was at the root of his humiliation. And he was going to pay. Elliott wanted Matthews alive, but he wasn't too fussy about his condition, and in Skinner's experience, what Mr Elliott wanted, Mr Elliott got. The youth's lips curled in a smile, remembering the last time Mr Elliott had taken what he wanted. On Saturday night, Elliott had appeared at the door of his flat unannounced and uninvited. Neither spoke, the routine and ritual formulated over six years. They had showered together, standing in Skinner's stained and cracked bath, Elliott the master, being soaped and washed by his slave. Only when he was satisfied would Elliott turn to wash Skinner, his short hard fingers biting into the youth's flesh, tracing the puckered glass scars across his shoulders, the knife scar across his stomach, the circular ridges of cigarette burns. They were all Elliott's doing; an artist signing his work. He'd once boasted that he had signed – with knife and glass and fire – nearly thirty young men and five women in London alone. There were times when Elliott allowed Skinner to take the dominant role, but not tonight. Using the leather wrist and ankle cuffs he had spread-eagled Skinner on the bare wooden floor, and then, with molten wax, razor blades and finally his own teeth and nails, had marked Skinner's body. The older man's frenzy had warned Skinner that another killing had been authorized, and the thought of taking another life had aroused him even more. Expertly, exquisitely, Elliott had taken him to the limits of his own endurance, and then beyond, transmuting the pain of cuts and bites, the sting of hot wax, the hair-thin agony of razor slits into absolute pleasure. It had been close to dawn before Elliott had finally pulled on the ribbed condom, turned the skinhead over and entered him. As he pounded at his flesh, his chin on

Skinner's shoulder, sometimes biting into the skin, nipping savagely at his ear, he had whispered the details of the next killing. As he described the tortures they had been ordered to inflict on the next victim, he allowed Skinner to touch himself, stroke at his flesh in rhythm to the words of pain and suffering. When he had hissed how their victim would eventually die, both men had orgasmed almost simultaneously, and then collapsed in an exhausted bloody heap on the floor.

When Skinner had awoken stiff and sore in the late afternoon, Elliott was gone as usual and as usual, neither man would ever speak of what had occurred.

'What now?' Larry drawled. He twisted in the passenger seat to look at the skinhead. The red line where the window had cut into his throat was still visible on his flesh.

Skinner swallowed hard, the action painful against his bruised windpipe. 'We find Matthews,' he grunted, his voice harsh and rasping. He swallowed and tried again. 'We find Matthews, and the bag. And we take him to Mr Elliott.'

'He could be anywhere,' Larry muttered.

'He's just out of hospital, he's on foot. He can't have got far. Mr Elliott suggested that we watch the tube station. The nearest one is Highbury and Islington.'

'He could have taken a bus or a taxi,' Larry suggested, brushing dirty long hair out of his eyes.

'As far as we know he's never been to this part of London before. He won't know the buses. He won't go for a taxi in case the cabby remembers him.' Skinner shook his head quickly, repeating everything Elliott had said. 'He'll go for the tube.'

Larry shrugged, unconvinced. He was tired, wired and jumpy; all he wanted to do now was to head back to his flat and crash, do some hash and mellow out. The old woman had died hard, and while Larry had no problems with that, he had found her silence disturbing, almost threatening. He loved listening to the screams . . . but the old woman hadn't screamed. Her cold grey eyes had continued to stare at him even as he stripped the flesh from her muscles with the flensing knife. When he couldn't bear the expression in those eyes – chilling and mocking – he had put them out with a hot blade. And then the gaping weeping wounds had mocked him.

Traffic lights changed to red and Skinner stopped the van, rear brakes squealing loudly. He twisted in the seat to look at the two blank-eyed young men in the back seats. They were passing a crack pipe back and forth, oblivious to everything else, their memories of their bloody morning's work already fading, mingling with the crack cocaine dreams. By nightfall they would have forgotten what they'd done. They made the perfect tools. Skinner snatched the pipe away, watching as they both reached blindly for it. Dropping the glass pipe on the floor of the van, he ground it underfoot; he had nothing but contempt for druggies. 'That's enough of that shit. I want you two inside the tube station watching for Matthews. You do remember what he looked like?' he demanded.

They looked at him blankly.

'Jesus! You take one of them with you,' he said to Larry. 'I'll baby-sit the other one.' The light changed to green and he turned into the Holloway Road. 'And don't let Matthews get past you. Mr Elliott would be very upset.'

'And we wouldn't want that.' Larry bit the inside of his cheek to prevent himself from smiling.

Greg followed the tube signs. Street signs told him he was in Islington, in Upper Street, a part of London he had only driven through before. He walked slowly, head down, clutching the shopping bag to his chest, feeling his heart thump solidly against the hard metal of the sword. He stopped once, turning to look in a shop window as a pair of uniformed bobbies strolled past. He ignored the ambulance and police cruiser that sped down the road, sirens blaring; maybe they were going to Judith Walker's . . . and he found he didn't want to think of the old woman again, because thinking of her brought back the images of the pitiful creature in the cellar . . . And suddenly there were tears in his eyes, the world dissolving into rainbow-hued patterns. He blinked them away, feeling the moisture trickle down his stubbled cheeks. He glanced up but no one was looking at him except for a child holding her mother's hand. The little girl pointed at him and the mother looked up quickly, catching his eye, then quickly turned away, eyes clouded with embarrassment.

Greg dragged his sleeve across his eyes, suddenly realizing what he must look like: wild-haired, red-eyed, dirty clothing. He was just another lost soul, one of thousands that wandered London's streets. Only he was more lost than most.

Through shimmering tears he spotted a BR logo and headed towards it. All he had to do was to deliver the bag to Judith's niece, and it would all be over then.

CHAPTER TWENTY-TWO

'I've been nineteen years on the force, and I've never seen anything like it,' Tony Fowler admitted shakily. He was staring at the windscreen, mesmerized by the bloody handprint on the glass. 'I've seen the Yorkshire Ripper's handiwork, I was part of a special contingent of officers who went to the States in '74 to observe the Ted Bundy killings first hand. I've seen Chinese choppings and Mafia hits, I've seen the aftermath of a Jamaican posse's handiwork, I've cleaned up after IRA bombers . . . but I've never seen anything like that poor woman. How she must have suffered.'

'Why would someone do that?' Victoria asked softly. She had been a police officer for seven years and in that time thought she'd seen everything. She could hear sirens approaching, the sounds tinny and sharp on the still air. An ambulance, more police, forensics. 'How could someone do that to another person?'

Tony Fowler shrugged. 'Because after a while they stop thinking of their victim as a person. It's no longer a living human being any more, it's simply an object, a fleshy body to play with.' The detective reached up to place his hand on the inside of the windscreen, matching the bloody print on the glass. 'And once they start, once they get a taste for it, they cannot stop. The killings get worse, more brutal as the killer slips out of control.'

'But Matthews seemed so . . . so normal.'

Fowler grunted. 'So did Ted Bundy. I saw the

aftermath of one of his killing sprees. He attacked four girls sleeping in rooms on campus in Florida State University, bludgeoned two of them to death with a log of wood, battered another two until they were almost unrecognizable. Within the hour he'd beaten another girl to pulp in an apartment a couple of blocks away. And yet, everyone who knew him, said what a really nice guy he was.'

The ambulance turned into the street, siren wailing and the detective flashed his lights. Police cars and a white police van filled the road behind it.

'At least this should be a relatively simple case. We've caught him red-handed.' He grimaced at the unintentional irony. 'This shouldn't have happened,' he said quietly, climbing out of the car. 'We shouldn't have left him alone in the hospital.'

'We weren't to know . . .'

'We should have known,' Fowler snapped. 'We made a mistake. And because of that, this poor woman has died. But I'll make sure it doesn't happen again,' he added grimly.

CHAPTER TWENTY-THREE

The air smelt hot and stale and metallic in the train station . . . the same metallic sweetness of spilt blood. Greg felt his gorge rise and swallowed hard, images of wet meat appearing before his eyes, an advertisement for the Tate on the tiled wall opposite dissolving into patterns of raw flesh.

Next Train Two Minutes.

The train station was almost deserted, in the early evening lull between rush-hour traffic and the night-time crowd, less than half a dozen people waiting in the station. Greg moved away from them, walking towards the end of the platform, convinced they'd be able to smell the stench of death that clogged his own nostrils. He glanced back over his shoulder, checking the electronic notice board . . . and spotted the two men as they stepped on to the platform. One wore his hair cropped close to his skull and was dressed in faded army vest and combat trousers, while the second was wearing nondescript jeans and tie-dyed t-shirt. Greg recognized the young man's hair; he had seen the same mop of matted blond hair the day Judith Walker had been attacked, and again, this morning, he'd seen the young man amongst the group at the house.

Next Train One Minute.

He stepped back into the shadow of an arch and prayed that they weren't looking for him . . . but knew that they were. It couldn't be coincidence.

The train appeared in the distance, clicking over the

points. It seemed to take an age to reach the station and at any moment he expected to feel a hand on his shoulder. He daren't look around in case either man saw him. The train clattered into the station and double doors hissed open almost directly opposite him, and a tiny Malaysian woman stepped off, pulling a huge shopping bag behind her. A young woman pushed a toddler into the carriage before her as she folded a buggy flat and lifted it aboard.

Stand Clear of the Doors.

At the last moment Greg darted forward and on to the train, barely squeezing through as the doors hissed shut. He managed a single glance down the platform, but the two young men had vanished. Had they left the station or were they on the train? He flopped into a seat, staring straight ahead, heart thumping, chest heaving, stomach cramping. He was bathed in sour sweat and when he rubbed his hand across his forehead, it came away greasy and stained. When he caught the young mother staring at him with an expression of disgust, he immediately stood up and turned his back to her, staring intently at the Underground Map on the wall above the window. He kept glancing back down the train. It *would* have to be a train, rather than a tube, he decided grimly. A tube wouldn't allow people to move from carriage to carriage, whereas a train ... He turned back to the map; he needed to work out the shortest route to Earls Court Road. If he changed at Moorgate and got on to the Circle Line, he could change again at Paddington and transfer to the District Line, which would take him to Earls Court. Once he had given the bag to Judith Walker's niece – he pulled out the envelope and checked the name and address again, Elaine Powys, Scarsdale Villas – he could go to the police. He started to look at his watch before he remembered that it had stopped. As he wound it, he thought the journey wouldn't take more than a hour.

They had spotted him the moment they stepped on to the platform. He'd been slinking down at the far end of the platform, head bent, arms wrapped protectively around a bulging shopping bag, hugging it close to his chest.

'Get Skinner,' Larry snapped. He brushed strands of his long hair out of his eyes and eased his glassy-eyed companion towards the stairs. 'Get Skinner. Tell him we've found Matthews.' He saw Matthews duck into the shadows and guessed that they'd been seen. Larry chewed the inside of his cheek, trying to formulate a plan, regretting the dope he'd smoked earlier. It had mellowed him out, sure, but right now he simply couldn't think straight: should he tackle Matthews now and maybe cause a scene, or wait until Skinner arrived when he'd probably claim all the credit for himself.

He was still dithering when the train arrived and he knew that Matthews was going to dart aboard at the last moment. There was still no sign of Skinner: where the fuck had he got to? He allowed himself to be carried by the small crowd on to the train and then hovered in the doorway, watching intently for Matthews to make his move.

Stand clear of the doors.

He'd been just about to step off the train when Matthews appeared, moving fast and jumping aboard.

As the doors had hissed shut and the train lurched off, Larry had turned to see Skinner and the others come running on to the platform. Larry grinned at their expressions, but the smile faded when he realized that he didn't know where the train was going . . . and when he dug into his pockets he discovered he had exactly one pound and fifty pence on him: hardly enough for a phone call, and definitely not enough to get back to his flat. So he was trapped on the train with Matthews, and with nothing to do but follow him. Straightening, he looked down the train. He wondered how much the reward for Greg Matthews was.

Later, shocked eye witnesses would describe the incident in almost identical terms. Martha Hill, who was on her way to visit her mother in Old Street with her three-year-old son, Thomas, told how a blond-haired young man had come through the adjoining doors and approached the wild-haired dirty-looking young man who was sitting hunched over, arms wrapped tightly around his chest. She thought he might have been drunk or stoned. The two young men seemed to know one another; Martha Hill had got the impression that the blond had called the other young man by name: Matthews. She saw them speaking briefly together.

Walter Kassar had come off a thirty-six-hour shift and was dozing in his seat when he heard the doors between the compartments open and a young man with long, dirty blond hair stepped through. He'd moved unsteadily through the compartment, even though the train ride was smooth, and Kassar had got the impression that he was drunk. He'd stopped before another young man, who'd stared at him with red-rimmed sunken eyes. Walter Kassar dismissed them both as junkies. He too had heard the blond-haired youth call the other by name, and watched while they chatted together.

Suddenly the blond was standing in front of him, and Greg realized that he'd been dozing in the heat. Wild-eyed, the blond had licked cracked and scabbed lips and smiled, revealing dirty teeth. 'Matthews,' he said simply. He turned his hand, displaying the surgical scalpel held flat along the palm of his hand. 'Matthews . . .' he whispered again.

In a sworn statement, Martha Hill claimed that the seated man had pulled what looked like a hammer from a shopping bag on his lap and struck the blond-haired youth. Walter Kassar had seen an iron bar, possibly a crowbar or a pry bar.

'Move and I'll take your eye out,' Larry whispered, tilting the knife, allowing it to throw a sliver of metallic sunlight on to Greg's face. 'You won't need your eyes where I'm taking you.'

'What do you want?' Greg mumbled.

Larry raised his left hand, red evening sunlight running liquid and bloody along the length of metal. 'We're getting off at the next stop, and you're going to come along nice and quietly. Now give me the bag – real slow.'

Greg didn't move.

'Stubborn? The old woman was stubborn too . . . and you saw what we did to her, didn't you?' Larry grinned. 'I took her eyes out myself. Just sliced them down the middle like grapes . . .'

Abruptly, the lump of metal was a solid weight in his lap. Greg almost imagined he could feel it throb against his body. He could feel its chill through his clothing, a numbing sensation that spread through his chest, tightened his lungs and set his heart racing. Reaching into the bag, his hand closed around the rusted pommel, fingers sliding into the ancient well-worn grooves.

And then the broken sword came out of the bag in a smooth movement and caught Larry on the temple. The snap of bone was clearly audible above the clatter of the train over the points.

The blond youth swayed, eyes rolling back to white in his head, and then Greg hit him again, catching him low on the face, shattering his left cheekbone, the force of the blow fracturing his skull. A long ribbon of bright blood spurted, dappling the window and ceiling. Although almost unconscious on his feet, animal instinct drove Larry staggering back, but Greg rose to follow him, the blood-smeared broken sword gripped so tightly his knuckles hurt, rusted metal biting into his hand. Larry was turning and falling when the final blow caught him on the back of the neck at the base of his skull, snapping his spine, sending him head-first into the window. The heavy laminated glass shattered with the force of the tremendous blow, razor sharp shards almost completing the task of decapitating him.

Both witnesses then described how the young man had calmly pulled the emergency cord, bringing the train to a screeching halt. He had used the manual door levers to open the doors and leapt out on to the track. Witnesses estimated that from the moment the blond-haired youth had spoken to him to the time the murderer had left the train was less than one minute.

He had killed him. Killed him without a second thought. Without compunction. As he raced down the line, gravel crunching underfoot, he shoved the remnants of the broken sword into the bag. He didn't realize that there was no blood on the metal, though he himself was spattered with crimson.

CHAPTER TWENTY-FOUR

It had been a long time since it had tasted blood. Fresh and salt, warm and meaty.

Memories stirred.

Memories of the time when it had first taken on a consciousness, when the sorcerer-smiths, following a thousand-year-old tradition, had driven the inanimate lump of gleaming metal into the bodies of a score of slaves.

The moment of pain.

Of awareness.

Consciousness had come then.

That blood sacrifice had sent ripples out into the Otherworld, calling a score of spirits, inviting them to enter into the crafted object.

The sorcerer-smiths thought they were imbuing the artefact with life; they were wrong. They were merely opening a door, and only the strongest could pass through.

In the time that followed, it had feasted off flesh and blood and souls aplenty. This was a time of Chaos when men ruled by the sword, when justice was bought on the edge of steel. It had never regretted its decision to animate the sword.

And then it had been changed, fettered. One who wore the flesh of humankind, but who was more than human had altered it, binding its spirit, forcing it to another task. It chafed against the bonds, but they were powerful indeed.

It was still used as an instrument of death, it still feasted off flesh and souls, but it took little sustenance from the killings. That energy was directed elsewhere. Those who wielded it had changed too, primitive, gnarled hands had given way to leather and then mail gloves. It drank the souls of men and women of learning and intelligence, it supped off those who worshipped strange gods in dark lands . . .

And then it had been broken.

The two men fighting in the churned field considered themselves knights on opposite sides, fighting for causes which they themselves did not truly believe in, but fought because they were expected to fight, and because they knew no other trade. Nor did they know that they were fighting with weapons that were claimed by entities older than the race of mankind. While the men hacked and hewed, the metal blades sparking and blunting, another battle, bloodless but far more savage was being enacted in the place known to the humankind as the Otherworld.

And because one sword had been fed with innocent blood – sweet and clean – and the heady elixir of virgins, because the wielder was a despoiler of women, who took pleasure in rape and butchery, he was victorious. Battering his opponent to his knees, with a final blow his demon-blessed weapon had hewn through the other weapon, shattering it into two pieces. The same scything blow had taken the head from the kneeling knight. The sword had keened its triumph.

And later generations would name the demon sword Excalibur; the broken sword was Dyrnwyn.

CHAPTER TWENTY-FIVE

Greg pulled out the envelope and checked the address again – Elaine Powys, Scarsdale Villas – before turning into the side street off Earls Court Road. 'Miss Powys, my name is . . .' He shook his head. 'Miss Powys, your aunt Judith Walker sent me . . .' He nodded quickly. 'Yes, have to mention Judith's name to get her attention . . .' He stopped, becoming aware that a young couple on the opposite side of the road were watching him closely, and realized that he'd been speaking aloud, head nodding, shoulders twitching. Ducking his head, he hurried away.

When he reached the house, he couldn't find a bell for Elaine Powys.

Greg ran his finger down alongside the lighted bells on the white-painted door. Against the white paint, the blood engrained into his fingers and beneath his nails stood out vividly. All the bells had names on the white cards beneath them. Two were doctors, the rest went by first initials only . . . and there was no Powys. Digging into the bag he checked the envelope again, then stood back to look up at the number on the door. They matched.

He jumped when the hall door suddenly opened and a tall Asian woman, wearing a nurse's uniform beneath a light coat, stepped out. She gave a tiny gasp when she saw him standing there.

Greg attempted a smile, then stopped as he felt his face tighten into a grimace. 'I'm sorry I startled you. I have a package for Miss Elaine Powys.' He showed the nurse the envelope. 'I thought she lived at this address.'

'She does. But in the basement fl. . .' the nurse started to say, then stopped. She stepped back into the hall and closed the door slightly, obviously prepared to slam it shut. 'I'm sure she's not in right now; maybe you'd like to leave the parcel with me. I'll see she gets it.'

'I'm sorry. I have to deliver it into her hands.'

'It's no trouble,' the nurse said quickly.

'Thanks, but I promised her aunt that she'd get it.' He smiled and the nurse slammed the door.

There was a single bell on the basement door which was hidden directly beneath the steps. The faded biro on the sliver of white paper stuck on to the bell said *Powys*. Greg raked his fingers through his hair, and smoothed his stained clothing before pressing the bell. It buzzed deep in the flat. Moments later the curtains to his right twitched. The windows, he noted, were barred. Through the yellowed net curtains he thought he could make out a woman's face, hair wild and tousled, eyes dull with sleep. Again, he held up the letter, showing the address. 'I've a parcel for Miss Elaine Powys.'

The face disappeared from the window.

Footsteps padded in the hallway, a floorboard creaked, and then he heard the rattle of a chain. The door opened, but only to the extent of the safety chain. He realized then that she'd been putting the chain *on* the door, not taking it off. 'Are you Elaine Powys?'

'I'll take that,' the woman said, without answering his question.

'I can only give this to Elaine Powys, no one else,' he said, squinting to make out some details of the figure who was keeping well back into the shadows. She was wearing an oversize tracksuit that successfully concealed her figure.

'I am Elaine Powys.' There was a trace of a Welsh accent, he thought.

'Can you give me some proof?'

'What!'

'Proof. Can you give me some proof? Judith made me promise that I'd give this to her niece and no one else.'

'Judith? Aunt Judith?' The door closed, chain clattered, then the door was reopened.

'Aunt Judith gave me this to give to you.'

A young woman stepped out of the shadows, copper-red hair dull in the evening light. Hard green eyes narrowed as they took in Greg's dishevelled appearance, his ashen features, the deep shadows beneath his eyes.

Greg stuffed the envelope back into the bag and stretched out his hand, but the young woman made no move to take it. 'She told me to give you this and say . . . and say . . .' He suddenly stopped, energy draining away, leaving his legs rubbery, icy sweat on his forehead, his tongue thick in his mouth.

'Are you all right?'

He tried to lick his dry lips, but his tongue felt huge and swollen. 'I'm fine,' he mumbled, reaching out to grip the wall. 'Just a little faint. I'm just out of hospital,' he added.

The woman caught him as he fell, expertly turning him, one arm across his back, supporting his spine, her left hand catching his, holding him tightly, keeping him upright. 'Just take it easy. Take it easy.' She walked him into the tiny hall, then turned to the right into the small sitting-room. Easing him into a battered fireside chair, she disappeared into a kitchen. He heard a tap running, then Elaine reappeared with a glass of water. Greg accepted it gratefully, sipping eagerly.

'Take your time,' Elaine advised, 'you'll get stomach ache.' Folding her arms across her chest, she observed him critically. 'You said you were in hospital. What for?' she asked quickly.

Greg shrugged. He still felt light-headed and disso-ciated, but at least the world had stopped swaying. 'Observation . . . shock . . . I don't know.'

'You don't know why you were in hospital,' the woman asked incredulously. 'Which hospital?'

'Royal Free . . . I think.'

'You think!'

Greg shook his head. 'I'm not sure. The events of the last few days are confused.'

'When were you discharged?'

'I discharged myself today.'

Elaine crouched down facing Greg and lifted his left wrist, pressing two fingers against his wrist. 'I'm a nurse,' she said. 'Your pulse rate is high,' she said moments later, 'and you look close to collapse. I think you should go to the nearest Accident and Emergency or even back to the Royal Free and see will they readmit you. I could take you . . .' she added.

'I'm fine,' Greg said quickly. 'I just wanted to get the bag to you.'

The woman reached over and pulled across the bag from where he'd dropped it on the floor. She grunted in surprise at the weight. Pulling out the envelope that was on top, she glanced at it quickly, then looked back at Greg, eyes narrowing. 'Where did you get this?'

'I told you; Judith Walker gave it to me. She told me – she made me promise – that I'd give it into your hands. And she told me to say . . . she told me to say . . .' Greg could feel the burning at the back of his throat, the sour acid in his stomach. He stood up suddenly, and Elaine came quickly to her feet and backed away in alarm. 'She told me to say that she was sorry, so sorry,' he said in a rush. Then he turned and staggered from the room. Elaine watched in astonishment as he ran past the window and up into the gathering night.

CHAPTER TWENTY-SIX

Robert Elliott struck Skinner sharply across the face, the sound echoing in the underground carpark. The signet ring on his index finger caught the skinhead on the cheekbone, opening the skin in a wide, deep cut. For an instant, rage sparked behind the skinhead's muddy eyes and his fists clenched. Elliott laughed. 'Touch me and I'll kill you.' Then he deliberately turned his back on the skinhead, leaving him to dab at the wound on his cheek with his sleeve, and walked back to his car.

'It wasn't my fault,' Skinner said plaintively. 'I wasn't even on the train. Larry was probably out of his head on something . . .'

Elliott pulled out his car keys and pointed the remote control at the black BMW. The lights flashed and the door locks thumped. 'I told *you* to find Matthews . . . I told *you* to bring him back . . . I told *you* . . . *you* . . . *you* . . .'

'I'm sorry Mr Elliott, I'll find him.'

The small man opened the car door and climbed in. 'I know you will, because if you don't, then our association will be at an end,' Elliott snapped and pulled the door closed. The BMW pulled away with hardly a sound.

Skinner waited until the car had turned and vanished before he whispered, 'Fuck you.' Then he dug his hand into the back pockets of his jeans and went to look for Greg Matthews. He didn't know where he was going to begin.

Robert Elliott cruised London's streets in the BMW desperately trying to work out how he was going to tell his mysterious employer that he had failed – again – to bring him Gregory Matthews. The boy led a charmed life. And, unlike Skinner, Elliott knew exactly how Larry had died. He hadn't slipped and fallen, as Skinner speculated. Elliott had used a police connection to get an up-to-date report on Larry's death. According to eye-witness reports, Matthews had struck the boy with what had variously been described as an iron bar, a metal bar, or a hammer.

Elliott knew it had been the sword.

He finally made the call from a phone box in New Cavendish Street. He'd driven around for thirty minutes, trying to think of a good excuse, finally deciding that honesty – he smiled wryly – was the best policy.

This time the call was picked up on the first ring. As usual, no one on the other end responded. 'It's me,' he said shortly.

'The boy?' The harsh arrogant voice on the other end of the phone demanded.

'We haven't found the boy yet – he evaded us on the tube. One of my men was with him, but there was some sort of accident; it looks as if Matthews killed him.'

'An accident. How?'

Elliott took a deep breath. 'With the sword.'

The phone was slammed down so hard it hurt his ear.

'Bad news?' Vyvienne asked. She slithered up on the bed and knelt behind the naked man, wrapping her

118

arms around his chest, pressing her breasts against his shoulders.

'The sword has tasted blood. Tasted blood . . . but not the blood of its keeper.' Saurin surged to his feet and strode across the room, then swung back to face the woman. 'Do you know what this means?'

'Another of the Hallows has become active?' she suggested. 'But you've been firing the artefacts with the blood and pain of the Keepers . . .'

'Of the Keepers – yes. But the boy Matthews has killed with the sword, allowed it to taste blood.' The Dark Man's voice was thick with emotion, his cultured accent momentarily slipping. He realized he was trembling with a mixture of rage . . . and fear? 'But do you know what this means?'

She shook her head, long dark hair trailing across her eyes.

'The power within the Hallow has been dormant for centuries. The blood of the Hallow Keepers fires the artefact and simultaneously calms it, leaving it replete with power. But Matthews has given it a soul to drink. Now it is awakened. It will begin to renew itself . . . not only in this world, but in the Otherworld also. Even now, it is probably rippling through the astral.' He stopped suddenly. 'Could you find it? Could you follow a disturbance in the astral?'

'Probably . . .' she said, sounding doubtful.

'Then do it. Do it now!'

The woman smiled lasciviously. 'I will need your strength if I'm to go adventuring . . .'

The phone buzzed in the BMW. Startled, Elliott nearly crashed the car. No one – *no one* – had the car number. He only used it for outgoing calls. Maybe it was a wrong number. It buzzed a dozen times before he finally picked it up. He recognized the husky voice immediately and felt again the trickle of fear. How had this man got the number?

'Judith Walker had a niece, an Elaine Powys. The girl lives alone in a flat in Scarsdale Villas. Matthews has been there, he has given her the sword.'

'But how do you know . . .' Elliott blurted.

'I know.' There was a dry rasping chuckle 'I know everything, Mr Elliott. Everything.'

CHAPTER TWENTY-SEVEN

'It would seem like an open and shut case,' Victoria Heath said tiredly, heels clicking as she walked along the tiled morgue floor. It was close to ten-thirty and she'd been on her feet for nearly sixteen hours.

'There's a *but* in your voice . . .' Tony Fowler said.

The sergeant brushed her hair out of her eyes. 'I don't believe he had the time to do all those terrible things to Judith Walker.'

'I agree.'

'You do!'

'Sure I do.' Tony Fowler fished in his pockets and produced the cologne-impregnated handkerchief he kept for visits to the morgue. 'I think Matthews may have had help. A friend or friends who started the proceedings, as it were.'

'And you think this corpse was one of those friends?'

'I'll lay money on it. The witnesses on the train said they both knew one another. Maybe this friend was trying to blackmail Matthews . . . and Matthews killed him.'

'But why? None of this makes sense.'

Tony Fowler grinned sourly. 'After a while you'll realize that there's a lot of police work that will make very little sense: the killings, the muggings, the rapes, the robberies. Sometimes – *rarely* – there's a pattern. Usually, it's just a mess.'

Victoria Heath shook her head. 'I don't want to believe that.'

'You will.' Fowler pushed open the heavy swinging doors 'You will.'

'The subject is a white male, early twenties, twenty-two, twenty-three, six feet, ten stones or one hundred and forty pounds . . . which is underweight for this height,' the pathologist added, glancing across at the two police officers. Fowler was staring at the pathologist, deliberately avoiding the naked body on the metal tray. Heath was staring fixedly at the corpse.

'The subject shows extensive puncture marks along both arms, indicating systematic drug usage . . .'

'McCall,' Fowler said suddenly, 'we've both had a long day. Do we have to stand here while you do the full routine. Just give us the highlights, eh? In layman's terms.'

'Sure Tony,' Gavin McCall grinned. He reached up and turned off the dangling microphone. The enormous Scotsman called them forward, until they were almost at the edge of the table. 'What you have here is a wasted junkie. He's been shooting up for two, maybe three years.' He turned the arms, showing the track marks, some healed to black spots, others still scabbed and crusted. 'When he ran out of veins on one arm he moved over to the other. And if you check between his toes, you'll see he tried shooting up there too. He's underweight, as I noted, probably jaundiced, hepatitis, maybe even HIV positive.'

'I don't want his medical history. I want to know how he died.'

The Scotsman grinned. 'Someone damn nearly cut his head off – that's how he died.'

'That was the glass in the train window . . .' Sergeant Heath said tightly.

McCall shook his head. He turned the young man's shattered head to one side; Victoria Heath felt her stomach flip: the head was attached to the body only by slivers of flesh. 'He was struck three times, here . . . here on the face and . . .' McCall turned the head, 'here at the back of the neck. These two blows were struck by a flat, blunt object, the third blow was from an edged weapon. This blow severed his spine and drove him forward and into the window. Falling glass severed flesh and tendons, but the youth was dead by that time. We excavated the wound and discovered slivers and flakes of oxidized metal. Rust to you and me. In my opinion, this young man was killed by three blows from a sword. A rusty sword.'

'A sword!' Fowler snapped. 'None of the witnesses reported seeing a sword.'

'They said it was an iron bar,' Victoria added.

'A sword is an iron bar . . . with an added edge,' McCall said. 'The two blows here were caused by the flat of the sword. The killing stroke was with the edge of the sword. I think your murder weapon is a rusting sword.'

'This is getting too weird,' Victoria whispered.

'We haven't even got to the weird part,' McCall grinned. 'Look at our friend here: what's missing . . . besides most of his head,' he added.

Tony Fowler looked at the body and shook his head. Victoria Heath swallowed hard. 'Blood,' she said finally. 'I would have thought there'd be more blood.'

'Bravo. There are eight pints of blood in the human body. In a traumatic wound such as this, you would expect to lose quite a lot, until the heart stopped beating and circulation ceased. But there would still be some blood left in the corpse.

'The train carriage looked like an abattoir,' Tony observed.

'A little blood goes a long way.' McCall jabbed a finger at the corpse on the table. 'Our friend here has no blood in his body. None. It's as if he's been sucked dry.'

CHAPTER TWENTY-EIGHT

Elaine Powys came out of the kitchen carrying a cup of tea. She stood in the doorway, leaning against the jamb, sipping the Earl Grey, looking at the bag the wild-eyed stranger had given her. It was still on the floor where she'd left it. She'd been half tempted to contact the police, but dismissed the idea as ridiculous. What was she going to tell them: a weird-looking guy brought me a message from my aunt? She had tried phoning Aunt Judith, but the phone had been engaged. She'd glanced at the contents of the bag quickly; it seemed to be manuscript papers, some old letters. Why would her aunt send her a bag of papers? And why didn't she use the regular post, or even take the tube. Elaine put her cup on the mantelpiece and sank into the battered balding fireside chair. When was the last time she had visited her aunt?

Elaine reached for the telephone and hit the redial button. The digits sang their electronic chirping . . . and then the engaged tone cut in. Elaine frowned. On the off chance that she might be phoning the wrong number, she checked it in her tiny address book, then dialled again. It was still engaged.

She glanced at the clock, and was shocked to discover that it was ten forty-five. She'd thought it was earlier, but in July it would not get fully dark for another thirty minutes or so. Who would her aunt be speaking to at this time of night? She dialled the number again. Still engaged, or maybe the phone was out of order?

Elaine looked at the clock again. She'd try the number again at eleven, and if it was still engaged, then she'd take a taxi across the city.

She was reaching for her aunt's bag when she heard footsteps on the stairs leading down to her basement flat. A shadow passed her window, and then a second and a third.

The bell rang long and hard.

This time Elliott was taking no chances.

Although his employer hadn't threatened him, Elliott had *heard* the threat in his voice, understood it and knew that this time he couldn't afford to fail. He still didn't know how the other man had got his number, nor how he knew that Matthews had given the sword to Judith Walker's niece. There were times when he bitterly regretted getting involved in this whole affair – not that he'd had any choice in the first place – but he had the feeling that it was time he started thinking about a holiday, a nice long holiday.

He had driven to Scarsdale Villas in Skinner's van; Elliott wasn't going to risk having someone see his car in the vicinity of what could turn out to be a murder site. He was dressed in army surplus trousers and jacket, cheap runners, and had pulled on a pair of surgical gloves before he had climbed into the van. And even if anything should go wrong and he was spotted, he had a cast-iron alibi: he was playing bridge with friends in Chelsea; three solid citizens would vouch for him. Robert Elliott was a man who did not believe in taking chances. The only people who'd know he was there were his two companions, Skinner and a blank-eyed youth, whom Elliott suspected was Skinner's slave or lover, or possibly both. And if necessary – and Elliott was beginning to suspect that it might be – he would dispose of them both without a second thought. Lovers' suicide pact . . . carbon monoxide poisoning in the van, possibly?

'You're in good form, Mr Elliott,' Skinner said, watching the small man's thin lips curl in a smile.

'This should be an amusing evening,' he murmured. He glanced along the row of houses, checking the numbers. This was a quiet street; they would not be able to let the girl scream. 'Get in quick, get the girl under control,' he ordered as they strolled down the street, taking their time, drawing no attention to themselves. 'We want the bag Matthews gave her, and the sword. And let's see what other information we can get out of her.'

'How do you know Matthews was here, Mr Elliott?' Skinner asked quietly.

Robert Elliott grinned. 'I have my sources.'

Elaine Powys peered through the curtains. There were three men standing outside her window. A skinhead, another man, younger with a tight-cropped haircut, and a short, bulky man. She saw him reach up to press the doorbell again, noted the signet ring on his index finger . . . and then realized that it was indistinct, the pattern blurred and she recognized the effect. She saw it every day in the hospital: the short man was wearing flesh-coloured surgical gloves. The image terrified her.

Elaine jerked back from the window, but not before the short man had turned and looked directly at her, and smiled. Reaching into his pocket he pulled out some pliers.

Heart thundering, Elaine scrambled for the phone, sending it flying off the table. Dropping to the floor, she hauled it back by the wire, listened to the dial tone, and was stabbing for the nines when the phone went dead, no sound from the earpiece. When she looked up at the window, she saw the black wire dangling against the glass.

And all the time the bell rang continuously.

Elliott kept his finger on the bell to intimidate the woman while Skinner worked on the lock. It was a simple Yale, and he was reasonably confident that she hadn't locked up for the night. Most people never expected to be mugged, never thought they'd be attacked in their homes, or that they'd be burgled. That sort of thing always happened to someone else, so when it did happen, they were completely unprepared for it. Right now Miss Powys was probably rigid with fear. She would have discovered that the phone was dead, and the constant jangling of the bell would have set her nerves on edge. Maybe she was looking for a weapon, a kitchen knife, a poker; Elliott hoped so. He always made a point of using their weapons against them.

The lock clicked open.

And the three men stepped into the hall.

This couldn't be happening. It couldn't be!

Elaine attempted to slow her ragged breathing, and think clearly. Her heart was thumping so hard in her breast that she could actually feel her skin tremble.

Catching the edge of the table, she pushed it up against the door, then snatched up a poker from the grate. There was no escape out the back, the basement flat gave on to a tiny walled garden, no way out through the barred windows and she knew the flat directly above hers was empty, so even if she screamed no one would hear.

There was movement in the hall, floorboards creaking.

Suddenly the sitting-room door moved, banged against the table she'd pushed up against it. The door was flung back, moving the table a couple of inches. Gripping the poker tightly in both hands, Elaine Powys swung it at the window, shattering the glass, slivers nicking her forehead, biting at her cheek. Pressing her mouth to the opening, she started to scream. 'Help me . . . please help me . . .'

And then the foul-smelling rubber-gloved hand pressed over her mouth, and she was dragged, kicking and struggling, away from the window.

'You should not have screamed,' Robert Elliott said softly. He brought his face so close to the girl's that his hair brushed her skin. She recoiled from the touch, the minty sweetness on his breath, twisting her head away, but the two youths holding her in the chair pressed down on her shoulders, ensuring that she couldn't move. 'No, you should not have screamed.' The gag they jammed into her mouth had torn the soft skin on either side of her lips, and she kept having to fight the urge to throw up. If she did, she knew she could easily choke on her own vomit.

The small cold-eyed man lifted the poker. 'And

what were you going to use this for, eh?' In the reflected street lights, his lips shone wetly. He licked them suddenly, a quick flickering movement.

Iron-hard fingers closed around her jaw, biting into the flesh of her cheeks. 'I would love to spend time with you – we could have such fun together.' He allowed his hand to trail along the line of her throat, down across her breasts. 'But time is something I don't have. So I'll be brief. Tell me what I want to know, and we'll leave you alone. Lie to me, and I'll hurt you badly. Maybe even blind you. Do you understand me? Do you!' he suddenly snarled.

Elaine nodded, blinking away tears. She wasn't going to give this animal the satisfaction of seeing her cry.

'Matthews came to visit you today. What did he give you?' He suddenly whisked away the gag, flesh from her cheeks and lips tearing. Blood oozed from dry, chapped lips. 'If you scream, I'll break your fingers,' he hissed, lifting the pliers, working the jaws inches from her eyes.

'Matthews . . . ? I don't . . .' she began, but the small man was shaking his head.

'Don't tell me you don't know. That will upset me. I know he was here. I know he gave you the bag. Now I want to know what he told you, where he is and where the bag is.'

Elaine continued to stare straight into Elliott's eyes. She knew now what bag the small man was talking about; it had to be the same bag the wild-looking young man had given her. The bag was on the floor almost directly behind Elliott, where it must have fallen out of the chair. All she had to do was to lower her eyes and she would be looking at it. But she knew he'd see and she wasn't going to give him the satisfaction.

'A young man came around a couple of hours ago. He had a bag with him, right enough. He claimed to have come from my Aunt Judith. But when I spoke to her, she said she'd never heard of him in her life.'

Elliott struck her, quickly, casually, expertly, the ring on his index finger catching her along the line of the jaw. A purple-black bruise appeared immediately. 'I told you not to lie to me. You couldn't have spoken to your aunt . . . and do you know why?' The small man's grin was fixed, his forehead greasy with sweat. 'Because these two young men were partially responsible for killing her. Slowly. Oh, so slowly. I believe she died hard.' His fingers tightened on her jaw again, forcing her head back, forcing her to look at him. 'I want the bag and its contents. I want to know if Matthews told you where he was staying.' Lifting the pliers he caught the soft flesh of the lobe of her ear and snapped the jaws shut. The pain was incredible, and she convulsed in the chair. Elliott had his hands on her throat now, squeezing tightly, fingers along the line of her windpipe. She could barely breathe. The scream died in her chest. 'Answer me, or I'll rip your ear off.'

Behind her one of the youths giggled, the sound high pitched and feminine.

'I'll tell you,' Elaine sobbed.

CHAPTER TWENTY-NINE

The one-eyed tramp huddled in the doorway and watched as the wild-eyed young man appeared out of the shadows, started across the street, then stopped, hovering indecisively, before darting back the way he had come and returning to the shadows.

The tramp eased himself to a sitting position and the paper bag in his lap hit the ground with a solid thump and rolled into the gutter, glass clinking and clunking. The tramp watched it, trying to remember if there had been anything left in it. His memory wasn't good any more. A shape loomed out of the shadows and the tramp drew back, but it was only the young man again. His foot hit the paper-wrapped bottle, sending it clinking further into the gutter.

'Who are you – what are you doing here?' the young man snarled crouching before him.

The tramp shook his head quickly, keeping his face down, not meeting the other's gaze, streetlight washing half of his face in yellow light, giving it an unhealthy cast. The thick bandage pasted over his left eye was filthy. 'I'm nobody. I was just kipping here . . .'

'How long have you been here?'

The tramp frowned, trying to make sense of time. 'A while,' he said eventually, then shook his head quickly. 'A good while.'

'Did you see three men pass by here a few moments ago?'

The tramp nodded again. He had seen them, and

instinctively recognized them for what they were, survival instincts honed on the streets driving him back into the safety of the shadows. He squinted his single eye at the wild-eyed young man. Was he with them? He didn't think so . . .

'Where did they go?'

The tramp pointed, long filthy finger-nails pointing across and down. 'Down there . . . down there.'

Greg Matthews straightened and looked towards Elaine Powys's flat. And then the window shattered.

CHAPTER THIRTY

He could hear one of them talking. A foul-voiced man, his words bitter, twisted, full of loathing and amusement. And then there was a choking gasp, high pitched, rasping, followed by the sound of someone giggling.

They were torturing her, Greg knew. Torturing her for the same reason they had killed her aunt. For the bag. And the sword.

He could just about make them out through the hole in the window. One man was blocking his view of the woman, but he could clearly see the skinhead standing in the background.

The front door gave to his gentle push

The sounds were clearer now, the girl's choked sobs, the skinhead's giggling, and the small man's bitter voice.

'. . . Greg Matthews.'

Shocked, he stopped, hearing his own name mentioned. How did they know him . . . unless . . . unless . . . unless these were the same men who had phoned him in his office, the same men who had butchered his family.

Rage – terrible, terrifying in its intensity – washed over him, and he was moving before he was even conscious of it, screaming wordlessly. He was aware only of images, frozen snapshots: the small man turning towards him, pliers in his hand . . . one of the youths releasing the girl, lunging for him . . . the shock of recognition on the girl's face.

And then the small man jabbed him in the chest with the blunt end of the pliers, pain blossoming and he crashed to the floor, lungs struggling for breath. He hit a chair and toppled sideways and the boot, which had been coming for his head, struck his shoulder, numbing his entire arm, spinning him around in a half circle to crash to the floor, rolling right over the familiar bag.

'Alive,' Elliott snapped. 'I want him alive.' He grinned. Suddenly everything was going to be all right again. He could trade Matthews to his employer, make everything right again.

He watched as the shaven-headed youth struck out at Matthews again, catching him high on the thigh with his steel-toecapped boot. He was moving in for another savage kick, when Matthews rolled over, pulling a sheaf of newspaper from a bag on the floor.

The bag.

Elliott raised his arm to point, but by then Matthews had come up on one knee, holding the newspaper tightly in both hands. He lunged straight ahead, catching the youth in the groin. Even before he saw the newspaper turn red with blood, Elliott knew what it concealed.

The broken sword punched through the soft flesh, destroying tissue, muscles and the delicate inner organs. Blood spurted, sizzling where it soaked into the newspaper, hissing when it touched the metal. Greg jerked the ancient weapon upwards, the rusty edge of the sword – dull and blunt – neatly shredding flesh, eviscerating the youth.

Somewhere, the distant call of a hunting horn, some-where the faintest clash of metal off metal, the song of the sword.

Greg jerked the sword free. The shaven-headed youth swayed, eyes wide and shocked, mouth open, both hands pressed against the gaping wound in the pit of his stomach. Stepping forward, still holding the sword in a two-handed grip, he brought it down in a short chopping motion, catching the youth below the line of the jaw. There was surprisingly little blood when the head tumbled away from the body.

The hunters were closer, their horns shrilling, the belling of the hounds louder.

Greg Matthews stepped over the butchered body and raised the sword above his head in both hands. The sword struck the lightbulb, plunging the room into darkness, sparks and tendrils of white fire curling down the blade.

Elliott and Skinner turned and ran.

'What happened?' He was sick to his stomach, and the pain in his head was so intense he knew if he moved he would throw up.

'I don't know,' Elaine Powys muttered tightly, press-ing a damp face-cloth to Greg's forehead. She was trying to breathe through her mouth; the stench in the apartment from the dead body was appalling, a mixture of excrement, urine and blood. 'They ran away when you . . . when you . . .' She jerked her head into the shadowy corner. 'When you did that.'

Greg struggled to raise himself on to one elbow. When he did what? He remembered bursting into the room, the pain in his chest as the small man struck him – rubbing his chest, he felt the egg-sized bruise – and the blows as one of the skinheads had punched and kicked him. He remembered falling, the shape and weight of the sword beneath his body, the pommel cold in his hand . . .

The hunters had not been human. And he was the quarry. A creature had reared before him, fantastical in its demon-armour . . . except that it had not been wearing armour. He had struck it, catching it a lucky blow, then dispatched it by removing its head.

'I don't remember,' Greg said slowly. There were fragments, images, vague and ephemeral. When he tried to concentrate on them they slid and shifted away.

'You killed a man,' Elaine said quietly. 'Stabbed him, then cut his head off.'

Greg shook his head, but Elaine caught it, holding his cheeks in both hands, staring into his eyes. Her eyes were very green, he realized. 'You did. But it's going to be all right. I'll tell the police you did it to rescue me. That's why you came back, isn't it?'

Greg nodded, felt his head throb and pound. 'I was afraid they'd come for you.' He struggled into a sitting position.

'I've got to phone the police . . . and then I've got to get in touch with my aunt. These men were talking about her saying . . . saying . . .' She suddenly remembered what they had been saying. 'They said she was dead,' she whispered hoarsely.

Greg reached out and squeezed Elaine's hand softly. 'Your aunt is dead, Elaine. These men killed her. They killed her for the bag and the sword I gave to you. She wouldn't give it to them, wouldn't tell them where it was. She was strong, so strong. She asked me to get the bag and the sword to you, and she told me to tell you that she was sorry.'

'Sorry?'

'I think she knew this would bring you nothing but trouble.' He groaned as he sat up, then pushed himself to his feet. 'I'm going to the police,' he said thickly.

'I'll come with you.'

Greg shook his head. 'I think you should take the bag and sword and hide them away somewhere safe. Then I think you should do exactly the same. These people have killed before; they killed my family, they killed your Aunt Judith, they were prepared to kill you today. Go away. Hide until these people are in custody.'

'But why, Greg, why?'

'I don't know,' he said tiredly. 'It has something to do with the sword.'

'What sword?'

Stooping, he lifted the chunk of metal off the floor. Much of the rust had flaked away, revealing shining metal beneath. 'This is Dyrnwyn.'

Elaine reached out and touched the metal with the tip of her finger. A spark snapped between the two and she jerked her hand back. 'When you fought that youth, and then later when you confronted the other two men, I could have sworn the sword was whole and complete.'

Greg shook his head. 'The sword is broken.' He turned his head suddenly, the movement sickening. 'Can you hear anything?'

'Nothing. What?'

'I thought I heard horns. Hunting horns.'

CHAPTER THIRTY-ONE

Reaction only hit them when they were well away from the flat, Skinner driving hard, clutching the steering wheel in a white-knuckled grip. Suddenly the skinhead swerved into the side of the road, pushed open the door, leaned his head out and vomited.

Elliott swallowed hard and turned away, wiping his sleeve across watering eyes and nose.

Skinner slammed the door. His breath was coming in great heaving gasps, and he pounded the steering wheel. 'I'll kill him. I'll fucking kill him.' He turned to Elliott. 'Just who the fuck is he? I thought he was a nobody, a nothing. You told me he was a nobody,' he said accusingly.

'He is a nobody,' Elliott said tiredly.

'This nobody's killed two of my people.'

'I know. I know. Find a phone box. I need to call someone.'

'You've got a phone in the car,' Skinner snapped. 'This is all your fucking fault.'

Elliott's hand closed over Skinner's throat, slender fingers squeezing, overlong nails leaving half moons in the pale flesh. Before Skinner could react, the small man produced the pliers and closed the ends – gently – around the skinhead's protruding tongue. 'Don't you *ever* speak to me like that again!' He squeezed the pliers for emphasis. 'Now do as you're told.'

Elaine stuffed clothes into a small suitcase. 'Are you

sure this is what you want to do?' she asked again.

Greg nodded tiredly He was slumped in the arm-chair staring at the corpse on the floor. Thankfully much of the body was in shadow, so he couldn't see the damage the broken sword had wrought. The smell was indescribable though. A noxious mixture of gas and excrement, the metallic odour of blood and an-other, almost indefinable odour, which he was coming to understand was the smell of death. He had killed a man. His second today . . . and both with the sword. He lifted the rusted lump of metal, turning it over in his red-stained hands. He assumed the staining on his hands was rust, but he suspected otherwise.

'Greg?'

Dyrnwyn, the Sword that is Broken.

'Greg?'

He remembered the weight in his hands, the perfect balance as he swung it at the monster, the sword a natural extension of his arm. In the moment when the sword had sunk into the body of the monster he had felt such . . . *power.*

'Greg?'

He looked up, suddenly realizing that Elaine was talking to him. Crouching before him, she rested her hands over his – small hands, neat hands, beautiful nails, he noticed – and squeezed gently. 'Greg. It's going to be all right. I'll talk to the police. I'll tell them it was an accident.'

'One might have been an accident.'

Elaine looked at him blankly.

'I killed another one today.' His voice was a mono-tone. 'I was on the way to see you when he attacked me on the train. I hit him. He put his head through the window.' He laughed quickly, the sound high and hysterical. 'We might be able to convince the police that one was an accident . . . but two? They've probably got me pegged as a serial killer.'

'Once we explain the circumstance . . .' Elaine began.

Greg suddenly lunged forward and caught her face in both hands, his fingers leaving red streaks on her pale flesh. 'Listen to me. The police already suspect me of killing my own family. They know I knew your aunt. They know I was in the house today. They probably even think I did that too,' he added bitterly. 'Now they've got a body in the train and another here. They're going to lock me up . . . and do you know what: I deserve it.' There were huge tears in his eyes and he was trembling so hard the chair was shaking.

Elaine carefully eased his hands away from her face. She squeezed his fingers until they hurt, and the pain registered. 'We will go to the police,' she said firmly. 'They'll believe us.'

'How?' he demanded.

'We'll make them. We'll tell them the truth.'

'What truth?' he laughed shakily.

'We'll tell them what happened. No more. Now, come on.'

Vyvienne had been in the astral, the Otherworld, watching them when the shaven-headed youth had been killed. As if from a great height she watched the monochrome figures haloed with traces of colour move in the Incarnate World and, with an ease born of long practice, she interpreted the spots and lines of vibrating colour. The cold blue-white of the girl's terror contrasted sharply with the bruise-green and ugly blue of Elliott and his two henchmen. The woman noted that Elliott's blood lust was tempered with the yellow of sexual arousal. And then the stranger appeared, flooding the other colours with his own: cold white, tinged with red and black. Terror. Anger. Then pain.

And then another colour had flooded the Otherworld. Yellow light blazed around the stranger. Gold and bronze lances of energy – ancient and incredibly powerful – pulsed through the astral, sending the woman reeling back. For an instant, she had seen into the Incarnate World below, seen Gregory Matthews lift the broken remnant of sword and plunge it into the skinhead . . . and then the ball of flame had engulfed her.

Vyvienne awoke screaming, hands flailing at the yellow fire that had washed over her, the wordless howling as the sword sank into the youth's stomach and drank flesh and blood and soul ringing triumphantly in her ears.

Saurin, the Dark Man, held her, soothing her, allowing her to draw upon a little of his strength. With her head pressed against his chest, he drew up the sheet to cover her naked body, so that she would not be able to see the puckered water blisters that were beginning to swell on her flesh.

'What did you see?' he whispered, stroking her temples.

'The broken sword. And the boy, Matthews, using it. It has killed again. Such power . . .' she muttered sleepily. 'Such power.'

'Where is it?' Saurin demanded.

'Such power,' Vyvienne mumbled and fell asleep.

In the bedroom, the phone started ringing.

Robert Elliott kept rubbing at the phone with the tissue in his hand while waiting for the call to be answered. It would be far easier to say that the girl hadn't been there, but he supposed he could always say that she *had* been there, but had known nothing . . . or that she'd told them everything she knew, and she simply knew nothing . . .

The phone was picked up, a hollow clicking echo on the line. Before Elliott could speak, the ice-cold voice hissed against the static. 'So you have failed me again, Mr Elliott. And lost one of your men too. I'm beginning to think I misjudged you.'

'But how . . .' There was no possible way that his employer could know. None. Unless, of course he had someone watching the house.

'You forget, Mr Elliott, I know everything there is to know about you. I know what you do, and who you do it with. I know where you go, who you see . . . I know everything. Now tell me you have the sword.'

Elliott frowned. If his employer knew everything, then how come he didn't know whether he had the sword or not. Or was this a trap, to see how much he would reveal? 'I don't have the sword,' he admitted. 'Matthews burst into the room like a madman. He ripped up one of my men and then attacked us. We barely got out with our lives.'

'Matthews is still in the flat with the girl?'

'Yes . . . as far as I know.'

'Then go back and get them both. I want them alive. Not necessarily unharmed, but I want them alive. And get me that sword. I must have the sword. Don't fail me again, Mr Elliott,' he added and hung up.

'We've got to go back and get them,' he said to Skinner, climbing back into the van.

'I'm not going back there!'

Elliott ignored him. Reaching under the seat, he pulled out a length of chain and dropped it in Skinner's lap. Then he pulled out a lump hammer. In the reflected streetlights his smile was ghastly. 'All we have to do is to deliver them alive. Condition doesn't really matter.'

The skinhead smiled and nodded in understanding. Without a word, he turned the van around. He was going to enjoy breaking Matthews' kneecaps.

CHAPTER THIRTY-TWO

'Where will you go?'

Elaine shook her head. 'I don't know.'

The couple stood in the shadows, watching the quiet road carefully, trying to see if anyone was watching them. With the exception of an old tramp huddled in a doorway, the street seemed deserted. Elaine pulled out her car keys and crossed to the seven-year-old Honda Civic badly parked by the side of the road. Greg hurried after her, holding Judith Walker's bag in one hand, the broken sword in the other. Elaine had the car running by the time he reached it, flung the bag on to the back seat and climbed in.

They both breathed a sigh of relief.

'Drop me at the nearest police station,' Greg said tiredly.

'Are you sure you won't change your mind?'

'There's no point in running. The longer I run, the more convinced they'll become that I'm guilty.' He stopped suddenly, then added softly. 'I am guilty.'

'Self-defence,' Elaine replied.

'I'm not sure the police will see it that way.' Glancing at Elaine he repeated his earlier question. 'Where will you go?'

'My mother's in Edinburgh. I could go there. And I've family in Wales. I suppose I could go and stay with them for a few weeks.'

'Do it!' Greg snapped.

Elaine pulled the car out on to the road. 'Aren't you

interested in the men behind this? The men who attacked me tonight . . .' Her voice broke suddenly. 'The men who killed my aunt. Aren't you interested in seeing them brought to justice?'

'These men killed my family. I want to see them rot . . . but I know that there's nothing I can do. These people have killed and will kill again; you can be sure they're hunting us now.'

'But why, Greg? Why?'

Greg Matthews lifted the remains of the sword off his lap. 'For this.'

'A broken antique.'

Greg shook his head. 'More than that. Much more.'

Skinner leaned across the steering wheel. 'There they are. In the red Civic.'

'I see them,' Elliott muttered. The car was pulling out of Scarsdale Villas on to the Earls Court Road. He swore gently. He'd hoped to catch them in the quiet street, where their screams wouldn't attract too much attention. 'Fall in behind them. We'll move when they stop at lights or turn into a side-street.' He lifted the hammer and allowed the heavy head to slap into his cupped palm. 'Alive,' his employer had said, 'but not necessarily unharmed.'

'I think . . .' Elaine Powys said, five minutes later, 'I think there's a van following us.'

Greg resisted the temptation to swivel in the seat and look. 'What makes you think that?'

'We're doing just under thirty. Everything else on the road is zooming past, but this van just sits there.'

'Make a couple of turns. Let's see if they follow us

. . .' Greg suggested. His fingers closed around the hilt of the sword, drawing strength from the rusted metal.

Without indicating, Elaine suddenly turned to the left. The car between them and the van braked sharply, the driver hitting lights and horn simultaneously. At the bottom of the street, she turned right, then right again. At the top of the road, she turned left, back on to the Earls Court Road. As they pulled back out into traffic, the van slipped in two cars behind them.

'She's made us!' Skinner snapped.

Elliott nodded. 'Pull alongside. Force them off the road.'

'Here? Now! In the middle of the city?'

'Do it.' Elliott was gambling that no one would want to get involved. They'd have a couple of minutes before someone phoned the police, another couple of minutes before the police actually reached the scene. Plenty of time to snatch Matthews and girl. And if any do-gooder wanted to take part, well, Elliott had the answer for them too. He tapped the hammer in his hand.

'It's OK.' Elaine Powys relaxed as the van indicated that it was overtaking and pulled out behind her.

Greg ducked his head to look across Elaine at the van. He caught a glimpse of the profile of the passenger, and then the man turned and looked down into the small car. There was a single moment of recognition, but then the van door was opening and the sharp-faced man was leaning out, a hammer in his left hand. 'Elaine!' Greg shouted.

The hammer smashed into the windscreen, spiderwebbing it, showering the front seats with tiny flecks of glass. Elaine screamed, jerking on the wheel, sending the Civic into the heavier Volkswagen van, metal crumpling, bouncing off, then crashing into it again, showering sparks across Elliott who was clinging on to the door. 'Keep driving. Keep driving.' Greg smashed at the windscreen with the broken sword, punching a hole through the frosted window. Skinner drove the van into the lighter car again, and Elliott slammed the hammer on to the car roof, rupturing the metal, triangular petals blossoming above Elaine's red hair. A third blow stove in the driver's window, crystalline shards speckling the woman's ashen face.

'Brake,' Greg shouted, 'brake!'

Elaine stood on the brakes, the Civic sliding and screaming to a halt. The Volkswagen shot past, Elliott leaning from the door, face a mask of fury. There was a sudden crash as a car ran into the back of the Civic, followed by a lesser crash as another car went into that. Twenty yards down the road, the van came to a screeching halt, white smoke cascading from its tyres. Its reversing lights flared white.

Elaine spun the wheel, cutting across the road, horns blaring, metal and glass crumpling and shattering as cars slammed on their brakes, most of them too late. She shot past the reversing Volkswagen and out on to Kensington High Street.

Skinner attempted to follow them. The Volkswagen mounted the pavement, scattering late-night strollers, and bounced back on to the road again. By the time they turned on to Kensington High Street, the Civic's tail lights were distant points of light. Skinner floored the accelerator and the van shot forward.

'Dump the car,' Greg said decisively. He pointed to the tube signs. 'Dump the car and take the tube; we can head into the heart of the city and lose them there.'

Elaine wiped the back of her face with her hand, blood from her nicked cheeks and forehead staining her hand. She could feel glass shards in her face. 'Forget it. I'm not leaving this car. I saved for two whole years to buy it.'

Greg swivelled in his seat to look through the rear window. He thought he could see the van moving through the light traffic behind them. 'You can buy another.'

'On a nurse's salary?' Elaine squinted through the shattered window. 'Forget it.'

'They're back,' Greg said quietly.

The van roared up and slammed into the back of the Civic, crushing the plastic bumper.

Elaine grunted, seatbelt biting into her chest and stomach, feeling the long muscles at the back of her neck tighten, knowing she'd suffered a mild whiplash. She was gripping the steering wheel so tightly she could feel her finger-nails digging into the flesh of her palms. Where were the police?

The van struck the car again, sending it careering across the road. The rear offside struck a lamp-post, metal buckling, the fluorescent bulb exploding in a shower of sparks. Elaine drove through a red light with the van in close pursuit. A white Mercedes coming through on a green light struck the van just above the rear wheel, the heavy car spinning the van through ninety degrees. Skinner straightened the van and screeched away. The middle-aged driver looked on in shocked amazement as the van drove off, leaving a litter of broken metal and glass in the middle of the street. He had just enough presence of mind to note the licence number before he phoned the police from the car.

'There!' Skinner pointed.

The Civic was parked at the entrance to Derry Street, lights on, right indicator flashing. Both doors were open.

Elliott leaped from the van even before it had stopped moving. He darted past the car, ducking to glance inside. It was empty. Holding the hammer in both hands, he hurried down the narrow street. Skinner drove slowly past, headlights – only one was working – on full beam. The narrow street opened out into Kensington Square. Skinner stopped and climbed out of the van, the chain dangling from his fist. He waited while Elliott came running up. 'They could have gone anywhere,' the skinhead mumbled.

Elliott raised the hammer and for a single moment, Skinner thought he was going to hit him.

'What are we going to do?'

Elliott shook his head. He didn't know. His employer was not going to be pleased.

'You can tell the boss we did our best. It's not our fault they escaped.'

'Then whose fault is it?' Elliott snarled.

The skinhead looked at him blankly. Then he shrugged. 'What are you going to tell him?'

'Nothing at all.' Elliott flung the hammer into the van and climbed in. He had a large sum in used notes in his apartment, a variety of passports. If he left now he could be far away before his icy-voiced employer even knew what had happened here tonight.

*

Moving quickly, huddled together like any late-night couple, the right side of her face pressed against his chest to hide the cuts and nicks, Elaine and Greg hurried down the steps into Kensington High Street tube station.

CHAPTER THIRTY-THREE

Thursday 29 July

'The call came in around midnight. Report of a disturbance, breaking glass, a woman screaming.' Victoria Heath leaned forward and pointed to the right. 'It's down there.'

Tony Fowler cut across the Earls Court Road without bothering to indicate, leaving horns flaring in his wake.

'However, last night was a hot time in the old town,' the sergeant continued, glancing down at her notebook. 'Chelsea lost two nil to the Villa, and there were a lot of disappointed fans. Then there was a multiple pile up on Earls Court Road which effectively closed off this whole section of roadway. So it was close to two-thirty before a unit drove by to investigate. When they checked out the complainant, it turned out to be a woman living in one of the flats above the basement apartment, the landlady. Turns out she'd been talking to one of her tenants earlier who said she'd encountered a stranger on the step earlier that evening asking after the girl in the flat. Landlady hadn't thought too much of it until she heard the screams . . .'

'And by then it was too late,' Fowler sighed. 'When will the public ever fucking learn. Phone us sooner, not later.'

'Even when they do phone us, it takes us nearly two and a half hours to get there,' Victoria reminded him.

'What happened then?'

'When the officers reached the flat, they found the glass in the sitting-room window broken and when they shone a torch through they saw a pair of legs on the floor. They effected an entry and discovered the body of an unidentified male. He'd been disembowelled and decapitated by a sharp weapon. Possibly a sword,' she added with a sour smile.

'A sword?'

'A sword.'

'I don't fucking believe it.' Tony Fowler eased the car into the kerb before the coroner's car.

'The flat was rented to a nurse, an Elaine Powys.' She squinted, trying to read her own shaky writing. She'd copied the notes over the air from an officer already at the scene.

'Do we have an ID on the corpse. A boyfriend?'

'Not as far as we know. He was a skinhead . . . they discovered that when they found his head.'

'Any sign of the woman?'

'None.'

Gavin McCall was peeling off his rubber gloves when they entered the flat. The Scotsman's face was drawn, deep shadows under his eyes. He waved an arm behind him, taking in the mess and the dead body which was being unceremoniously loaded on to a stretcher. 'What's wrong with this picture?' he asked.

Tony Fowler stopped beside the body, pulling down the zip on the body-bag to look over the horrific wounds. Then he stood and looked around the room. 'No blood,' he said finally.

'Exactly!' McCall snapped. 'Where's the blood? He's been gutted like a fish. This place should be swimming in blood. He's had his throat cut while still alive. Blood, pumping from the arteries under pressure should have sprayed the walls and ceiling.' All heads turned to look up at the ceiling. 'So, what's the connection between this guy and the body I looked at earlier?'

'None, as far as we know.'

'Well, there is now. They were both killed by the same weapon and that generally means the same killer.' He smiled wanly. 'I'm glad I'm not a cop.'

The landlady's name was Anne Gale and although she felt sorry for the young woman in the basement flat, who seemed to have been kidnapped, or murdered – or possibly both – by a homicidal maniac, she was enjoying her moment in the spotlight. She was also keeping a tight rein on what she said; after all, surely one of the tabloids would be prepared to pay good money for the story and she didn't want to give it all away for nothing.

'I've given my statement to the other officers,' she said when the tired-looking man and the masculine-looking woman appeared at her door, both holding police ID in their hands.

'This will only take a minute, Mrs Gale,' Tony Fowler said easily, ignoring her and stepping into the hall.

'It's Miss, actually.'

'Miss,' Tony corrected. 'I am Detective Fowler, in charge of this case, and this is my sergeant, Victoria Heath. First I would like to thank you for your invaluable assistance. If more of the public were like you, our job would be made a lot easier.' He managed to make the words sound sincere.

They followed the woman into a tiny sitting-room that was dominated by an enormous television set. Smiling Breakfast Time announcers listed the overnight stories and crises and disasters in fifteen-second sound bites. Miss Gale turned the television off as the smiling weather girl appeared.

'Miss Gale, what can you tell us about the young woman who lived downstairs?' Tony Fowler said immediately.

'She was a nurse. All my tenants are nurses. I was a nurse myself . . .'

'Did she have any boyfriends?' Victoria Heath asked quickly.

'Well of course. She was a pretty girl; there were always young men coming and going. But no one special, if you know what I mean.'

'Any of them skinheads?'

'Absolutely not. Elaine was not that type of girl.'

'What about family?'

'There's some family I believe. Her father's dead, mother's still alive as far as I know. There is an aunt on the other side of the city. She visits her occasionally.'

'Do you have a name for this aunt?' Victoria asked. 'We'll need to contact her.'

The landlady opened the drawer of a hideous reproduction bureau and pulled out a ledger. 'There might be something in here. I usually ask my girls to give me a relative's address in case I need to get in touch after they've left, send on post, that sort of thing . . . Yes, here we are. Elaine Powys listed a Miss Judith Walker as an aunt . . .'

Anne Gale turned back to the room, smiling broadly.

The smile faded slowly from her face as the two police officers silently turned and walked from the room.

Tony Fowler paused at the bottom step and searched through his pockets looking for cigarettes he no longer smoked. Victoria Heath stared at him, saying nothing.

A uniformed officer approached and saluted. 'Excuse me sir, but there's a constable here I think you should talk to.'

The detective and sergeant followed the constable across to one of the police cars where a young red-faced officer was standing, shifting uneasily from foot to foot. 'This is Constable Napier, he's with the local station.' The young officer saluted.

'What can we do for you, constable?'

'I was on my way to this address to talk to the owner of a red Honda Civic, registration number . . .'

Fowler raised his hand. 'The point?' he snapped.

'The car registered to a Miss Elaine Powys was found abandoned at the corner of Kensington High Street and Derry Street. We believe, judging from the damage to the car that Miss Powys had been involved in a multiple car crash in the early hours of the morning. We initially thought she might simply have driven off, but we have established the existence of blood stains on the upholstery. We think she may have been injured.'

Fowler caught the older constable by the shoulder. 'Get McCall. Tell him to meet us there. You,' he grabbed the younger constable by the arm, 'take us there immediately.'

'It's Matthews, isn't it?' Sergeant Heath asked.

'Has to be. He's the link. He probably kidnapped

the girl, and was driving away in her car when she struggled, the car got out of control and crashed.'

Victoria Heath nodded. It made sense.

'Contact HQ,' Fowler added. 'Tell them to make an addition to Matthews' sheet. He should not be approached. Use extreme caution.'

'I'm just wondering where the girl is now,' Victoria Heath whispered.

Fowler grunted. 'Dead or if she's not dead, then he's probably torturing her to death right now.'

CHAPTER THIRTY-FOUR

The smell of roasting coffee and burning toast brought her awake. Elaine Powys rolled over and struggled to sit up in bed. She brushed hair out of her eyes, groaning aloud as her hand accidentally brushed against her cheek. The entire right side of her face was hot and felt swollen to the touch, and she could feel hard points of glass beneath the skin.

So it hadn't been a dream.

The wild car chase had wandered through her dreams, only now the cold-eyed man with the hammer hadn't pounded the windscreen and bashed on the roof, he had been striking her directly with the hammer, the blows cracking bones, breaking skin.

She barely remembered the tube ride to Notting Hill Gate. She'd made the journey slumped up against Greg, numbed by the events of the evening, her face against his chest to hide the cuts. She'd taken Greg to the flat of a friend in Notting Hill, just off the Portobello Road. The young woman was away for the week and had given Elaine a set of keys so that she could feed the cats.

A shadow loomed in the door, and her heart lurched, remembering the shadowy figures of the previous night.

Greg tapped on the door with his foot before stepping into the room. He'd recently showered and shaved, his dark hair plastered close to his skull, and his eyes, which had seemed so dead and lifeless the previous day, were now brighter. He sat on the edge of the bed and waited until she had straightened the pillows and pulled the sheet up to her chin before placing a tray on her knees.

'I haven't had breakfast in bed for a long time.' She attempted to smile, but it pulled the skin on her face. Wrapping her hands around a mug of coffee, she sipped it slowly, feeling the scalding liquid sear her tongue. She sighed and sank back on to the pillows.

'How do you feel?' Greg asked.

'How do I look?'

He grinned quickly, his face suddenly boyish. 'Like shit.'

'Exactly how I feel.' She pressed her hand against the side of her face, wincing at the tender flesh.

'I cleaned it as best I could,' he said, 'but there may be some glass still in it.'

Elaine shook her head. 'I don't remember.' She suddenly lifted the covers and looked under them. She was only wearing her bra and panties. Colour washed up her face, and was instantly mirrored on Greg's face. He looked so ashamed that she had to laugh.

'There was glass all over your clothes . . .' he began. And then he smiled shyly. 'And after everything that had happened last night, I was in no state to do anything, not even look,' he added.

Elaine nodded. 'I didn't get a chance to thank you last night . . .'

'You can thank me by eating your breakfast.'

Greg chewed on a corner of toast and looked at the girl, seeing her properly for the first time. He could see some of her aunt in her features, the same determination in her eyes and in the strong jaw. She would never be beautiful, her green eyes were too close together, and perhaps her mouth was too small, but her face had strength and character.

'Who owns the flat?' he asked, aware that the silence was lengthening between them.

'A friend, a nurse. She's away for the week.' An ancient grey-haired tom cat hopped on to the bed, eyes fixed on the milk jug. 'I promised to feed Tom Jones and Delilah.' She tipped a little milk into her saucer and a second cat, a slender tabby, jumped on to the bed. Both cats squatted down to lap at the milk. 'Do you think we'll be safe here?' she asked, not looking at him.

'I don't know,' he said truthfully. 'It depends how organized these people are. Maybe they'll get around to checking out your friends. But you've probably got a few days.'

'Are you still going to the police?'

'I am.'

'I'll come with you.'

Greg started to shake his head.

'I'm coming with you,' Elaine said firmly. She finished her coffee. 'I want to grab a shower and try and clean up my face first.'

Greg stood up, picked up the tray, and carried it back into the cubby-hole of a kitchen. He had been watching the Breakfast Time news on a tiny television, but there had been no mention of the man he'd killed. There had been pictures of the pile up on Kensington High Street, half a dozen cars scattered across the road, the reporter's face washed blue and red in the lights of the emergency vehicles. There had been several serious injuries, but no one had been killed.

Emptying the tray into the sink, he heard Elaine climb out of bed and pad into the bathroom. Moments later the shower began thundering.

Greg wandered back into the sitting-room and sank into an overstuffed easy chair. Reaching into the bag at his feet, he lifted out the broken sword.

Hunting horns. Faint and distant.

Calling.

Greg blinked. For an instant the sword had been whole, a shining bar of silver metal, and then the sunlight had run liquid down it, blinding him, making his eyes water, and when he'd been able to see again, the sword was nothing more than a rusted bar of metal. Someone had killed to possess this chunk of metal; Judith Walker had died in appalling agony to protect its secret. Maybe it was solid gold beneath the rust; he picked at the rust with his thumb-nail, blood-red slivers of oxidized iron tumbled to his lap, but no shining metal shone through. And yet the sword was special, he knew it. Last night when he had plunged it into the skinhead he had felt . . . what had he felt? For a brief moment, he had felt strong, powerful, his terror had faded and he felt . . . *alive*. And earlier, when he'd struck the youth in the train, he'd reacted instinctively, bringing the metal bar up to crack across the side of his head. In the moment when the youth had smashed into the window, Greg had felt . . . what had he felt? Regret? Horror? Fear? No, he'd felt nothing but satisfaction.

Cradling the sword in his arms, Greg Matthews lay back in the chair and closed his eyes, the only sound in the flat the distant hissing of the shower in the bath-room. It sounded like rain.

'It's raining.'

'It's always raining in this cursed country.'

'God-forsaken place.'

A shadow fell across them. 'No place is forsaken by God.' Both men turned away and bent to their tasks as the raven-haired boy passed. They refused to meet his cold, empty eyes, and both surreptitiously touched amulets and talismans stitched inside their clothing. The boy looked back over his shoulder, thin lips curled in a wry smile, as if he knew what they were doing.

The grey-haired, white-bearded man standing in the prow placed his arm on his nephew's shoulder and pointed towards the distant line of the white cliffs. 'Our destination. We'll land before the night.'

The boy nodded. 'Are we far from home, uncle?'

'Far indeed, Yeshu'a.'

The boy leaned forward to stare at the white cliffs. 'The sailors think we've come perilously close to the edge of the world, and the Egyptian is predicting that if we were to sail a day further west we would fall off the edge.'

'The Egyptian, despite his learning, is a fool. If we were to sail a day west and north we would en-counter another land, a wondrous green land, peo-pled by savage war-like tribes. It is a land rich in gold, and its people are skilled in working the soft metal.'

'Will you travel there, uncle?'

'Not this time.' The older man pulled his woollen hood over his head as the wind shifted, driving sleeting rain into his face. 'We will trade for tin, spend a ten-day replenishing our supplies, and then return home.'

The boy Yeshu'a turned his face to the rain, closing his eyes, opening his mouth to catch the icy water. 'It tastes of cold soil and bitter herbs,' he said, without opening his eyes. Then he turned his head and his dark eyes fixed on his uncle. 'What will you trade?'

'Not the usual trade goods. These people are artisans and craftsmen; they only appreciate unusual, interesting goods.' He gestured towards the centre of the squat-bellied ship, where the trade goods were covered beneath an oiled leather tarpaulin. 'One of the reasons they will trade with me, when they refuse to do business with others, is because I always bring them something unusual. Sometimes I think they are like children, desiring only the newest toys . . .' He stopped suddenly. The boy had wandered away, moving sure-footedly down the length of the ship towards the covered goods. The Master Mariner shook his head and turned back towards the land. Yeshu'a was his sister's child; a strange boy who had done nothing but bring disgrace on to the family almost from the moment of his birth. He looked and acted far beyond his years, preferring the company of adults to children, but his very presence made many adults nervous. He was given to wandering off by himself for days at a time, and although he had reached the age where he should have been beginning to learn a trade, he showed no interest in any of the crafts. Josea was hoping that this trip to the edge of the world would excite the boy's interest; if it did then he would take him as his apprentice, teach him the way of the sea and show him wonders: the lands of the Yellow Folk of the far east, the hairy demon breeds of the south, men with hair the colour of fire, skin the colour of chalk. It would be enough to capture any man's imagination.

It had his. Josea had been about the same age when his father, Joshua, had first taken him to sea. It had been a short journey, north and west to the countless isles of the Greek Sea. Joshua had shown him the cities beneath the waves, perfect streets, paved roads, houses, glittering palaces, ornate statues, and told him the tales of the civilization that had thrived there, a mighty race. And then he had given him a dagger, plucked by a diver from one of the houses beneath the waves. He had told him there were other civilizations, other races, other mysteries and treasures to be found. Josea still carried the knife, an extraordinary creation of banded metal and copper wire, long bladed and ornate, incised with a spiralling pattern that he had not encountered again until he had come to the Tin Lands.

When this trip was completed, he would take the boy to the Greek Sea. Together they would explore the many islands, search for treasures in the golden sands . . . and maybe Josea would be able to convince the boy to follow him. The boy Yeshu'a had a restless spirit; Josea too had possessed a similar spirit, though his curiosity was reserved for distant lands, whereas Yeshu'a was interested in everything.

Josea turned to look at the cliffs again. They were nearer now, and already fires were burning on the cliffs, warning of the approaching ship. This was not a bad life, though it was a hard one, that was true, but no harder than that of the craftsman, the farmer, the shepherd. Living was hard. Glancing over his shoulder, he watched his nephew examining the trade goods, then turned back to the approaching cliffs. All he had to do was to channel the boy's curiosity.

Yeshu'a's long fingers moved over the leather-wrapped bundles. Closing his mind to the countless thoughts and emotions buffeting him, concentrating on the endless hiss of the sea to clear his head, he picked up a package and undid the leather cord that bound it. Colour blazed on the grey morning air. Yeshu'a smiled his rare and wondrous smile. It was a cloak, a cloak woven of crimson feathers, the pattern and patina of the feathers marvellously placed and shaped to give the faintest impression of an ornate design on the back of the cloak. On impulse the boy pulled it on to his shoulders, holding it tightly at his throat. And then his smile faded and his lips twisted in a bitter grimace. A wave of terror rose up to engulf him. He was a bird, trapped in a net, struggling helplessly, bones snapping in a desperate effort to pull free . . . and was surrounded by countless thousands of its own kind. Red-feathered birds, squawking, screeching in terror. And creeping through the bushes were dark-skinned men. The boy pulled off the cloak and tossed it on to the deck.

'Yeshu'a!' He turned, eyes blank and expressionless. His uncle was glaring at him. 'Pick that up, wrap it before the sea water destroys it. It cost me a fortune.'

Yeshu'a reluctantly touched the cloak again and wrapped the leather sheet around it. He had the briefest glimpse of the struggling birds, but he savagely blanked the thought from his mind. Searching through the items, his slender fingers touched cold metal. When he unwrapped the leather covering, he discovered the sword.

Greg Matthews came awake with a start, convinced that he was holding a three-foot shining broad-bladed sword, the hilt wrapped in rich red leather, the blade etched and incised with spirals and intricate knot-work. He was almost disappointed to find he was holding the rusted chunk of metal. Lifting his hands, he discovered that the rust had come off and coated his sweating flesh in red dye the colour of fresh blood.

He looked up to find Elaine Powys standing in front of him, wreathed in steam. Her damp hair was plastered close to her skull, and she was wrapped in a thick towelling bathrobe. She was staring at his bloody hands. 'You should go and wash them,' she said softly.

CHAPTER THIRTY-FIVE

Skinner finished the last of the can, crumpled it in his fist and tossed it into the corner. Squeezing his eyes shut, he willed himself to weep, but he had no tears to cry, and yet he could feel the emotion bubbling inside him, acrid and bitter. Then slowly, almost imperceptibly, he curled up on the filthy mattress, turned his face to the flaking wall and thought of Karl and Elliott and Matthews. He could still see Matthews bursting into the room, Karl landing one or two good ones on him, then the briefest glimpse of the rusty metal in Matthews' hands, and then the sound, that awful sickening, crunching sound of the sword sinking into flesh. For an instant – the briefest of instants – he'd imagined he'd seen a gleaming metal sword in Matthews' hands. And as Karl had tumbled and fallen, Matthews had hit him again, and then Skinner truly had seen the sword blaze whole and complete in the moment it took Karl's head from his shoulders. The skinhead swallowed bile. He couldn't have seen the sword blaze with light, that had happened afterwards when Matthews had struck the lightbulb and sparks had flown everywhere.

And then everything had happened so fast. Suddenly he'd been running from the room, convinced that Matthews – now a terrifying shadowy figure silhouetted against the window – was coming for him. And then there'd been the wild car chase. Madness. Absolute madness. Chasing a car through the middle of

London, while Elliott smashed it up with a hammer. Someone must have seen something; no doubt they'd passed the registration on to the police . . . he'd better report the van stolen.

And Karl, dear dead Karl; he'd loved that boy, truly loved him. They'd had some great times together, but Skinner couldn't remember the times, all he could see now was his lover falling to the ground, his head spinning slowly away in the opposite direction. He would not even be able to claim the body.

Wrapping his arms tightly around his body, Skinner ground his teeth together. This was all Elliott's fault, and Matthews' – especially Gregory Matthews. And, by Christ, they were both going to pay.

On the ground floor, the phone started ringing.

Twice before in his life Robert Elliott had walked away. The first time he had been sixteen years old; the girl was fifteen, and the daughter of the village policeman, while he was the son of the local drunk. She was three months pregnant and suddenly claiming that he had raped her. She'd been willing enough at the time, but who were they going to believe? Easier to walk away, set up a new life with a new name in a big city like Manchester. He'd been twenty-four the second time he'd given up everything and disappeared. He had no conscious memory of killing the young man, in fact he'd no conscious memory of that entire night. But the body lying in the bed beside him bore all the marks of savage lovemaking, and his own flesh was also torn and marked from the whips and chains. Walk away, this time to London, another name, another start.

And now he was about to walk away again.

Previously, when he'd been forced to leave, he'd come away with nothing, but this time he was prepared. There was money salted away in a dozen accounts in banks all across the world. He had credit accounts for another half dozen names, and authentic passports in four nationalities.

The small man pulled the leather suitcase out of the wardrobe and tossed it on to the bed. It was kept permanently packed.

He had no illusions that his employer would come looking for him. Nor had he any illusions about the man's capabilities. Although Elliott, along with Skinner and his crew had accounted for five of the men and women, he suspected that there were others that the voice on the phone took care of personally. Only last week he'd read something in the paper about an old woman found dead in her bed. Most of her flesh had been removed. And his employer had been very particular about that. The old people had to suffer.

The first call had come in six months previously. Three o'clock in the morning, and Elliott was just getting in from the clubs when the phone had rung. The answering machine had clicked on, and then the voice had spoken. 'Pick up the phone, Mr Elliott, I know you're there. You are wearing your grey Armani suit, a blue silk shirt, midnight blue tie and matching handkerchief, Dubarry loafers, black silk socks . . .'

He'd picked up the phone, knowing – in that instant – that it was trouble. Anyone who knew that much about him had to be trouble. The mysterious caller told him that there was an envelope in the top drawer of his desk – and yet the flat should have been impregnable – and then hung up. Robert Elliott felt then the first touch of fear. The caller was demonstrating his power: not only did he know everything about Elliott, even down to his underwear, he'd shown he could get into his flat at any time. The envelope had contained a single sheet of paper bearing the name and address of a man living on the outskirts of London. He had been reading the name and address when the phone had rung again. The caller told Elliott what he wanted done to the man, Thomas Sexton; he'd been quite precise. The man had an artefact, a whetstone, a flat circular stone with a round hole in the middle, which the caller wanted. Thomas Sexton was to be killed in a particularly bloody manner, his body opened from throat to crotch, heart and lungs removed, and then the stone was to be placed into the bloody cavity, and left there until it was completely coated in blood. Elliott had hung up without saying a word, then unplugged the phone from the wall when it started ringing moments later. The first post brought a parcel. When he'd cut through the packing, and the plastic bag, he'd recoiled from the noisome stench that filled the room: he was looking at the left arm – complete with tattoo – of a young man he'd been forced to dispose of six months previously. The parcel was accompanied by photographs – remarkably clear photographs – of Elliott digging the grave in the New Forest, tossing the naked body in and covering it up again.

Two hours later, a couriered parcel had brought Elliott an envelope containing a dozen detailed colour photographs of the face of his last victim. The sight of the rotting head had made him sick to his stomach. And then, at some time during the day, though he could never work out how, an envelope had been dropped into his letterbox. It contained a single sheet of paper showing most – but not all – of his accounts, and the current balance.

So when the phone rang in the early hours of the morning, he knew he had little choice but to obey the caller. He'd taken out his frustration and anger on the hapless victim Thomas Sexton.

But he'd always known that a day like this would come; a day when he'd fail and his employer would turn on him. He still didn't know how Matthews and the girl had eluded him. The only conclusion he could come to was that they had slipped into one of the houses in Kensington Square. What mattered was that he had lost them both . . . and the sword.

Opening the wall safe, Robert Elliott pulled out his passports and quickly sorted through them. He shoved the two English and the American passports into his briefcase, and pushed the wine-coloured Irish passport into his pocket. Today he was Patrick Mellet, computer salesman. He would not need a passport to fly to the Irish Republic and once there he could fly anywhere in the world. Elliott glanced at his watch; an hour to Heathrow, then an hour's flight to Dublin. He could be in Ireland before noon, in the States before nightfall.

'You are Nick Jacobs, but you are commonly called Skinner, so that is how I will address you.' The voice was soft and distant, powerful and commanding.

'Who the fuck is this?'

'I am Mr Robert Elliott's employer. Former employer.'

Skinner straightened. 'You're the guy he keeps phoning?'

'I am.' There was a long silence broken only by the line clicking and snapping. 'Tell me, Skinner, what happened tonight?'

'Matthews and the girl got away. Karl was killed,' he added bitterly.

'And you were close to Karl?'

'I was. Elliott's fault. We should never have gone in there in the first place; we should have snatched the Powys bitch on the streets.'

'I would agree. You should take your revenge on Elliott and Matthews.'

'I will.'

'Do you know that Mr Elliott is planning to flee the country?'

'When?'

'Within the hour. If you're going to catch him you will have to be quick.'

'I don't have his address. He never told me.'

'Mr Elliott was a very cautious man.' There was a pause, then the voice asked: 'Would you like his address . . . ?'

'Yes sir.'

'Good. Very good Mr Jacobs. Need I remind you that you're now working for me.'

'Yes sir.'

'When I've given you the address, I'll give you a phone number. You may reach me there at any time.'

Robert Elliott strode across the underground parking

lot, heels tapping on the ground. The air was heavy with petrol and carbon monoxide fumes and he held his breath as he walked, unwilling to breathe in such a concentrated dose of carcinogenic air. Since he wasn't coming back he'd drive the BMW to the airport. He hated having to leave the car, but he'd buy himself another in America. A Trans-Am. Black.

The smell of petrol was stronger at this end of the garage, strong enough to make his eyes water. He used the remote control to open the car doors from a distance. He walked up to the car, pulled open the door and slid into the leather seat.

'Fuck!'

The interior of the car was reeking of petrol fumes. And then Elliott was aware that moisture was soaking into his trousers and back. Reaching out he touched the passenger seat . . . and put his hand in a puddle of liquid. He didn't have to bring his hand to his face to realize that it was petrol.

A shape moved alongside the car, and then the passenger window burst inwards, shards of glass raining around Elliott. 'Skinner?' he whispered.

'Your former employer told me to tell you that running was a mistake.' Skinner's broken yellow teeth gleamed in the sulphurous flare of a long kitchen match.

And then the match was falling, slowly, slowly, slowly, on to the leather seat.

On the other side of the country, the naked woman spread-eagled on the silken sheets grunted when the car erupted into flames. Elliott's agony was a vague and distant discomfort, nothing more. If she heightened her consciousness, she could experience his pain, but she had no love of pain. 'He burns. He is in agony.'

'Remember, do not allow him to die, chain his spirit to his body as long as possible. Let him suffer.'

'He is suffering.'

'Good. Now show him this.'

Vyvienne opened her eyes and looked at the man standing at the end of the bed, wrapped in a red cloak woven of birds' feathers. Then he opened his arms wide, spreading the cloak. 'Let him see me.'

Robert Elliott opened his mouth to scream, and vomited flames on to the bubbling glass. The windscreen melted, a hole appearing, curling outwards. A shape moved in the underground garage, a towering man-bird wreathed in flame, but the pain was too great and he closed his eyes moments before he lost them. His last impression was the smell of burning meat, and by then there was no pain.

CHAPTER THIRTY-SIX

Gavin McCall had been a pathologist for twelve years. Handsome, charismatic and witty with a soft Scots accent made acceptable by Sean Connery, he was a regular on late-night television talk shows and radio phone-ins. He had a wealth of amusing and moral stories about his job, but whenever he was asked what was the most awful part of the job, he liked to say the smells. And sometimes to prove his point, he would bring the interviewer into the morgue and bring them face to face – or nose to face – with a particularly ripe corpse. The mixture of decomposing flesh and decaying gases was indescribable. However, if the truth were known, after twelve years he now never registered the smells. It was as if his olfactory senses closed down once he stepped into the building.

But McCall was smelling something rotten now.

He had been leaving the building for an early luncheon appointment with a charming magazine editor when he'd caught the faintest hint of an odour. Something bitter and sweet, like a rotten fruit, sticky with juice and flies. He wandered back down the tiled corridors, head thrown back, broad nostrils flaring. He'd worked in this building for so long now that he knew it intimately, knew its peculiarities, its smells and creaks, the rattling doors and shaky windows that gave the building its haunted reputation. There was mildew in one of the basements, dry rot in another corner of the building, but here . . . here there should only have been the sharpness of disinfectant, perhaps the faintest sweetness of decomposition, or the touch of metallic blood.

McCall threw his briefcase and coat on to the desk in the outer office and pushed through two sets of double doors into the morgue. He brought up the lights. Most of the staff were out to lunch and the building was quiet, only the distant hum of the air conditioning disturbing the silence. The smell was stronger here. McCall breathed deeply. It was decomposition. Advanced decomposition. That state of decay when rotting flesh turned the consistency of soap and sloughed off brittle bones. But there was nothing in that state here unless something had come in and he hadn't been informed.

McCall wandered down the ranked and numbered freezers, nostrils flaring, identifying the corpses by odour before he read the tag on the door.

Raw bloody meat: road-traffic accident.

Rancid sea-weed and salt: drowning.

Burnt meat and petrol: just come in, suicide in a car, doused it in petrol then set it alight.

Cheap perfume; McCall grinned, no matter how often the body had been washed he could still get the faintest odours of cheap perfume off the prostitute, found dead in an alley off Soho. No obvious cause of death. A dozen diseases however.

The smell was stronger here. McCall blinked, eyes suddenly watering.

Unknown/male/44. Unknown/Male/45.

The young men struck down by the sword-wielding maniac. Neither had been positively identified yet. McCall pulled open the drawer of Number 44, the youth from the train, and recoiled, pinching his nostrils shut. The smell was appalling. The meaty, fruiting smell of advanced decay. And yet it shouldn't be . . . McCall tugged back the sheet . . . and then the hardened pathologist spun away and vomited.

The body was a mass of wriggling white worms. Much of the flesh was missing and the bones were already beginning to show the characteristic yellow-white of age. What flesh remained was black and leathery.

Squeezing his watering eyes shut, McCall pushed the drawer closed, and pulled out Number 45, the headless body which had been taken from the flat off the Earls Court Road. The smell here was even more intense and the sheet which covered the body was lying almost flat on the metal tray, only the curve of the skull, the jut of ribs indenting the sheet. The white sheet was stained yellow and black and tendrils of sticky black ichor dripped on to the tiled floor. McCall staggered back and stumbled out of the morgue. The bodies looked as if they had been dead for years, not hours.

CHAPTER THIRTY-SEVEN

Greg Matthews folded his arms and leaned against the door-jamb looking at Elaine Powys. She was sitting on the floor with her back against the couch going through the contents of her aunt's bag. Seeing her now, with her hair pulled back off her face, exposing her fine high cheek-bones, emphasizing her eyes, he realized that she was actually pretty.

She looked up suddenly and he was shocked to discover her bright green eyes magnified by tears. She held up a single sheet of flimsy paper. 'It's a letter, from Aunt Judith.'

Greg sank on to the floor facing Elaine. The big cat immediately climbed on to his legs and Greg's fingers started moving over the sleek fur.

'Have you read it?' Elaine asked, almost accusingly.

He shook his head. 'I went through the bag to get an address for you. That's all. I didn't read anything.'

Elaine looked at the page, then taking a deep sobbing breath she read slowly, struggling to decipher the crabbed, often hurried writing.

'My dearest Elaine, If you are reading this then there is a good chance that I am dead or missing. You must not grieve for me. Everything dies, but only so that it may be reborn. This I truly believe. If you know I have been killed, then I pray that this note accompanied the sword. The sword may look like nothing more than a piece of rusty metal, but I must ask you to treat it with all the reverence of a holy relic.

The sword is Dyrnwyn, the broken sword, once the Sword of Rhydderch.' Elaine stumbled over the names. 'The sword is older than the land, and forms part of the Hallows, thirteen sacred objects that are the Sovereignty of the Land of Britain. When I was a child I was entrusted with the sword and created a Keeper of the Hallows, and now I pass this Keepership on to you. This is not a task I do lightly, but you are of my blood line and there is no other. Guard the sword well, for its power is terrible indeed and in time you will be able to wield a fragment of its power.'

Elaine looked up, eyes burning. She suddenly crumpled the page and tossed it to one side. Then she buried her face in her hands and her shoulders shook as she wept piteously.

Greg leaned over and retrieved the letter, smoothing it out without a word.

'We knew she was mentally ill,' Elaine sobbed, 'but she wouldn't let anyone help her. She lived alone; she would not let us put her in a home. A couple of years ago she fell and had to have a hip replaced. She'd lain for two days in the hall before someone found her. She'd written children's books for years, lovely, charming books that had won all sorts of awards. Lately her books had become wilder and darker. She started writing what her publishers called dark fantasies and erotic horror.' Elaine nodded towards the letter in Greg's hands. 'She was obviously slipping further and further into her fantasy world.'

'The men who flayed her alive, who blinded and abused her were no fantasy,' Greg said quietly. 'The men who broke into your flat were no fantasy.'

Elaine stopped and stared at him. 'Are you saying you believe her?'

Greg bent his head and continued reading the letter aloud. 'I have spent much of my life researching the Hallows, their forms, identities and powers. Much of what I have learned or conjectured is contained in these notebooks. How I came to be a Keeper is also contained in the smaller, separate notebook. It is a diary of a young girl evacuated from the city to a farm in the heart of the country. It is my diary.

'In the last few months my work has taken on an additional urgency. I have learned that the Keepers of the Hallows are being killed, horribly, cruelly. There are – *were* – thirteen of us; I am unsure how many survive now, and only the Lord knows how many will still be living by the time you read this. I have listed the names and the last addresses I had for them. I am convinced that the Keepers are being killed for their Hallows. I am convinced that someone is collecting the Hallows.

'My dearest Elaine, this must never happen. The Hallows must never be brought together. Never.

'I am sorry, truly sorry, that this burden has passed to you. From father to son, mother to daughter, the Hallows have been passed on through the generations, though if the lines die out, then a Guardian is reputed to come to redistribute them. You are my nearest female relative. You are all I have. Do not fail me.' Greg turned the page over, but it was blank. 'Well?' he asked.

'Well? What does *well* mean? Are you telling me you believe her? Ancient artefacts. Keepers of the Hallows? It's like something out of one of her novels.'

Greg lifted the padded envelope off the floor and

shook everything on to the worn carpet between them. There was a notebook, faded and tattered, JUDITH WALKER written in large childish script on the brown cover, a small gilt-edged address book, and a fat scrap book. A piece of paper curled from the edge of the scrap book.

PENSIONER AND GOOD SAMARITAN SLAIN

Police in Edinburgh are investigating the brutal slaying of Elizabeth Clay (64), and the neighbour, Evelyn Saville (26), who went to her assistance. Investigators believe that Mrs Clay, a widow, disturbed burglars in her flat, who tied her to the bed and gagged her with a pillowcase. Mrs Clay died of asphyxiation. Police suspect that Mrs Saville, who lived in the flat upstairs, heard a noise and came to investigate. In a struggle with one of the burglars, Mrs Saville was fatally stabbed.

Greg opened the book to push the cutting back inside. The pages were covered with neat extracts clipped from newspapers with wavy-edged scissors.

PENSIONER HIT BY TRAIN

A coroner has returned a verdict of accidental death on Miss Georgina Rifkin (63), with an address at the Stella Maris Nursing Home. Miss Rifkin was struck by the six-thirty Intercity. The coroner dismissed as 'malicious' press allegations that she had been tied to the track.

GANGLAND SLAYING

Police fears of an upsurge in gangland crimes were repeated today as criminal mastermind,

Thomas Sexton, was slain in one of the bloodiest killings Tyneside has ever seen. Sexton, whose links with organized crime were well known to the police, was killed in what a police spokesman described as a 'particularly brutal manner'. This reporter has learned that Thomas Sexton (62) was laid open from throat to groin with a knife or sharp sword.

Greg closed the book with a snap. He picked up the diary and turned it over in his hands before opening it. On the inside front cover was a list of names. Some of them leapt up at him. Nina Byrne . . . Elizabeth Clay . . . Georgina Rifkin . . . Thomas Sexton . . .

Closing the diary he picked up the small address book, flipped it open and thumbed through the pages. Most of the book was empty, little more than a dozen names in the flimsy pages, all of them written in black splotched fountain-pen ink that had now faded to purple. Nina Byrne . . . Elizabeth Clay . . . Georgina Rifkin . . . Thomas Sexton . . .

'You should look at this,' he said, his voice sounding thick and numb.

'I don't want to.'

'Look at it!' he snapped suddenly, shoving the book into her face. 'Look at it.' He could feel the rage bubbling inside him now, a burning, trembling rage. 'Look at these names, here and here and here. And now look at your aunt's diary. And now the address book. Here. And here. And here.' The anger subsided as quickly as it had begun, leaving him drained and exhausted. 'Judith knew all these people, Elaine. And they're all dead. And your aunt is dead.' Crouched on the floor, he reached across and cupped Elaine's face in his hands. 'If she wasn't dreaming, or fantasizing or raving . . . what then Elaine? What then?'

Elaine Powys looked into his eyes. She licked dry lips. 'She was raving.'

Greg stared at her, saying nothing.

'She was raving,' Elaine insisted. Her eyes fell on the papers on the floor. 'She was . . .' she whispered, but much of the conviction had gone from her voice. Then she picked up Judith Walker's diary, opened it at random and began to read aloud.

'Monday. The tramp Ambrose returned to the village today. Bea and I saw him hiding in the woods. We know he saw us, but he would not come out, merely stayed in the trees, staring at us with his one eye. Everyone says he's harmless, but I'm not so sure. He scares me, and Bea told me she was frightened of him too. Bea also said that she'd been dreaming the strangest dreams about him; I wonder should I tell her that I was dreaming about him too?

'Tuesday. Dreamt about Ambrose again, last night. The strangest dreams, only this time all the others were in the dreams too. We were in the middle of the wood and none of us were wearing any clothes, not even the boys, except Ambrose and he was wearing some sort of gown. We had gathered in a semicircle around Ambrose who was standing before a tree stump with his back to a tree. And on the tree stump were lots of strange objects. Cups, plates, knives, a chessboard, a beautiful cloak. One by one we were walking up to Ambrose and he was giving each of us one of the beautiful objects off the tree stump. I was last up, and there was only a piece of rusty metal for me. I didn't want to take it, but Ambrose insisted, and he leaned so close I could see the burst veins in his single eye. "This is the most precious of my treasures," he said, "guard it well."'

Elaine closed the book with a snap. Greg was turning the sword over in his hands, absently stroking the broken blade with the back of his fingers. 'Read on,' he said softly.

Elaine shook her head. 'I don't want to. It seems . . . too personal.' She reached for the scrapbook, and silently read through the catalogue of death and suffering. When she was finished she looked across at Greg who had picked up the diary and was reading the large rounded childish hand. 'My aunt knew all these people?' she said.

'From childhood.' He tapped the diary pages with the sword. 'Listen to this. They were all evacuated together. Thirteen children from all parts of the south of Britain. They were billeted on a farm in Wales, where they met an old one-eyed tramp called Mr Ambrose. Mr Ambrose gave them all the objects known as the Hallows. This is from close to the end of the diary.

'It happened. It was so like my dream, I thought it might have been a dream. But now I know it really happened. But I'm still not sure when I stopped dreaming and everything started happening for real. I dreamt I woke up in the middle of the night and climbed out of bed, and slipped out into the night. Some of the others were already there, and the rest were hurrying up from where they were staying in the village. When the thirteen of us had gathered, Mr Ambrose appeared. He didn't say anything, and we followed him into the heart of the woods. I think I must have been dreaming as I walked through the woods. Sometimes I thought I was an old, old woman, wearing ragged clothing, then I was a short man shivering in the cold, then was a knight on horseback, then a lady wearing a fabulous gown, then a crabbed old man with hands twisted by arthritis, and there were more, but the dreams slipped past, too quick to follow. Finally I was just myself, but my night-dress had vanished and I was naked, and so were the other boys and girls but none of us minded. And then my dream came true. We gathered around Mr Ambrose in a half circle, and he called us forward one by one to take the little objects he gave us. I was last, only this time I didn't refuse the sword. Mr Ambrose seemed surprised. "I thought you would not want this?"

'"This is Dyrnwyn, the broken sword," I said and lifted up the object.

'And Mr Ambrose seemed pleased. "Truly, you are a Keeper of the Hallows. The blood of the ancients flows in your veins, diluted certainly, but it is there. You, and these others, are descended from the first Keepers of the Hallows, only you are worthy enough to keep the sacred Hallow."

'Then he whispered the special words in my ear and told me that whenever I was in trouble, I was to hold the sword in both hands and call it thrice by name, Dyrnwyn. What does thrice mean?'

Greg closed the book, laid it on the floor and lifted the sword in both hands. 'Dyrnwyn,' he said strongly.

'Greg . . . what are you doing?'

'Dyrnwyn.'
'Greg!' Elaine's voice was high with alarm.
'Dyrnwyn!'
No sound broke the long silence that followed.

CHAPTER THIRTY-EIGHT

Beyond the physical world exist realms of experience undreamed of by the vast majority of mankind. These are the Ghost Worlds, sometimes known as the Astral Plane or simply the astral.

A score of religions and beliefs accept that the human spirit, the soul, travels to the astral while the physical body sleeps, and renews itself. The spirits of the newly dead linger on the astral before they take the final journey into the Light. Powerful emotions in the living world, the Incarnate World, echo into the astral, tiny pulses of colour in the grey landscape. Words of power, either prayers or curses, once fired with emotion, can penetrate the astral. Places of special worship, holy shrines, revered artefacts leave their mark in the astral.

A solid cone of light burst through the shifting pattern of clouds, lancing into the upper reaches of the Ghost World. Higher and higher it soared, slicing through realms accessible only to a rare few. The sleeping spirits of humankind roamed the lower levels, more highly developed souls had access to the middle levels, those who had dedicated their lives to the acquisition of arcane knowledge and had subsequently gained the necessary skill could gain the highest levels.

The grey landscape lit up as the beacon throbbed in the sere nothingness, washing away the shadows, muting the lights of human emotions and dreams that specked the grey astral.

And then the cone took shape, streamers of light flowing liquid and chill, giving the creation form and substance, angles forming, lines appearing, the beam of light tapering from the lowest levels, rising to a slender point high in the astral.

The sword formed.

It pulsed and throbbed in the Ghost World for less than a handful of heartbeats and then it winked out of existence. The greyness, darker now, slipped back, the pastel lights of human consciousness sparkling in the astral.

But the sudden appalling burst of power had attracted the attention of those within and without the astral. Such power – raw, naked, uncontrollable power – had not been witnessed in a score of generations, and those who once tapped the power, twisting and shaping it to their own ends, those whom people called great or good or evil, had not walked the world for nearly two thousand years.

The curious gathered. Lights and spots of fire, bright primary colours, solid dark pigments, mirrored whites, reflective blacks, raced across the astral landscape towards the last location of the sword.

In the Incarnate World, those with the power to see and travel in the astral recoiled from the blinding, deafening power, while those who were sensitive, but untrained, awoke from terrifying nightmares.

On a London backstreet, an old man awoke.

Vyvienne's cold grey eyes snapped open. She was leaning heavily against an ancient stone wall, staring out towards the grim mountains. It was raining in the distance, heavy clouds banked to the horizon, slanting sunlight lending the scene a quality that was almost pretty. But the unseasonably icy wind robbed the day of all charm.

She had felt the pulse of raw power, heard the words echoing clarion-like across the astral, 'Dyrnwyn Dyrnwyn . . . Dyrnwyn . . .', felt the ripples of energy bubbling the surface of the grey landscape. Superimposed over the distant mountains she saw the image of the sword suspended against the lowering sky. Then it vanished in a roar like the thunder of the surf on a rocky shore as the wash of power blinded her.

When she could see again, Vyvienne turned and ran back towards the house.

She had always been psychic, she had grown up in a family of what the Sunday papers called witches, but who in actuality worshipped something far older and wilder than the horned god or the mother goddess of the Wiccans. By the time she was ten she had walked the myriad lower levels of the astral; when she gave up her virginity at the age of twelve to Marcus Saurin, the Dark Man, her skills had been honed by techniques and rituals centuries old. Saurin had come for her when she was fifteen, and then together they had embarked upon the Great Work. Enhancing her natural skills with the ancient power of sex, the Dark Man had encouraged her to seek out the artefacts, to read their sleeping signatures in the astral, and then trace them to their source. It had taken them nearly ten years, though once she had the initial astral *shape* of the first object they were seeking, the rest came quickly. Men and women had died, but humankind was born to die, and at least these died with purpose; they had given their blood to fire the ancient objects.

Vyvienne found Saurin in the tower room, sitting in the carved wooden seat, staring out across the village towards the mountains. He was naked save for the red cloak, the Hallow known as the Crimson Coat, and his black eyes were flat and expressionless as he turned to look at her. 'What happened?'

'He's called the sword by name, fired it. It has appeared in the astral.'

The Dark Man stood and spread his arms, gathered the trembling woman into them. 'Why do you fear?'

'Such power, you never felt such power.'

'A fragment of what we will eventually control.'

'But we cannot proceed without the sword . . .'

He slapped her quickly, casually, huge hands cracking her head from side to side. 'That is for me to decide.' Holding her at arm's length, he began unbuttoning her coat. 'But it is true that a new urgency must enter our work. We must seek out the next Hallowed artefact.'

CHAPTER THIRTY-NINE

Detective Tony Fowler walked away from the burnt-out wreckage of the car, a dirty handkerchief pressed to his mouth. The underground carpark was still thick with smoke and Fowler's face was smudged, black spots on the starched white collar of his shirt.

Victoria Heath smiled at the handkerchief. 'Didn't think you were squeamish.'

'I'm not. But the smell of petrol makes me throw up. No need to ask what happened here,' he added. 'Someone doused the car and occupant with petrol and tossed a match inside.' He looked sharply at the sergeant and started smiling. 'I've a feeling you're about to make an old man very happy.'

Sergeant Heath smiled. 'The piece of burnt meat is Robert Elliott, aka about a dozen different names. Small-time pimp, dealer, fixer, fence. Owner of a couple of bondage clubs, half a dozen cafés, two peep joints, porno cinema. Occasionally he imported a little coke, some heroin. Definitely small time, but liked to think he was connected. We've been keeping tabs on him on and off over the past couple of years, waiting for the right moment to take him.'

'Someone's already taken him,' Tony Fowler said grimly.

'Mr Elliott swung both ways and liked his sex with a little pain. In general he preferred boys. A lad called Nick Jacobs, commonly referred to as Skinner, possibly because he sported a skinhead haircut, was a long-term boyfriend. Skinner in turn was involved with another skinhead youth called Karl Lang.'

Fowler stopped. The name was familiar.

'Mr Lang was the headless body we took out of Elaine Powys's flat this morning.'

Fowler stared at her, horrified.

'It gets better. Elliott supplied dope to a Lawrence Cloake, aka Larry. Larry managed the porno cinema and did odd jobs for his boss.'

'Larry was the body in the train,' Fowler suggested.

'The same.'

'Jesus Christ – what is going on here?'

'And just so as I make your day complete,' Victoria Heath added, 'I got a message from McCall at the morgue. The two bodies, Lang and Cloake have melted. Advanced state of putrefaction he said was the technical term. Melted was what he meant.'

They stood and watched in silence as the ambulance crew removed what remained of Robert Elliott from the car. Victoria gritted her teeth when they started scraping the driver's seat with the blade of a knife; she didn't even want to think about what they were scraping off. The surprisingly small plastic bag was loaded on to the stretcher and wheeled through the crowd of police and forensics. None of them gave it a second glance.

Fowler and Heath fell into step behind the ambulance crew. 'Matthews is the key, you know that.'

Sergeant Heath nodded. 'What about Elaine Powys? Is she dead?'

Tony Fowler shook his head. 'I'm inclined to think not. Matthews likes to leave his bodies lying around. I think if she was dead Miss Powys would have turned up. Did you get me the list of her friends?'

'Mostly nurses from the hospital,' the sergeant said passing across the single sheet of paper. 'I talked to all of them, except this woman here, who's away for a few days.'

'Would Elaine know that?' Fowler asked sharply.

'Undoubtedly. The two women are very close; the nurses in the hospital said that Elaine usually feeds the cats.' She stopped suddenly. 'You don't think . . .'

'It's a straw. It's all I've got to clutch at.'

CHAPTER FORTY

Greg lowered the sword, suddenly feeling foolish. He thought he could still hear the echoes of his voice ringing in the flat, and his arm was trembling with the effort of holding the sword high, even though it didn't weigh much.

Elaine was staring at him solemnly, green eyes wide and staring, then suddenly she smiled. 'You look like an idiot.'

'I feel like an idiot.'

'What did you expect: thunder, lightning?' she smiled.

'Yes. No. Something like that. I don't know. It just seemed like the right thing to do.'

The hunting horns were louder, sharper, clearer.

'I think we should warn some of the people on this list,' he said abruptly. He tapped the address book with the sword, flakes of rust rattling on to the page. Elaine gently blew them off. 'Let us assume that there is some truth in what your aunt says . . .'

'Said,' Elaine corrected him.

'Said,' Greg murmured. 'It's got to be more than coincidence that some of the names on this list have turned up dead.'

'They were old people,' Elaine reminded him. 'Old people die.'

'They were into their sixties, as far as I can see. That is not old. Also, they didn't die of natural causes.
~~e~~ articles Judith cut out pointed to unusual

deaths.' Spreading out the scrapbook, diary and address book on the floor, he tapped each in turn with the sword. 'Judith Walker spent some time during the war with these people. There she – and they – were entrusted with these Hallows, whatever they are. Now someone is killing each of the Hallow Keepers to gain possession of the objects.' He glanced up at Elaine. 'Do you agree?'

'It certainly looks that way,' she muttered. She rubbed her hand across the back of the diary, rust flakes smearing like blood on the dusty surface. 'But why are they brutalized, killed in such a bizarre manner?'

'I don't know.' He tapped the address book with the broken end of the sword. 'I wonder how many of these people are still alive?'

Elaine reached for the phone, lifting it off the small coffee table. Picking up the address book, she opened it at the first name and address. 'There's an easy way to find out.'

Ninety minutes and twenty-two phone calls later, Elaine replaced the phone and looked into Greg's troubled face. 'Not counting Aunt Judith, six are dead – one of them natural causes – and four are missing. By missing, I mean I cannot trace them, and no one knows where they've gone. One old man is in hospital; I spoke to his nephew however, but the only name on the list I actually got to speak to, a woman, lives not too far from here.'

Greg jumped up. 'We should go there immediately.'

Elaine looked up. 'And what?'

'We'll tell her what we know.'

'You're mad!'

'If she's a Hallow Keeper, then we're telling her nothing new. If she's not, then she'll probably think we're nothing more than disturbed kids.'

Elaine climbed to her feet and pushed strands of red hair off her face. Wrapping her arms tightly around her body, she looked at the white-faced young man. 'You believe all this don't you?'

He took a deep breath before answering. 'I don't want to . . . but yes, I do. Don't you?'

'I'm not sure.' She smiled at him. 'Are we in danger?'

Greg returned her smile. 'I think we're in terrible danger.'

Elaine's smile broadened. 'You didn't have to tell me the truth.'

Elaine was buttoning up a borrowed denim shirt when Greg burst into the bedroom. The look on his face stilled her protest. 'Police have just pulled up in front of the building.'

Brushing past Greg, Elaine crossed to the window and looked down. 'Where?' she demanded.

'The blue car; it's an unmarked police car. I spoke to the two officers, a man and a woman, in hospital. They turned up again outside Judith's house. We've got to get out of here now.' Greg turned back to the room and began shoving Judith Walker's papers back into the bag. When he picked up the sword, rust flaked off it, revealing a hint of bright metal beneath. With no time to examine it, he shoved it into the bag.

Elaine cracked open the door and stepped out on to the narrow landing. Voices echoed up from below, and she heard her friend's name being mentioned, and a man's voice asking for the number of the flat. 'We're trapped,' she hissed. 'There's no way past.'

Greg pushed her out on to the landing. 'Upstairs,' he whispered. 'Quickly.'

They hurried to the end of the corridor and then crouched on the stairs leading to the third floor, praying none of the doors on the next floor would open.

Soft footsteps hurried up the stairs, and a man and a blonde-haired woman appeared and stopped outside the flat. Greg put his mouth close to Elaine's ear, his voice moist against her flesh. 'Detective Fowler, and the woman is Sergeant Heath, I think.'

They watched as the man produced a key and carefully inserted it into the lock. Then, holding the key in both hands, he turned it with infinite care, ensuring that it made no sound. The detective then eased the door open, and the couple stepped inside.

'Now!' Greg hissed. Catching hold of Elaine's hand, he pulled her down the stairs and they crept past the door. They could hear voices from inside, the woman speaking. 'The bed's been slept in, and there's two sets of dirty dishes. The teapot's still warm.'

'Let's go. They can't have got far.'

Greg's eyes widened in alarm as he looked desperately around . . . and then Elaine pulled the door shut and turned the key in the lock. By the time they reached the hall door, the police officers were pounding on the door, and other doors to flats were opening one by one, heads appearing.

Tony Fowler hammered on the door, rattling it in its frame, knowing instantly what had happened.

'Inspector!' Victoria Heath called. She was standing by the window, pointing down to the street.

In his report, Detective Fowler wrote that he saw Greg Matthews holding Elaine Powys tightly by the arm, pulling her down the street. He added that the side of Elaine Powys's face was cut and bruised and looked as if she had been punched.

What the detective didn't add was that at one point, Greg Matthews had turned and looked back up at the window where the officers were framed against the light, and smiled mockingly. Then he savagely jerked the terrified girl away. In that instant, Tony Fowler decided that Mr Matthews might have a very serious accident before he was taken into custody.

'What now?' Elaine demanded as they rounded the corner. 'We'll have every policeman in the country after us.'

'After *me*; you're just an innocent victim.' Greg shook his head desperately. 'I don't know what to do.' He reached into the bag to adjust the sword which was protruding over the top, then hissed as a tiny spark of static electricity leapt from the metal to his fingertips. And suddenly he felt confident. Straightening, he pointed down the road. 'First we'll buy a change of clothes for both of us. The cop in the flat saw us, knows how we're dressed.' He ran his fingers through his hair. 'And I'll get a haircut. Then we'll go to the Hallow Keeper, Brigid Davis, warn her, talk to her, maybe she'll know something that could help.'

'Let's hope we're not too late,' Elaine muttered.

CHAPTER FORTY-ONE

Someone – *something* – had awoken him.

This was always the hardest part, the time when the memories returned, flooding into him like water into a vessel. Coming to his feet, he nudged the empty paper-wrapped wine bottle at his feet and shuffled away. Well . . . maybe not water into a vessel. Wine had always been his failing.

He was . . . *he was* . . . names whirled through his head, and he stopped suddenly in the middle of the busy street, trying to focus on the letters, attempting to work them into a shape and pattern, to make a word. But the words wouldn't come and he wandered on, moving aimlessly, content to allow his instincts to control his actions, the same instincts that had taken him into so much trouble . . . and usually out of it again.

Shifting his focus, he looked around him, trying to determine where he was. The buildings were strange, identical, characterless. There were no obvious land-marks to guide him.

He looked at the faces of the people whirling by him, seeming to move so fast. So many races, white to black and all shades in between, so many costumes and dresses. He looked down at his own body, grimacing when he discovered that it was dressed in foul rags, the oversized shoes on his feet held together with twine, a cord around his waist, holding up two pairs of trousers. He rubbed the back of his hand against his face. It tangled in whiskers, rasping, and he could actually feel the vermin crawl through his hair and beneath his clothing.

Dear gods, how had he ended up like this?

He wandered on, stopping to stare at himself in a shop window, then slowly raised and lowered his arms, to ensure that the image he was seeing was, in truth, himself. He was foul; a vagabond, filthy, degenerate, even evil looking, the patch over his left eye crusted with filth.

He was . . .

Almost. He almost had a name, an identity. He was unconcerned. He knew that the names and places and everything else would come, and while he needed the knowledge, he also knew on an instinctive level that the knowledge would bring pain. And his aged and tired body recoiled from pain; there had been so much pain in his life. So much pain, so many deaths . . .

Deaths.

There had been a death.

Was it a death that had awoken him?

Images flickered at the corners of his vision, and then with appalling swiftness the people and place around him faded, becoming insubstantial, the landscape grey, speckling with tiny winking lights. And now the demons gathered, shadow shapes with crimson eyes and snarling beast-like faces. He blinked, and the images faded, leaving him shaken and trembling. He never doubted that the beasts were real.

Something had called him . . . something powerful, something ancient.

Digging into his voluminous greatcoat pockets he pulled out a small bottle of vodka. Snapping off the red cap, he raised it to his mouth, felt the fiery liquor brush his lips, a tiny trickle of sour liquid ease past his cracked lips and down his throat, burning all the way to his stomach, but cleansing the sourness from his mouth. He shuddered and pulled the bottle away from his mouth and screwed the cap back on.

The world faded again, and now he was watching letters tumbling, falling, making shapes and sounds and words. Some of them he understood.

Ambrose.

Hallows.

Keepers.

CHAPTER FORTY-TWO

In his time, Skinner had tried both male and female lovers and always seemed to end up with a male. It had taken him a long time to admit that he was gay, it was a difficult and confusing process and so, when he discovered that he was attracted to women also, he became hopelessly confused. Then he met Robert Elliott; Elliott too was attracted to men and women, but Elliott had liked his sex spiced with pain and domination. So the small man had taken the impressionable sixteen-year-old youth and shaped him, first introducing him to the shadowy world of bondage and pain, then beginning to teach him to enjoy the heightened sensations that pain brought, and the infinite pleasure of inflicting pain. And Skinner, in turn, had gone on to teach others, become master to their slave, just as he had been slave to Elliott, the master. But Elliott was gone now. And for the first time in his life, since he had run away from a brutal father and uncaring mother, and come to London, Skinner was free.

He had stood before the car and watched the small man twist and writhe in agony, mouth open, leaking smoke, eyes running molten down his face, blue flames licking from his ears. He still couldn't understand why Elliott simply hadn't opened the door and jumped out . . . if he had, Skinner had been ready for him. The voice on the phone had told him that there were to be no marks on the body, no visible injuries. Elliott had taught him how to do that, how and where to strike and inflict pain, but leave no mark. He had brought along a nylon stocking filled with sand; a blow to the temple would render Elliott unconscious, and the fire would burn away the bruised flesh. But in the end, he didn't need to use the cosh. And watching Elliott burn had aroused him.

Now he lay on the filthy mattress and watched the woman moving in the bathroom, the flash of naked skin in the light arousing him again.

He couldn't remember how or where he'd picked her up. He had the vague idea that he'd gone to one of the clubs afterwards, drinking to take the taste of petrol and the stench of overdone meat and burnt rubber from his mouth. He didn't remember coming back to the flat – though that wasn't too unusual. Pushing up on the mattress, he laced his fingers behind the back of his head and watched the bathroom door, wondering if the woman was any good, wondering if he'd remembered to take precautions, realizing that if he'd been too drunk to remember where he picked her up, he'd been too drunk to remember to wear anything.

The woman stepped out of the bathroom, and flicked off the light before he had a chance to see her clearly. It took his eyes a few moments to adjust to the gloom. The curtains were long rectangles of light; obviously it was late in the morning, but this morning he was his own boss, in charge of his own destiny, he had nowhere to go, no errands to run, nothing to do. Except the woman, he leered.

The woman moved around to stand before the curtains, a naked silhouette against the light, turning slowly, allowing him to see her profile, her high forehead, straight nose, long neck, proud breasts tipped with hard nipples, flat belly, with the faintest hint of curls at its base, long thighs. She tilted her head back and long hair cascaded down her back to the small of her spine.

Skinner grinned. He knew now why he'd chosen this woman: long hair. He had always been attracted to men and women with long hair. Sometimes, when he thought of his mother, he remembered that she'd had long hair; he couldn't remember her face any more, but he remembered the hair.

Crouching low, the woman moved slowly, sensuously across the floor, then dropped to her knees at the foot of the mattress and crawled towards him. Grinning, he threw back the single sheet to greet her. Pressing her breasts against his feet, she slithered up him, deliberately shifting her body to allow her hard nipples to brush against his thighs, his groin, across his belly, his chest. He was reaching for her when she reared up, pressing her breasts against his face, her nipples against his lips.

And the phone rang.

And Skinner woke up.

He was sitting up on the mattress, his naked back against the flaking wall, arms behind his head, elbows aching, pins and needles tingling in his forearms . . . and incredibly aroused. Moving his arms was agony; he must have fallen asleep in this position. When he allowed his arms to drop into his lap, sensation flooded back, setting his muscles trembling and cramping. The pain was incredible . . . and enjoyable.

The phone continued ringing.

Skinner rolled off the mattress, wrapped the sheet

around himself, and padded barefoot out into the hall. The insistent ringing was setting his teeth on edge, beginning to pulse in time with the headache that was gathering behind his eyes. He snatched the phone off the hook, hearing the static howl of a long distance call. 'Yes?'

'Were you enjoying the dream, Mr Jacobs?'

Skinner stared at the phone, recognizing the voice. Elliott's employer, the man who had given him Elliott's address.

'She is a particularly accomplished lover, you will enjoy her in the flesh, Skinner, I promise you. And her hair – like silk. She can arouse a man in a hundred ways, she can give you such pleasure with that hair.' There was a long pause, while Skinner tried to make sense out of what he was hearing. Was the man suggesting that he knew what Skinner had been dreaming about? 'You should know, Skinner, that there is very little I do not know about you. Now the late unlamented Mr Elliott also knew this, but he chose to ignore it. There is nothing you can do, nowhere you can go to escape me. And do you know why, Skinner? Because you must sleep, and while you sleep you dream, and no one can run from their dreams.' There was another pause, and then a rasping chuckle. 'Now why don't you wake up . . .'

The phone rang.

And Skinner woke up.

He was sitting up on the mattress, his naked back against the flaking wall, arms behind his head, elbows aching, pins and needles tingling in his forearms. Suddenly nauseated: confused, his heart hammering madly, he scrambled off the mattress, groaning aloud as his cramping arms protested. Naked, he darted out into the hallway and snatched up the phone. Static howled on the line.

'So you see, Skinner,' the male voice said, continuing the conversation he had begun in the dream. 'I don't want you making the same mistakes that Mr Elliott did. You cannot run, you cannot hide from me. However, obey me and I will reward you well. Now, here's what I want you to do . . .'

Vyvienne opened her eyes and smiled at the Dark Man. 'The poor boy is dreadfully confused. He's still standing by the phone, wondering if this is a dream also, waiting to wake up.' The smile faded. 'Why are you using him?'

'He is a useful tool. And he knows Elliott's methods, he knows what we require, he's done this work before . . . it does not *disturb* him. But when we're finished you can have him. He's young, strong, and has learned to enjoy pain. You could toy with him for a long time.'

The grey-eyed woman sat up on the bed, and started twisting her thick black hair into a simple braid. 'You should know that the astral is in turmoil. Matthews calling with the sword has unleashed all manner of shadows on to the plane. I have felt peculiar . . . echoes.'

'Are we in danger here?'

'Not yet. But with so many of the Hallows around us, I'm sure even a tiny leakage of their power must be trickling through to the astral. Sooner or later some *thing* will come to investigate.'

'They will come too late,' he said confidently. He suddenly leaned forward and cupped the woman's small face in his large hands. 'Do not doubt me now . . .'

'I don't . . .'

'We have ten of the Hallows. We know Matthews has one and the woman Brigid Davis has another. And we will have the location of the final Hallow within the day. However, I'm unsure we want the sword . . .'

Vyvienne tried to shake her head, but the hand clutching her jaw squeezed tightly. 'I'm sure. We should have them all . . .'

'Matthews has tainted the sword feeding it unsanctified blood,' he snapped. 'And with Judith Walker dead, we cannot fire it clean again.' He spun away in disgust, and stood before the arched windows, arms folded, staring out towards the mountains.

Vyvienne opened a cardboard folder on the bedside locker and shook out a picture of Elaine Powys. The picture had been taken at a Christmas party the previous year, and the woman's cheeks were flushed, her forehead gleaming with sweat. The camera had painted her eyes red. Vyvienne could find nothing remarkable about the face. Lifting the picture of Gregory Matthews which Elliott's men had stolen from the Matthews home, she looked into his dark eyes, noting the weak jaw and nervous wrinkles around the eyes and mouth. A man who smiled his way out of trouble. It was ludicrous that they were opposed by this pair. 'Matthews is now with the woman, Elaine Powys, Judith Walker's nearest blood relative,' Vyvienne suggested softly, an idea forming at the back of her mind.

The Dark Man turned to look at her.

'Matthews is the sword-wielder now. He does not know it. He has no idea of the forces he has unleashed.

But if he were to slay the Hallow Keeper . . .' she suggested.

The Dark Man smiled. 'An unsanctified sword-wielder slaying a Hallow Keeper,' he said softly. 'What would that do to the sword?'

'Make it powerful indeed.'

'Do it!'

The woman spread her arms. 'I will need energy; you must feed me your power.'

CHAPTER FORTY-THREE

'I've been expecting you.'

The tiny woman opened the door wider and stepped back. Greg and Elaine looked at one another blankly. They had rehearsed their opening conversation with Brigid Davis, trying to devise a gambit that would get them past the door without the old woman calling the police. But the door had been opened on the first ring, the woman smiling as if she knew them.

Brigid Davis lived in one of the faceless tower blocks that had been built on the fringes of the city in the sixties and early seventies. Greg and Elaine had spent the best part of an hour wandering around the apartment blocks, trying to trace the old woman; all the spray-painted blocks had names – Victory House, Trafalgar House, Agincourt House – but Judith Walker had not recorded the name of Brigid's building in her address book. Most of the letter boxes in the sour-smelling hallways were hanging open, and Greg suspected that the few closed boxes had been glued shut. No one seemed to know the woman, nor did they know the address, or if they did, they certainly weren't going to give it to a shaven-headed youth with the intense stare and a red-haired young woman with the bruised and bandaged face. One person did ask what had happened and she told him she'd gone through a windscreen; it was close enough to the truth. They had been on the verge of quitting when they had spoken to an aged West Indian woman who had directed them to a flat on the top floor of Waterloo House. 'An architect with a sense of humour,' Greg muttered as they climbed the eight floors to the top of the building. 'Probably never came back to look at the building he designed.'

'I've been expecting you,' Brigid Davis repeated, closing the door behind them, then ramming home two bolts and sliding a heavy chain into place. Catching hold of the couple's arms, linking them both, she manoeuvred them down the narrow hallway and into the small sitting-room.

'Please sit, sit. Oh, don't look so surprised,' she smiled at their expressions as they eased into the over-stuffed settee. She sat down opposite them on a scarred rocking chair. When she sat back into it, her feet didn't quite touch the ground, making her look almost child-like.

In her youth, Brigid Davis must have been spectacularly beautiful, Greg decided. Although he knew she was a contemporary of Judith Walker's and therefore into her sixties, her skin was smooth and unlined, almost alabaster-white in its clarity. Her sparkling blue eyes were wide set and her teeth strong and white. Yellow-white hair was pulled straight back off her face, knotted into a thick rope that hung along her spine. She was dressed in a simple black dress, unrelieved of any colour, and she wore no jewellery.

'Mrs Davis . . .' Elaine began.

'Miss,' the old woman corrected gently. 'You are Elaine Powys, dear Judith's niece. I was saddened to learn of her death.'

'You know?' Elaine was surprised.

Brigid nodded.

'I didn't realize it had been on the news,' the young woman said.

'Perhaps it was, but I didn't hear it. And you are Gregory Matthews.' The old woman turned to look at him, and he was suddenly conscious of her intense scrutiny. 'I did hear about *you* on the news,' she added with a wry smile. 'The police seem very eager to interview you.'

'A misunderstanding . . .' Greg began, but the old woman raised a hand, silencing him.

'You need make no explanations to me.' Folding her hands in her lap, she concentrated on them for a few moments, and when she looked up again, her eyes were magnified by unshed tears. 'You were coming here to warn me about the deaths of the other Keepers. I've known about those deaths for a while now.'

'You have!' Elaine whispered. 'Why didn't you tell the police?' she demanded.

'I'm not sure the police would consider my sources reliable,' Brigid said softly.

'What are your sources?' Greg asked.

'Tea?'

Elaine and Greg looked at her. 'I beg your pardon?'

'Tea?' she asked again. 'Would you like some tea? Of course you would,' she said, standing up. 'I'll make us some tea, and then we'll talk. I'll answer your questions then.' She hurried out into the kitchen and moments later water thundered into a kettle.

'Is she mad?' Greg whispered.

Elaine shook her head. 'I don't know. I don't think so.'

'I'm not mad,' Brigid said, popping her head around

the door, 'though I can understand how you would think so.'

Greg opened his mouth to reply, but Elaine pressed her hands to his lips, silencing him. She stood and crossed to a small table below the window where a dozen framed photographs were laid out. Some were of Brigid herself: in a ball gown, graduation robe, bridesmaid's dress, others were of small children – nieces, nephews? – but one at the back was a faded sepia photograph of a group of children.

'The Hallow Keepers,' Brigid said returning with a laden tray. Greg stood to take it from her and she smiled her thanks. 'Your aunt is there; second from the left, middle row. I'm standing in front of her.'

'You haven't changed much,' Elaine smiled.

'It's sweet of you to say so. That photograph was taken more than fifty years ago.' Lifting the photograph from Elaine's hands, she tilted it towards the light. 'That was the last time we were all together. Do you know,' she said suddenly, 'there are only three of us alive now. Barbara Bennett and Don Close . . . and I'm not sure how much longer poor Babs and Don can last,' she added enigmatically, still staring at the photograph, her index fingers moving across the faces. She glanced sidelong at Elaine and Greg. 'He has them, you see. And every day he tortures them to get them to reveal the location of their Hallows. They haven't yet, but they will, it's only a matter of time.' The old woman smiled again, and this time Greg realized that she was quite mad, quietly and dangerously mad.

'Are you saying that two people are being held prisoner?' Elaine asked cautiously, unsure if she had heard correctly.

'Yes.' Brigid Davis sat down and began pouring tea.

Greg sat down opposite her. 'Why haven't you told the police?' he asked.

'And what am I to tell the police?' she asked gently. 'Two people are being held prisoner, I don't know where they are nor do I know who has them. I simply *know*. What do you think the police will do about that?'

'You obviously know a lot more about what's going on than we do; what can you tell us?' Greg asked.

Brigid smiled brilliantly. 'Enough to terrify you. Enough to convince you that I am truly quietly and dangerously mad,' she smiled again, her eyes locked on his face.

'You're playing with us!' Greg snapped. 'For Christ's sake if you know something that could help us, tell us, please. Right now, the police are convinced that I've killed two men, probably butchered my entire family and kidnapped Elaine. I'm locked in some sort of living nightmare and you're playing mind-reading tricks!'

'Milk, sugar?'

'Oh for Christ's sake!'

'Language!' Brigid snapped. 'Thou shalt not take the name of the Lord, thy God, in vain.'

'I'm sorry,' he mumbled. 'I didn't mean to offend . . .'

'You didn't offend . . . it is simply that there is a power in names, and it is foolish to call upon them unnecessarily.' She waited until they were both sipping the scalding tea, before speaking. 'It is difficult to know where to begin and we have so little time left. I could begin fifty years ago when thirteen children were drawn from all parts of this island to the tiny village of Madoc, almost in sight of the Welsh border. I could begin four hundred years ago, when the first Elizabeth ruled England, or I could begin it five hundred years before that, when history and mythology met . . . or I could begin it nearly two thousand years ago when the Hallows were first brought to the land that would one day be called England.'

'Yeshu'a,' Greg breathed.

Brigid hissed, teacup falling to shatter on the floor. 'What do you know of Yeshu'a?'

'I dreamt . . .'

'Yeshu'a was a man, blond, blue eyes . . .' she suggested.

Greg shook his head. 'I dreamt of a boy, dark-haired, dark eyes . . .'

Brigid Davis smiled thinly. 'So you did dream of the boy.' She suddenly reached out. 'Give me your hand.'

Glancing sidelong at Elaine, Greg put down the cup and stretched out his hand. The old woman caught his hand in both of hers, finger-nails digging into his flesh. 'Who are you?' she whispered.

'I'm Gr . . .' The grip tightened painfully on his hand, silencing him.

'Who are you?'

The sound of a hunting horn, hounds belling . . .

The boy Yeshu'a turning, looking at him, dark eyes lost in shadow, thin lips twisted in a smile . . .

An old man turning, looking at him, half his face washed in the light of a setting sun, the other half in shadow . . .

A powerful warrior, mail clad, turning, looking at him, blood on his face, a broken sword in his hand . . .

Judith Walker's face, bloody and broken . . . The small man with the evil eyes . . . the skinhead with the leering smile. Elaine's face. Brigid's.

'So . . .' the old woman murmured, releasing his hands.

Greg blinked, the images fading. He felt sick to his stomach, a dull headache throbbing behind his eyes, a sour taste in his mouth. Elaine reached over and squeezed his arm, and he could actually feel the warmth flowing from her touch into his flesh, moving through his body, easing across his chest, settling into his stomach. He exhaled explosively, abruptly realizing that he had been holding his breath. When he brought the teacup to his lips, his hands were trembling so badly he could barely hold it.

Elaine broke the long silence that followed. 'Why don't you begin with the Hallows,' she said.

CHAPTER FORTY-FOUR

Skinner eased the battered van into the kerb and turned off the ignition. Draping both hands across the steering wheel, he stared at the blocks of flats, mirrored shades reflecting the grey towers. The voice on the phone had given him precise instructions, and there had been the unspoken threat if he failed. But he wasn't going to fail. Reaching under the seat, he pulled out the double-barrelled shotgun, the sawn-off barrels only a few inches in length. He had only ever used it once before, when he'd been sent out to frighten a client who owed Elliott money. Skinner was supposed to fire a shot into the ground and frighten him. Unused to the shotgun and the spread of the pellets, he had fired too close to the terrified man and blown most of his foot off. Skinner's lips twisted in a sour smile as he remembered; the client had paid up, Elliott had made the collection in hospital.

The skinhead shook his head and pushed his glasses up on to his forehead. When he thought back on his association with Elliott, he realized that he must have been mad. He did Elliott's dirty work, and all he got in return were crumbs and a lot of grief. Well, this was his big chance now, he was working in the big league, and although his new employers were terrifying and vaguely threatening, there was also the far more solid promise of a reward. If he did this job right, there would be more. Maybe in a year, two at the most, he could really be someone, money in his pocket, a car, a flat, people to do *his* dirty work. He nodded sharply, the sunglasses sliding on to his nose; that's what he wanted. In a year or two he would be someone.

Three blocks from the left. Waterloo House, eight floors up. The woman's name was Brigid Davis. When he had secured her, he was to make a telephone call – the number was written on the back of his hand – and he would receive further instructions. Tucking the shotgun under his long coat, he climbed out of the van, locked it and walked away.

Detective Tony Fowler was the first through the shattered door, moving quickly through the flat, even though he already knew that it was empty. Too many years breaking down doors.

Sergeant Heath padded silently beside him, a long-bodied torch held tightly in both hands. Behind her the hallway was filling with police.

'He's not here,' Fowler muttered.

'How do you know?' Victoria asked.

'What would you do if someone kicked in your door?'

'Start screaming.'

'And if you had something to hide, or a guilty conscience?'

'Make a run for it . . . or flush the evidence down the loo.'

'And what do you hear?'

'Nothing.'

Nick Jacobs – aka Skinner – lived in the top floor flat over an adult cinema on the fringes of Soho. The entire building stank of damp and the sweeter stink of mould, and the disinfectant used in the cinema below percolated into the flat. Amid the squalor of scattered clothes, fast-food cartons, crumpled beer cans, the wide-screen stereo television and matching stereo video were out of place. Alongside the filthy mattress that Skinner obviously used for a bed, an impressive sound system had been set up, massive speakers in the centre of the room, facing inwards towards the bed.

'I'll bet he liked to play them loud,' Sergeant Heath muttered, nudging the dozens of CDs and plastic cases scattered across the floor with her foot. 'A Grateful Dead fan,' she added.

'Is that a joke?' Fowler snapped. He turned to the six officers spread out around the room. 'Take this place apart. Bag everything. And if you find anything interesting . . .' He left the sentence unfinished.

Victoria Heath wandered around the flat. They had just come from Elliott's sumptuous place in Bayswater, and the contrast between the two was startling. Elliott had everything. The flat was decorated in the best of taste, was spotlessly clean, everything meticulously in place. And yet his lover lived in a pigsty. The only thing they both had in common was expensive sound and television systems.

Standing in the hallway, leaning on the banisters, she wondered where Skinner was. Was he dead; had Matthews killed him? And how had Matthews – who had never been in trouble with the law before – got involved with this crowd. They had no evidence that Matthews even knew these people, and yet two days ago he had butchered his entire family, and had then been involved in the deaths of at least another two people, possibly two more and the kidnapping of Elaine Powys. Where was he now and was the girl still alive?

There was a phone at the bottom of the stairs and she walked down to it. There were dozens of names and numbers scrawled on the wall behind them, but one address stood out. It had been scribbled in black marker on to the wall above the phone, overwriting most of the other names and numbers. She tilted her head to read it. 'Brigid Davis, Flat 812, Floor Eight, Waterloo House, Hounslow.' When she ran her finger across the writing, the fresh ink smeared.

'Tony! I think we've got something.'

CHAPTER FORTY-FIVE

'There is much I cannot tell you,' Brigid Davis said quietly, 'simply because I don't know,' she added quickly, watching the expression on Greg's face. She raised both hands. 'Let me speak, and then you can ask your questions.'

Elaine squeezed Greg's arm, stilling his protests. 'Let her speak,' she said softly.

'Thank you.' Brigid Davis took a deep breath, then turned her head to look through the window, across an irregular patchwork skyline, towards the west. 'Fifty-something years ago, at the height of the war, children were evacuated out of the major cities and sent to towns and villages in the country. Even today, I'm not sure how we were picked, or who chose our destinations. I ended up in a village called Madoc, on the borders of England and Wales. There were other children there, twelve others, boys and girls of around my own age, from all parts of the country. For all of us, I think, it was our first time away from home, and although I know our parents must have been terribly upset, we thought it was a grand adventure.' The old woman smiled, blinking quickly. 'It was a lovely time, and I can say now with complete honesty, that it was one of the happiest times of my life. The village was beautiful, the people were kind, the weather that summer was glorious, I had new friends . . . and we had the *secret*.' The old woman turned to look at Greg. 'That was the summer we were given the

Hallows.' She nodded towards the bag at Greg's feet. 'You've got Judith's with you. I can feel it. The Sword of . . . well, let's just call it the sword, shall we: there is a magic in names.'

Almost unconsciously Greg reached into the bag and pulled out the newspaper-wrapped sword. More of the rust had fallen off, hints of silver metal amidst the oxidization, the sword shape a little more distinct.

Brigid stretched out her hand towards the sword, then drew her fingers back as if they had been burned. 'It is strong, powerful: has it fed?'

'Fed?'

'Has it tasted blood?' she demanded.

'I used it to kill two men.'

The old woman's breath escaped in a long hiss and the fingers of her left hand moved in a complicated pattern which ended with the hand closed tightly into a fist, index and little fingers extended, thumb crossed over the folded fingers.

'You were telling us about the Hallows,' Elaine said quickly. 'In the village of Madoc, during the war . . . you were given the Hallows.'

Brigid's eyes slowly lost their glassy look. 'Yes. Yes, we were given the Hallows. An old man came to the village. He was a tramp and he'd been coming to the village for as long as anyone could remember; he was called Mr Ambrose. He would sharpen knives, mend pots and pans, help out on the farms, tell fortunes in the evening.

'All the children loved him. I suppose we all wanted to be like him. This was a different age, remember, when tramps were looked upon as somehow noble, gentlemen of the road we called them. They had a dignity that you don't often see in modern-day vagrants.

'He lived in a cave in the forest on the edge of the village. Over the years he had added wooden shelves and a makeshift bed of sorts and the local children would dare each other to creep in and lie on the bed.

'The cave fascinated us townies.

'Because we were all strangers to the village we tended to stick together, though in normal circumstances, we would never have mixed. We were from all classes and backgrounds, and in those days that simply did not happen. Naturally, we all went out to look at the cave.

'And that's where we met Ambrose.' Brigid Davis fell silent, remembering her first encounter with the one-eyed tramp. When she spoke again, her voice was soft, distant.

'I think we all realized the moment we set eyes on him that we had known him before. Impossible, of course. But we knew him. And he knew us. He called each of us by name, knew our ages, even knew where we were from. It should have been terrifying, but even now, fifty years later, I can remember that he felt so safe.' Brigid took a deep shuddering breath. 'In the weeks that followed we got to know him very well; soon we all – though none of us realized it at the time – started dreaming about him. Strange, curious dreams in which he would be sitting surrounded by mirrors, talking, talking, talking. But his words were incomprehensible, the sounds strange and garbled. Wild dreams. It was only when we discovered that the others were also experiencing the same dream that we started to suspect that something very strange was happening.

'We took to gathering outside his cave in the late afternoons. Golden afternoons with the sun slanting in through the trees, and the air still and heavy, rich with forest smells. It is something I have never forgotten . . . though nowadays the woods terrify me,' she added with a smile.

'Ambrose started telling us stories, rich, magical tales of legend and folklore. And once, he told us about the Hallows. The Thirteen Treasures of Britain. A week later he produced the artefacts themselves.' Brigid fell silent.

'What happened, Brigid?' Elaine asked softly.

The old woman smiled. 'I'm not sure. That day is confused in my memory, though many of the others have remained vividly clear. I do recall that the day was heavy with thunder, the air moist and electric, it had rained the previous day, torrential rain that had turned the forest tracks to muddy quagmires, making them impassable, and we were confined to our various homes. That night it clouded over early. These were the days before television, so we were sent to bed . . .'

'You keep saying we,' Greg interrupted. 'Who is we?'

'All of us.' Brigid smiled. 'I'm telling you what happened to me . . . but it was happening to the other twelve at the same time. We were all dreaming the same dreams, thinking the same thoughts, doing the one thing.'

'What happened?' Elaine asked.

'We awoke about midnight filled with the compulsion to go to Ambrose.' Brigid laughed shakily. 'What a sight we must have been: thirteen naked children moving through the empty streets and back lanes and then down the muddy forest tracks.

'Ambrose was waiting for us. He was wearing a long grey gown, belted around the middle with a white knotted cord, a hood thrown over his head. He was standing before a moss-covered tree stump which was piled high with lots of strange artefacts. One by one we stepped forward . . . and he would reach around, without looking, and press one or other of the items into our hands, and whisper its name into our ears. Then we would step back and the next person would come forward . . .'

Elaine stared at the old woman, suddenly remembering the pieces she'd read from Judith's diary:

We were in the middle of the wood . . . gathered in a semicircle around Ambrose. On the tree stump were lots of strange objects. Cups, plates, knives, a chessboard, a beautiful cloak. One by one we were walking up to Ambrose and he was giving each of us one of the beautiful objects off the tree stump . . .

She suddenly realized that Brigid was staring at her. 'What's wrong my dear?'

She shook her head. 'My aunt described the events you're talking about, but she wrote that they were a dream.'

'At first it was a dream: every night for ten days, the same dream, the same sequence of events, and Ambrose would whisper the same words. On the eleventh night it came true, and by that time of course, we were word perfect in the ritual.' She gave a gentle shrug. 'I think the dreams were sent by Ambrose to prepare us for what was to come.'

'It wasn't a dream?' Greg asked.

Silently Brigid pointed to the sword in his hand, then, reaching into her pocket she pulled out a curved hunting horn of old, yellowed ivory, capped with wrought gold: inlaid with intricate patterns in stone. 'This is the Horn of B ∴ . . R . . . A . . . N,' she spelled out. 'I dare not say its name. And no, it wasn't a dream.' Holding the horn in a white-knuckled grip, she took a deep sobbing breath. 'When it came to my turn, I stepped up to the one-eyed old man and he pressed this into my hand. And when he said its name I knew – I suddenly knew – everything about this object . . . and indeed all the other Hallows. I knew what they were, where they came from and, more importantly, their function.

'I'm not sure how the others reacted to their gifts. It was something we never spoke about. I got the impression that some of the others simply didn't believe – or didn't want to believe – what Ambrose had told them. When the war ended, we all went our separate ways, and we were all, in minor ways, successful. Some, those who believed in the Hallows, instinctively understood their power, were more successful than the others. But that had little to do with us; that was the residual power of the Hallows working through us.'

'Did you ever meet up with any of the others?' Elaine asked.

'No. We were under strict instructions that we were not to meet with one another. Ambrose was insistent that the Hallows must never be brought together.'

'Why?' Greg asked. He thought he could feel the sword becoming warm in his grip, and he knew instinctively that it was the proximity of the Horn of Bran.

Brigid's smile was icy. 'Too dangerous. There are

thirteen Hallows. Individually, they are powerful. Together, they are devastating. They must never be brought together.'

'This Ambrose had brought them together,' Greg said quickly.

'Ambrose was powerful; he was the Guardian of the Hallows, he could control them.'

Elaine leaned forward, hands locked tightly together. 'You said you knew the function of the Hallows. What was it?'

Brigid's smile was cold, distant. 'I'm not sure I should tell you.'

'Why not?' Greg demanded.

'When Ambrose gave me the Hallow, he opened my mind to the ancient mysteries. I came from a deeply-religious background and what I learned that night shocked me to the core, making me doubt everything I had learned from childhood. I have spent my entire life in pursuit of religious knowledge, looking for some sort of answers. But the more I learn, the more I discover that I do not know.' Her smile twisted. 'I know that in the last few years your aunt also delved into the area of arcane lore and folklore, seeking answers in the past.'

Elaine shook her head. 'You're not making sense.'

'Tell us what the Hallows do?' Greg insisted.

'They are wards, protections, powerful barriers. They were put in place to contain ... .' She stopped and sighed. 'I cannot. It is far too dangerous. You are unprotected. Even the knowledge renders you vulnerable.'

'Tell me ...' Greg surged to his feet, the sword clutched before him, towering over the tiny woman rocking in the chair. He suddenly stopped, his breathing ragged, heart hammering, aware that Elaine was shouting at him, pulling at his arm.

Brigid reached out and touched his hand, and he felt the sudden red rage flow away, leaving him weak and trembling. Shaken, he sank back into the chair. 'You see the danger of the Hallows,' she murmured. 'You are not a man prone to anger . . . and yet see what it did to you? if you hold on to the sword, in another few days it will control you . . . and the paradox . . . the paradox is that you will enjoy it. That is what happened to some of the Hallow Keepers. They began enjoying the power . . . and the power corrupted them.'

'I'm not a Hallow Keeper,' Greg said sullenly.

'No,' Brigid agreed, 'but you are much more, I think.'

'What?' Greg demanded belligerently. Brigid smiled and shrugged her shoulders. 'The sword belongs to Elaine,' he continued. 'Judith asked me to take it to her.'

'Then give it to her,' Brigid suggested.

Greg turned to the young woman sitting beside him, abruptly alarmed by the idea of giving away the rusted piece of metal. He tried to lift his right hand, the hand holding the sword, but he found he couldn't lift it. A vice closed around his chest, squeezing the air from his lungs, acid burning in his stomach.

'You see?' the old woman smiled. 'You see the hold it has on you?'

Greg slumped back into the chair bathed in sweat, muscles trembling. 'What can I do?'

'Absolutely nothing.'

CHAPTER FORTY-SIX

Skinner climbed the stairs slowly, heart hammering, lungs burning. He hadn't realized he was so out of condition and the lift wasn't working. He never liked lifts anyway, it wasn't that he was claustrophobic, but he remembered a story he'd read as a child about a man who gets into a lift, presses 'down' ... and it carries him straight to hell, and all the floors he passes are highlights in his life. He'd been ten years old when he read that story, and it had brought him awake night after night screaming in terror ... and then his father would come in, reeking of sour drink, with the leather belt in his hand ...

As the skinhead climbed up through the building, he thought that living in a place like this must be a living hell. Identical flats, identical lives, no jobs, little money, identical grim futures. At least he had a future. Technically, he was unemployed, and he collected his unemployment benefit, but Elliott had always made sure he had more than enough in his pocket. Skinner's grin faded. With Elliott gone who was going to run the clubs, the cinema; who was going to pay him? His new employers had said that he would be well rewarded, but they hadn't mentioned money. On the way over here he'd filled up the van with petrol; usually Elliott would pick up the tab for that, but this time it had come out of his own pocket. He had twenty-two pounds in cash at the moment, but what was he going to do when that ran out?

Skinner stopped at the eighth floor, breathing heavily, leaning against the greasy wall. His heart was tripping madly and he had the feeling that he was going to throw up. Breathing in great gulps of the sour urine and cabbage-tainted air, he tried to work out where he was going to put his hands on some cash. Elliott must have had money put by, but he had no idea where or even how much and he knew no one who'd lend him any. He looked at the door at the end of the hall and wondered how much the old woman had in the flat. Old people didn't trust banks; they always kept their savings with them. And then abruptly he wondered how much his employers would pay him for this hunting horn they wanted. If they wanted it that badly – and they obviously did – then they would pay.

'Thinking back on it now, I realize that Ambrose told us remarkably little about the Hallows.' Brigid Davis stood before the window and stared out across the rooftops. 'Much of what I discovered I found out through my own researches. Individually, they appear again and again in one guise or another in English history, the property of kings and queens, or those closest to them. They are linked with all the great figures of legend, and they turn up, directly or indirectly, at all the great crisis points. Their last appearance was during the dark days of the war,' she added. 'The Hallows have been used – and abused – down through the centuries and in turn I think that they have used and shaped the Keepers to their own ends.'

Elaine smiled tentatively. 'You make it sound as if they are alive.'

Brigid turned from the window, her face in shadow. 'They are sentient,' she said simply. 'I believe they form a symbiotic relationship with the Keeper. They become rather like an addictive drug; you cannot bear to be parted from it.' She smiled at Greg. 'As you've discovered.'

'But I'm not the Keeper,' he said desperately.

'But you fed the sword,' she said simply. 'You are linked to it. Since you've come in here, you've not let it out of your hands.'

Greg looked at the sword in his rust-stained hands. He hadn't realized he'd been holding it.

'Someone is collecting the Hallows,' Brigid continued, turning back to the window. 'Sometimes, at the very edge of sleep, I think I see him: a tall, dark man, powerfully built and occasionally there is an image of a woman, beautiful, deadly, her hair blowing around her like a cape ... but I'm not sure if these are true seeings or just a dream. I'm inclined to think that they are shadows of real people. I don't know who these people are or why they are collecting the Hallows, but they are powerful ... they must be to control the energies of the collected Hallows. They are firing them, bringing them to magical life by bathing them in the blood and pain of the Keepers, channelling the dark emotional energy of pain and fear into the individual Hallow.'

'But why?' Elaine asked. 'Surely you have some idea?'

Brigid nodded. 'Yes, I have thought of a reason ... possibly the only reason someone would want – need – all the Hallows. But it is so abominable as to be incomprehensible.'

'Tell us,' Greg said softly.

'Why don't *you* tell us?' Brigid suggested.

'Me!'

'The sword is at the heart of the legend.' The old woman's voice dropped to a sibilant whisper. 'Look at it, feel it, listen to it . . . listen to it Greg.'

Greg attempted a smile – the old woman was mad – but the sword was suddenly a leaden weight and he had to grip it in both hands. His whole body shuddered, muscles twitching, the vibration working down through his arms into his wrists, The sword jerked in his hands, flakes of rust sliding off, revealing more of the sword-shape beneath, and he was suddenly able to see what it must have looked like when it was whole and complete.

An armoured man bearing down on him, leaf-shaped sword held high over his head in mailed fists, sunlight running molten off the metal. He blocked the first blow, but the force of it drove him to his knees, the second shattered his sword, the third clove through his helm . . .

The flat swam into sharp focus and then faded again.

The sword, whole and complete, was in his hands, gore dripping from its blade. He was standing on a dyke, while below him a wild-haired, wild-bearded warrior wielding a chipped battle-axe was scrambling up the dyke. He took the warrior's head from his shoulders . . . and never felt the pike that erupted through his chest . . .

Brigid's words were incomprehensible now, just sounds that pulsed in time to the trembling that shuddered through his body.

A warrior, in the armour of the Iron Legionaries struggled to pull out his pitiful short sword. He was dead before the gladius cleared the sheath. The sword smashed into another's throat, severing his head from his body, slashing away the standard, the eagle and the pennant bearing the legion's number − XII − fluttering into the mud . . .

The vibrations shook off the last of the blood-red rust, revealing its true shape.

Mist swirled, moisture beading on the metal, and then the creature appeared, jaws gaping, talons flashing, yellow eyes blazing in the grey light. And the boy Yeshu'a lifted the sword and pointed it at the creature.

'What are they?' Yeshu'a's voice was calm.

Josea placed a hand on his nephew's shoulder, taking comfort from the young man's almost unnatural calm. 'Demonkind,' he said simply, 'the local people call them Fomor.'

Yeshu'a watched the creatures swarm on the beach, angular misshapen figures moving through the early morning mist. They were taller than men, but green-grey and scaled like the crocodil from the Dark Southlands, with the same long tooth-filled jaws. Unlike the blank-eyed crocodil, the eyes of these creatures burned with cold intelligence. Appearing out of the morning mist, they had fallen upon the merchants and mariners and simple townspeople waiting on the beach, butchered them in sight of the approaching ships, killing some instantly, playing with others until their screams became too terrible and the sailors pressed wax into their ears. The Fomor had feasted. And now they waited on the beach, moving restlessly to and fro, waiting for the boats to land.

The young man allowed his consciousness to soar,

travelling across the waves to hover over the carnage on the beach, and then slowly – tentatively – settled into the minds of one of the creatures . . . only to spin away, revolted by the brief images. '*Fomor*,' he agreed. 'Demonkind.' The boy shuddered. 'Spawn of the Night Hag and the Shining One, the Fallen Spirit.'

'They hold this land in thrall,' Josea said quietly, forcing himself to keep his hand on his nephew's shoulder, willing himself to say the words calmly, quietly, even though he knew that no boy – no ordinary boy – should know the legend of the creation of the demon-breed. But Yeshu'a was no ordinary boy.

'When the First of Men spurned the Night Hag and cast her out into the Wilderness, she mated with the Fallen One who had also been cast from the Garden. In time, she brought forth the race known as demons.' The boy's eyes were blank and unseeing, his face an expressionless mask. When Josea looked at him, he had a glimpse of the stern face of the man the boy would become . . . and found that it frightened him.

'Once they ruled the world,' Yeshu'a said softly, 'until the coming of man. And then they were forced out, into the mountains and the marshes and the barren places. Sometimes they remained, or bred with the humans and created other abominations, eaters of flesh, drinkers of blood. Over the centuries they have been pushed out of all civilized lands, and that is why they have ended up here, at the edge of the world. This is their domain, this is the Realm of Demons. Let us leave it to them. This is an island; in time they will squeeze the life out of it, and perish.'

Greg.

Josea squeezed his nephew's arm. 'There are people here, good people. Are we simply to abandon them to the Demonkind? And what happens when the Demonkind find a way to leave this island and strike out across the mainland into the lands around the Middle Sea?'

Yeshu'a nodded. 'You are correct of course, uncle. What would you have me do?' he asked simply.

'Can we destroy the beasts?'

Greg.

'We can kill those who exist in this world. But they will return again and again unless we can seal the door to their world.'

'How?' the Master Mariner demanded.

The boy turned to look at him. 'Why would you do this, uncle?' he asked. 'These people are nothing to you, neither blood kin nor bonded.'

'If I was cold and ruthless,' as you are, he silently added, 'then I would tell you that I am simply protecting my investment. If we do not stop these creatures now, then sooner or later, when they are stronger, much stronger, they would come south, and destroy everything I have spent my life building. But I am neither cold nor ruthless, and all I can tell you is that the Lord, my God, told me to love my neighbour as one of my own.'

Greg.

'And yet there is much that your Lord tells you that will contradict what you have just said,' the boy said quickly.

Josea nodded, but said nothing. He knew better than to argue points of philosophy or religion with the boy. Several summers past he had been found, following a frantic search, arguing with the Elders in the Temple.

'Every creature must be destroyed, none must be allowed to remain alive. Then we must trace them to their lair and close the doors between the worlds . . .'

Greg.

Greg opened his eyes, and found he was looking into the cavernous barrels of a shotgun.

CHAPTER FORTY-SEVEN

This was the oldest of all magics, the simplest, the most powerful. When male and female joined together in the ultimate union, the forces, the energies generated could be focused, controlled, shaped.

Vyvienne was the vessel, the conduit through which the power would be channelled. The Dark Man would feed her his power. Lying flat on his back, the woman sat astride him, moving in a gentle rhythm, while his lips and tongue and fingers worked expertly at her body, arousing her coldly, deliberately, without passion. When he saw the flush creep across her breasts, felt the hardness of her nipples beneath the palms of his hands, he knew she was close, and he closed his eyes to concentrate on the ritual that would focus his power. Greg Matthews' face appeared before him, sharp and clear, and for an instant, it was not the woman Vyvienne atop him, but Matthews, his naked flesh sweat soaked.

Vyvienne's fingers bit into his shoulders, the signal that it was time.

The woman opened her eyes. The photograph of Matthews had been taped above the bed, and she was looking directly at it. Pressing both hands against the wall, supporting herself on rigid arms, she stared into the face and imagined it was Matthews beneath her. She felt her orgasm building deep in the pit of her stomach, felt it trembling in the Dark Man's legs and stomach muscles.

Vyvienne allowed the images to come quickly then: Matthews and Elaine . . . naked in a field of tall, waving grass, making love, he moving atop the woman, hands squeezing her breasts . . . and then his hands slid up along her throat, across her face, into her hair, into the long grass beyond. The woman transformed, her face and body twisting into that of a demon. Greg's scream was soundless as he reared up, the broken sword clutched in both hands, truncated blade pointing downwards . . . and the sword was falling, the broken blade biting into the demon's throat, blood spurting upwards, hissing where it touched the metal sword, splashing on to his body, coating him in red, and his orgasm was flooding through him as she twisted and writhed in death . . .

The Dark Man exploded into her as her own orgasm shuddered through her. They clutched one another, quivering, until the spasms passed. When they were quiet again, the Dark Man ran his large hands through her hair. 'Well?' he whispered.

'It is done,' she murmured, 'the seed is planted. He will kill her with the sword,' she said and fell asleep, still locked around his body.

CHAPTER FORTY-EIGHT

Skinner rested the shotgun on the bridge of Greg's nose, the rough-cut metal harsh and rasping. 'So we finally meet, Matthews. This is one really pleasant surprise.'

Greg blinked at him, confused, lost. Where had the skinhead come from? He tried to turn his head to look at Elaine and Brigid, but the weight of the gun on his face made movement impossible. Fragments of his dreams whirled and spun, images of the demons' snarling faces settling on to the skinhead's, the two becoming one.

Skinner thumbed back the hammers on the shotgun, the noise bringing him back to the present. 'I should blow your fucking head off right now!' he hissed.

'What do you want?' Elaine demanded loudly.

Skinner turned, and the weight of the gun lifted from Greg's face as he pointed the short-barrelled weapon at the girl. 'You shut the fuck up. I haven't come for you this time.' His twisted smile turned into a leer. 'You're just the icing on the cake.'

'What do you want?' Brigid repeated Elaine's question.

'Shut up.' Skinner backed into the centre of the room, holding the shotgun close to his chest, watching the trio, suddenly unsure. Getting into the flat had been childishly easy. He had simply knocked on the door and when the old woman had called out, 'who is it,' he had replied, 'parcel for Brigid Davis.' When she had opened the door he had put the shotgun into her face and walked in. Discovering Powys and Matthews had been a pleasant bonus. The girl had been shocked to see him, but Matthews had been staring straight ahead, mumbling softly, filthy hands wrapped around a dirty piece of metal. Skinner had seen that blank-eyed, loose-lipped look before; he hadn't realized Matthews was a junkie.

But right now he had an opportunity to get in with his new employers, big time. They couldn't fail to be impressed with this haul. He pointed the shotgun at Brigid. 'Where's the phone?'

'In the kitchen.'

'Get it.'

Brigid stood and moved carefully past the wild-eyed young man, her eyes on his face, watching the tension in the muscles of his jaw and neck. She could see the dark delight dancing in his eyes and knew he was enjoying this, knew he took pleasure in pain. She lifted the phone off the wall in the kitchen and carried it as far as it would go into the sitting-room, then placed it on a small sideboard. 'It won't go any further.'

The skinhead gestured her back to the chair with the gun. Then, checking a scrawl of numbers on the back of his left hand, he lifted the phone and dialled slowly and carefully. It rang twelve times before it was picked up, the line clicking and popping.

'Hello?' Skinner said.

There was silence at the other end of the line.

'It's me, Ski . . .'

'I know who it is.' The voice was chill, arrogant.

'I've got the woman . . .' he paused, savouring the moment. 'And a little bonus. Matth . . .'

'No names!' the voice snapped.

'The male and female you were looking for are here also.'

There was a long silence. 'You have done very well, very well. I am pleased.' There was another pause. 'Would you be able to take the three of them from the flat without being seen? Answer truthfully. This is no time for arrogance.'

Skinner turned to look at the trio sitting on the couch facing him. An old woman, a terrified female and a drugged male. 'It would be possible . . .' he said cautiously. 'Possibly later, under cover of darkness. I could bring in some help . . .'

'No help. You must do this yourself, or not at all. Be realistic. Could you manage the three of them?'

'Probably not,' Skinner admitted.

'Could you manage the two women?'

'Yes,' he said confidently.

'Then take care of the other. Bring the two women back to your flat. You will receive further instructions there. The old woman has the hunting horn, the younger, a broken sword. It is imperative that they bring along both objects.' There was a click and the line went dead before he could ask any more questions.

Skinner replaced the phone on the cradle. 'Seems only the women are needed.' He pointed the shotgun at Greg. 'You're superfluous.'

Greg looked at him blankly. The youth's features were still wavering, caught between their human face and the demon skull. He turned his head slightly, the walls of the flat were shifting, dissolving, white cliffs gleaming in the distance and he could smell the tart salt of the sea.

'What the fuck is he on!' Skinner snapped.

Elaine shook her head. 'Nothing. He's . . . not well. Hasn't been since the death of his family.'

The skinhead's thin lips curled. He nodded very slowly. 'I remember them,' he whispered. 'We took them before your aunt. I enjoyed his sisters and his mother. I'd never done it with an older woman before . . . of course, I tried it again with your aunt,' he added.

Elaine's scream tore her throat as she lunged for the skinhead's eyes, fingers curled. Her attack caught him off guard and he hesitated a moment too long before using the shotgun – he'd been told to bring her in alive – and then she was before him, nails raking his face, tearing the skin of his cheeks, pulling at the corner of his eye. Swinging the shotgun around, he hit her in the stomach with the stock, the force of the blow dropping her to her knees. Towering above her he gripped the shotgun in both hands, prepared to bring the stock down on her shoulder. He hadn't been told to bring her in in one piece.

The sound shocked him motionless.

It vibrated up through the floor, thrummed through the air, solid, insistent and terrible. There was such pain in the sound, raw endless despair overlain with unendurable agony. The sound went on and on, terrible, terrifying, calling for release, for ease.

Pressing both hands to his ears he staggered away from the crouching girl, and then realized that the old woman was holding a curious object to her lips. It was shaped like a ram's horn, yellowed with age, one end encircled with a golden band. For a moment he didn't realize what it was, until he saw her cheeks swell and then the sound increased. With a tremendous effort he lifted the gun.

Somewhere, the distant call of a hunting horn, somewhere the faintest clash of metal off metal, the song of the sword.

The sound of the horn.

Calling.

Greg opened his eyes, saw the demon before him, Elaine at his feet. The creature's bestial face was twisted in pain, ropy saliva drooping from gaping jaws.

The scene shifted. Greg was in a forest and the horn was sounding again and he could hear the distant belling of the hounds ... only now he knew they weren't hounds, they were Fomor, approaching fast through the trees, falling on all fours to scurry through the undergrowth. Putting his back against a tree, he drew the sword.

Skinner felt the pain behind his eyes and suddenly there was hot moisture on his lips. Salt and sweet, he knew the taste of blood. Then there was an icy penetrating coldness in his ears, and they both popped, and he heard a rushing, roaring sound, and warm sticky liquid trickled down the side of his neck. The pain was intense; he felt as if his head was about to explode. Pointing the gun at the woman, he squeezed the trigger.

Clutching her bruised stomach, Elaine was looking at the skinhead when Brigid blew the hunting horn. She heard a distant, almost ethereal sound, high and thin and sweet. She saw the look of agony on the youth's face and guessed that he was hearing something far different. Twisting her head, she saw Greg's face twist with fear, eyes wide and unseeing, turning as if he heard something. Then suddenly he straightened and gripped the broken sword in both hands . . . and froze.

A hot splash of moisture on her hand made Elaine look up. Blood was pumping from the skinhead's nose and then dark, sluggish blood trickled from his lips. His lips drew back from his teeth in a howl of agony as he raised the gun and fired, both barrels blazing.

And in the silence that followed, Greg Matthews stepped forward and calmly drove the broken sword through the youth's chest.

CHAPTER FORTY-NINE

Ambrose stopped in the middle of the street, the sound of a hunting horn ringing in his ears, memories whirling, echoes and images dancing before his eyes and then he almost doubled over as the agony lanced into his chest. He squeezed his eyes shut, tears of pain trickling down his lined cheeks, as the fire burned through him, now moving down to his stomach in a ragged tear, as if a blade were slicing through his flesh. He pressed both hands to his stomach, and for an instant imagined he could feel the warm wetness of the wound, the gaping hole where his flesh had been torn. When he opened his eyes, he could actually see the ghostly image of the sword protruding from his stomach, the ragged wound cut from his chest to his navel.

Dyrnwyn.

The sword was Dyrnwyn, once the Sword of Rhydderch, now the broken sword.

Echoes of the hunting horn.

The Horn was Bran.

And he was Ambrose.

And with the name came the memories, and with the memories, the pain.

'Shots fired in the vicinity of Waterloo House, Hounslow. All cars in the vicinity . . .'

Victoria Heath glanced at Tony Fowler as she leaned over to raise the volume. The senior detective's face was set in a rigid mask, and he refused even to acknowledge the radio report.

'All cars in the vicinity . . .'

Sergeant Heath lifted the radio. 'Mobile Four responding.'

'Location, Mobile Four?'

The sergeant took a deep breath. 'Directly outside Waterloo House.'

'Say again, Mobile Four.'

'You heard me first time.'

Elaine cradled the dying woman's head in her lap. Brigid Davis had taken the full force of both barrels in the chest and stomach, shredding most of the flesh, glints of bloody bone peeping through the wounds. A smattering of pellets had bitten into the soft flesh of her neck and face. Elaine examined the wounds coldly, professionally, and knew that there was little that could be done for the woman. By rights she should be dead; only her will and determination kept her spirit clinging to her body. Her eyes flickered, then bubbles of frothing blood formed on her lips. 'Is he dead?'

'Yes,' Elaine said softly. Against her will she turned her head to see Greg still standing motionless over Skinner's eviscerated corpse. Thick ropes of blood dripped from the broken sword adding length, giving it the appearance of wholeness. 'Yes, he's dead,' she whispered. 'Greg killed him.'

Brigid's ice-cold hands found hers, pressing the ancient hunting horn, the yellow ivory now splashed with her blood, into them. 'Into your hands I commend it,' she breathed.

Elaine bent her head, pulling her hair off her

ear as she brought it close to the old woman's face.

'Madoc,' Brigid whispered. 'Madoc. That's where it started. That's where it ends.' She was trembling now, and Elaine's fingers could barely find a pulse.

Vyvienne reared upright, pulling herself off the Dark Man's body, damp flesh parting stickily. 'What is it?' he hissed.

'The Horn of Bran has sounded.' Closing her eyes, tilting her head to one side, she listened, but all she could hear now were the faintest echoes of the hunting horn.

The Dark Man sat up, his broad back to the wall and watched the woman carefully. 'Find Skinner.' Placing both hands on her naked shoulders, he poured strength into her. 'Find Skinner.'

Vyvienne's eyes rolled back in her head . . .

. . . And she opened them again on the astral. She had walked this grey shadowy landscape since she was a child, not knowing then that her talent was remarkable and unusual. She had learned early on how to interpret the colours that danced in the greyness, knew which colours to avoid, or those places from the world below which sent dark echoes into the astral, usually ancient sites, old battlefields, certain graves, which were capable of catching and holding a spirit, like an insect against fly paper. She knew Skinner's colour and shape – the abstract criteria by which she identified him in the astral world. She knew Skinner better than anyone else; she had seen inside his soul, watched his dreams. He was a petty soul, dark and angry, soured by much bitterness and resentment. Willing herself to his spirit, she rose over the astral landscape, and then fell towards the countless pinpricks of light that were London.

The sounds of the horn were audible now, faint trembling echoes of the magical sound that had only recently soared across the greyness. Vyvienne found herself following the receding sounds, tracing them to their source. In the dreamstate, she dropped into the flat . . .

Greg stood over the body of the demon. In death the creature seemed diminished, its scales softer now, the sulphurous yellow of its eyes lighter, its savage rows of teeth retreating into its mouth. Its features melted, twisted, subtly altered and became almost – but not quite – human. And then Greg felt a sour bitter wind across his sweat-damp face, a heartbeat later he smelt it, tasted it on his tongue . . . and then another demon stepped into the room, materializing out of thin air. With a howl, Greg leaped at it.

Elaine watched in horror as Greg cut at the empty air, the broken sword slashing a picture from the wall, the metal leaving a long groove in the embossed wallpaper. 'Talk to him,' Brigid mumbled, 'call him by name, bring him back before the sword subsumes him.'

'Greg . . .' Elaine whispered. 'Greg . . .'

Vyvienne jerked awake with a shriek, her eyes wild and staring, heart hammering wildly. She suddenly scrambled off the Dark Man and raced into the bathroom where she leaned over the toilet expecting at any moment to be sick, stomach roiling, bile flooding her mouth. When nothing happened, she straightened and turned to lean on the washhand basin and stared into the mirror, shocked at her exhausted appearance.

The Dark Man filled the doorway. 'What happened?' he asked softly, his Welsh accent, which he took so much pains to hide, obvious now.

'Skinner is dead, his soul fed to the sword. The sword-wielder killed him . . . and he saw me.' She turned to look at the Dark Man. 'He saw me, struck out at me! How is that possible?' she asked. 'I've looked at his aura; he is nothing special. And yet he wields the sword . . .' She shook her head at the paradox.

'Skinner dead. And Davis?'

'Dead or dying. Skinner had shot her.' She had briefly glimpsed the undulating grey-black envelope around the woman's head as her spirit prepared to leave her body,

'The horn?'

'In the girl's hands.'

The Dark Man swore, using an oath that was five thousand years old. 'So they now have the sword *and* the horn.' He was unable to hide the tremor in his voice.

'Oh Christ!' Victoria Heath stopped in the doorway, pulled out her radio and called for an ambulance, although she knew instinctively that the old woman lying on the floor was beyond help.

Tony Fowler moved quickly through the flat, ensuring that it was empty before he returned to Skinner's corpse. He nudged it with his foot, though he knew that the skinhead could not possibly have survived the massive wound to his chest and stomach. 'Matthews' handiwork again; though I can't say this one causes me too much grief.'

'What happened here?' the sergeant asked. She was kneeling in front of the old woman, her fingers desperately searching for a pulse.

Tony glanced from Skinner to Brigid Davis. 'Looks as if Matthews shot the old woman, and then cut up Skinner.'

'Why?'

'Who knows?' he breathed tiredly.

'Skinner could have shot the woman . . .' she suggested.

'He could, but it's unlikely. He'd have no reason to and I'd lay money that Skinner has never met her before today.'

'Then what was he doing here?'

'How do I know?'

'How do you know it was Matthews; how do we know he was even here?' she asked.

Fowler bit back a sharp retort. 'How many maniacs do we have running around London cutting people open with a sword?' he asked mildly.

Victoria Heath nodded. 'And where is he now? These bodies are minutes old. Any sign of Elaine Powys?'

'None. But she was here.' He pointed to the three teacups lying on the floor with the toe of his shoe. 'Our friend Matthews is getting attached to her.'

'At least she's still alive.'

'I'm not so sure that's a good thing.' He turned to look out of the window. The sky was deepening towards twilight, lights appearing in some of the shaded tower blocks. Clouds boiled on the horizon, made darker, more ominous by the setting sun behind them. 'He's going to kill her, sooner or later, he's going to use the sword on her,' he said without turning around, and Victoria wasn't sure if he was talking to her or not. 'All we can do is wait.'

'Maybe we can find some connection between the women he's killed that will give us some clue . . .'

Fowler turned to look at the sergeant and she fell silent. 'We're only waiting for him to kill again.'

CHAPTER FIFTY

Today was . . . today was Thursday, the 29th of July. Was it only two days ago his family had been butchered? Had so much happened in that short space of time? Events of the last two days shifted and flowed, images and impressions, fragments of sentences, snapshot scenes, bits of dreams – or were they memories? – sliding together to become a confused jumble where he found it almost impossible to distinguish the reality from the fantasy. On a casual, almost unconscious level, he was aware that he was sitting on an underground platform with Elaine holding tightly on to his arm, fingers digging into his flesh. He was also aware of the bag on his lap, the weight of the sword in it.

Greg's last clear thoughts and images were of standing before his home on Tuesday afternoon, then pushing open the door and stepping into the gloom. After that everything had dissolved into a terrible unending dream.

'Greg?'

He turned his head to look at the young woman sitting beside him: was she real or another dream, was she likely to turn into a slavering demon, was she . . .

'Greg?'

She looked real, forehead shining with sweat, red hair plastered close to her skull, a graze on her cheek, her bottom lip bruised where she had bitten into it. He lifted a hand and squeezed her forearm; it felt real enough, the material of her denim shirt rough beneath his fingers. And she smelt real: a mixture of sweat and stale perfume, fear and the faintest hint of blood and gunpowder.

'Greg?' There were tears in her eyes now, magnifying them hugely, enormous green pebbles.

'Are you real?' he asked, his voice sounding lost and distant.

'Oh Greg . . .' Her fingers dug into his flesh, squeezing as hard as she could. 'Does that feel real?' She pinched the soft web of flesh between thumb and forefinger, her nails leaving half-moons in his skin. 'Does that feel real?' Then she leaned forward and kissed him gently on the lips. 'Does that?'

A train thundered into the station, stale, metallic air billowing around them, disgorging passengers in a brief and noisy frenzy. Neither Greg nor Elaine moved. When the train pulled out of the station a few moments later, there was a brief lull when the platform was empty and silent.

'Yes,' Greg said, into the silence, 'it seems real.' There were tears on his face now, though he seemed unaware of them. 'I thought it was a dream. I hoped it was a dream, a nightmare I was going to wake up from . . . but I'm never going to wake from this, am I?'

Elaine stared at him, saying nothing.

'I was hoping I was in hospital,' he said with a shaky laugh. He frowned. 'I *was* in hospital . . . I think, or was that a dream too?'

'You were in hospital.'

He nodded. The faces of his family, bloody and torn, with dead, staring eyes, started forming. 'I kept hoping I was going to wake up and discover that it had all been a dream, and I'd find my family standing around the bed. But I didn't.' He reached into the bag and touched the cold metal of the sword. 'And it's because of this sword.' Warmth flooded through him, tingling up from where his fingers rested on the rusted metal, doubts and fears dissolving in that moment, scattering the faces.

'What do you want to do, Greg?'

Lying atop Elaine in a field of grass, the sword held high in his hands . . .

The metal of the sword beneath his questing fingers felt soft and flesh-like. 'I was going to give myself up to the police, remember?' He glanced sidelong at the young woman. 'Should I do that now? It would end all this madness.'

Elaine looked away, staring deep into the tunnel, knowing how she would answer, knowing that Greg knew it too. 'I'm not sure it would,' she said quietly. 'The madness would continue . . . more elderly men and women would die for these curious objects.'

'But at least the police would know what's happening . . .' Greg protested. 'I could tell them . . .'

'What would you tell them?'

'Everything. About the Hallows and the dreams and . . .' He stopped suddenly.

'The police think you did it,' Elaine reminded him. 'And the only way for you to clear your name is to solve the mystery. Avenge your family and my aunt.'

The sword vibrated softly beneath Greg's touch. He was about to say that they couldn't get involved, the old Greg would have shied away from any involvement. But now he was involved and had been from the moment he met Judith Walker. And lately he had been beginning to think that his involvement predated even that. He was beginning to suspect that the dreams were more than just dreams, that they were hints and clues to the Hallows' true meanings. The cold-eyed face of the boy, Yeshu'a, swam into view. 'I suppose I should have walked away from your aunt when she was being attacked,' he said quietly. 'Maybe if I had done my family would still be alive,' he added, unable to keep the bitterness from his voice.

'But you didn't walk away,' Elaine said firmly. 'You were there when she needed you, and then later, you were at the house which enabled her to give you the sword, and then we were at Brigid Davis's flat when the skinhead turned up.'

'Coincidence,' he said shakily.

'I don't believe in coincidence, that's something I did inherit from my aunt. "Everything for a reason," she used to say. My aunt gave you the sword to give to me . . .' She grinned suddenly. 'Not that I've had a chance to hold it.' She could feel the weight of the Horn of Bran beneath her coat, the metal rim of the hunting horn cold against the flesh of her belly. 'Maybe I wasn't meant to have the sword. Maybe it was yours all along. Maybe I was meant to keep another Hallow.'

Greg started to shake his head, but Elaine pushed on.

'I think we owe it to your family, to my aunt, and to people like Brigid who died to protect these Hallows, to find out what's going on. We have to try and stop it. Maybe that way we can clear your name.'

He nodded tiredly. 'I know.' He took a deep shuddering breath. 'What do we do?'

'I think we should go to Madoc, the village where it

all started . . .' She stopped, seeing the surprised expression on his face. 'What's wrong?'

Greg raised his arm and pointed straight ahead.

Elaine turned her head, expecting to see someone standing behind them. But the platform was empty. 'What . . . ?' she started to say, and then she saw it. Plastered to the wall on the opposite side of the tracks was an enormous poster, the letters spiky and archaic, a bronze border of twisting spirals and curls. It was advertising The First International Celtic Festival of Arts and Culture . . . in Madoc, Wales.

'Coincidence,' Greg whispered.

'Sure.'

CHAPTER FIFTY-ONE

Friday 30 July

There were times when the pain subsided to a degree that would allow Don Close to think. Usually, it was impossible to concentrate on anything other than the excruciating fire at the ends of his arms, where his finger-nails had been torn out. Sometimes he thought that they had broken his fingers too, he could no longer move them, and the skin had swollen and split.

Don had lost track of the time he had spent in this dungeon, but he thought it might have been ten days, though it could easily have been longer, for he suspected that he had been unconscious for much of that time.

He had thought about escape when he'd first woken up in this terrible place, naked and chained to a weeping, foul-smelling wall. The chains were rusty, the links flaking and frayed and he knew that with the shadow of his once great strength he would be able to snap the links. He'd lost much of his physique during the times when the cancer had eaten at his lungs and the therapy had stolen the rest, leaving him a shell of his former self. But he could still dream, and he dreamt of avenging himself on the Dark Man and the cruel-faced woman who accompanied him. He could easily imagine wrapping the heavy chain around the Dark Man's thick neck and squeezing, crushing the larynx, then snapping the spine. The last time he had done that he'd been escaping from a cell in Biafra. Foreign mercenaries received little pity and no mercy and he'd killed four guards without remorse, knowing that if he failed, then he would face torture and a firing squad. Those killings and all the others he had committed, first for his Queen and country, later as a paid mercenary and finally as a security consultant, had all been necessary. He had killed without a second thought, without compunction and he took no pleasure from it. But killing this pair would be a special pleasure. The thought had comforted him in those first few days when the man and woman had done little to him other than humiliate and abuse him, torture him with hunger and thirst, leaving him to stand in his own waste. But the memory of his military service had served him well: he'd once spent a year in a Chinese prison, where he was tortured on an almost daily basis, until Her Majesty's Government had negotiated for his release. On the morning of the fourth day, the dark-featured man had quietly entered the dungeon and, even before Don had come fully awake, had shattered his two big toes with a hammer, and then walked away without a word. Don had screamed his throat bloody.

Later, much later, when the pain had abated, Don had realized that any plans of escaping had been effectively wiped away; any movement with a broken toe would be painful, and with his feet pulped to bloody ruin, now impossible. He was also forced to face the chilling fact that he was a sixty-seven-year-old man in poor health and not the robust thirty-year-old military specialist he had been when the Chinese had worked on him.

And always the questions were the same: 'Where is the Hallow . . . where is the Hallow . . . ?'

Denying that he even knew what they were talking about was pointless. The couple obviously knew that one of the ancient Hallows had been given into his sacred keeping some fifty years previously. He hadn't begged for mercy, hadn't even spoken to the couple, though this had driven them to a frenzy and they had taken out their frustrations on his frail body with clubs and canes. But they hadn't killed him. And he knew instinctively that so long as they did not have the location of the Hallow, they would not kill him. Even now, with his emaciated body covered in cuts and lacerations, he still held out some hope. Surely someone in the street on the outskirts of Cardiff, where he lived, would notice him missing and report it to the police. Deep in his heart, he knew it was a forlorn hope; old Mr Lewis who lived three doors away had been dead in his kitchen for the best part of a week before his body had been found.

Late at night, when the rats grew bolder and he could hear them skittering in the straw and occasionally feel their furred bodies brush against his ankles, Don Close knew he would never leave this place alive. All that was left to him now was to deny them the location of the Hallow for as long as possible. And if he could take the secret of its location with him to the grave, then so much the better.

They had taken him prisoner with surprising ease.

He had answered a knock on the door late in the evening to find a man and woman, well dressed, carrying briefcases, standing on the doorstep. The woman stepped forward, smiled, consulted a clipboard and said, 'You are Don Close?'

He nodded before realizing his mistake, old instincts coming to the fore, but too late. The man raised a gun and pointed it directly at his face. Then the couple had stepped into the hallway without another word. Neither had spoken again and ignored all his questions. When he had threatened to shout, the man had beaten him into semi-consciousness with the butt of the pistol. He'd awoken some time later in the back of a car as it bumped across a bad country road and managed to sit up and look out before the woman slapped him hard across the face, knocking him back down on to the seat. Lying with his face against the warm leather, he'd puzzled over the images he'd briefly glimpsed: purple mountains, the distant lights of a village, and a road sign in a foreign language. The lettering was English, almost familiar. Eastern Europe, perhaps, but there had been no accents on any of the letters. Besides, he knew he should recognize the letters. They were *almost* familiar. He was convinced then that someone from his chequered past had caught up with him; many of his old enemies would have long memories. He awoke some time later, and knew that he'd been looking at a sign in Welsh. He hadn't been in this part of Wales for . . . for more than fifty years. And in that instant he caught a glimmer of the reason he'd been snatched. When the car eventually stopped, a foul-smelling bag was pulled over his head and he'd been dragged across a gravel drive, down stone steps and into a chill room. His clothing had been torn and cut from his body, and then he'd been struck unconscious. When he'd awoken he'd been chained to the wall by his wrists and ankles and there was a thick bar around his neck.

The day after they broke his toes, they asked him

about the Hallow. Maybe they expected a quick answer; maybe they thought that the starvation, humiliation and pain would have weakened him to such a state that he would blurt out the secret without a second thought. They had been wrong, but he suspected that they weren't entirely unsurprised, nor were they displeased. It gave them a reason – if reason they needed – to hurt him. They would do it slowly and take great pleasure from his suffering. In a life spent in military service, he had come to recognize and despise the type: the pain lovers.

The door creaked open, but he resisted the temptation to turn his head and look. He would not give them the satisfaction.

Don caught the hint of perfume – bitter, acrid – before the woman stepped around him, a pitying smile on her thin lips, though her eyes remained cold and unfeeling. 'I am so sorry,' she said quietly.

'For what?' he demanded, trying to put as much authority as he could muster into his voice, but all that came out was a hoarse croak.

'For all this,' she smiled,

'I notice it didn't stop you laying into me.'

'I have to; Saurin would kill me if I didn't.'

Don filed the Dark Man's name away in case he ever got a chance to use it. However, he thought he recognized the scam. This was the honey pot. The couple were playing good cop, bad cop routine; when he'd served in the Military Police in Berlin it was a ploy he'd often used himself. He'd play the bad cop while Marty Arden – poor dead Marty – would play the good cop. He knew the script almost by heart. Next she'd be telling him she wanted to help.

'I want to help you.'

She was terrified of Saurin.

'Saurin frightens me.'

She had no control over him.

'I've no control over him. He's like an animal.'

But if he was to give up the location of the Hallow, she'd be able to help.

'But if you tell me where the Hallow is, then I'll take care of it, make sure he stays away from you.'

'I don't . . . I don't know what you're talking about,' he mumbled through cracked lips.

'Oh Don,' the woman whispered, sounding almost genuinely upset. 'He knows you have the Hallow. He already possesses nine of them. He has put in motion a plan to acquire two more, the Horn and the Sword. The only two outstanding Hallows are the Knife of the Horseman and the Halter of Clyno Eiddyn. You have one and Barbara Bennett has the other.' She smiled as he started at the name. 'You remember Barbara, don't you; she was one of the group of children Ambrose gave the Hallows to fifty years ago. She was a pretty girl with blonde hair tied back in two plaits and you two were inseparable that summer. Barbara is here too . . . in the next cell in fact. I'll try to keep Saurin from working on her, but I don't know how long I can keep him away. And he's worse with the women, much worse.' The woman shook her head and when she raised it, huge tears sparkled in her eyes. If he hadn't known the scam, Don might almost have believed that they were real. 'He's killed all the others,' she went on. 'Sexton and Rifkin, Byrne and Clay, and all the others. He has their Hallows. He's obsessed with them, and he's determined to own them all. If you give yours up, then he won't start on Barbara for a while, and in the meantime, I'll help you escape.'

'How do I know you have Barbara here?' he whispered. 'Let me see her.'

The young woman with the stone-grey eyes raised her head and smiled. 'She's here all right,' she said. 'Listen.'

A blood-curdling scream echoed off the stones, and then a woman began sobbing, the sound piteous, heartbroken.

And Don Close wept then, not for himself but for the woman who had been his first love.

They had always known that Close was going to be the difficult one. A professional soldier, sometime mercenary and criminal, who had served time for armed robbery. In prison he was known as a hard man and had been respected by prisoners and warders alike. Saurin had suspected all along that torture would not be enough, and that they needed to find a key to break him.

Saurin watched the monitor relaying pictures from the hidden camera set high in the wall, black and white images washing over his angular face, then he hit the play button again. Deep in the heart of the machine, digital tape spun reproducing perfect sound. The woman screamed again and again, reproducing the screams she had uttered before she died a month ago.

'Quickly,' the woman insisted, 'give me something so that I can make him stop it. I have to tell him something.'

It was only a knife, nothing more than an ancient sickle-shaped knife, the point snapped off, the edges dulled and rounded. Barbara had been given the miniature version of a horse's halter. He had never used the knife; the last time he'd seen it had been when he'd retired to Cardiff.

The scream that echoed down the corridor died to a dull sobbing.

Was it worth dying for, worth listening to Barbara – little Barbara, with her blonde hair and bright-blue eyes, exactly the colour of the summer sky – being tortured by this evil man. He should have married the girl; maybe his life would have been so different, so much better. Last he'd heard, she married an accountant in Halifax.

Barbara screamed again, and now Don heard a dry rasping chuckle.

'Tell me,' the woman said urgently. 'Tell me. Make him stop.'

Ambrose had said never to reveal the locations of the Hallows. Even now, fifty years later, Don could feel the old man's moist breath on his cheek. '*Individually they are powerful; together they are devastating. Once, they made this land; together they can unmake it.*' Did he believe it? There was a time when he would have said no, but he had fought in some of the most dangerous corners of the world, he had watched African witch-doctors, Chinese magicians, and South American shaman work their various spells. He had once fought alongside an enormous Zulu, the bravest man he had ever seen, fearless in battle, who had taken scores of minor wounds without complaint, but who had curled up and died without a mark because he had been cursed with juju.

'Don . . . ? Tell me!'

Raising his head, he looked at the woman, watching her sparkling eyes, saw her lick her lips in anticipation. 'You say he has the others?'

The woman visibly relaxed.

'Nine of the others. And the other two he will have before the night is out.'

'Swear this to me, Don Close. Swear that you will never reveal the location of the Hallow to any who might demand it. Swear to protect it with your life.'

Don Close had done much in his life that he was not proud of; he had lied, cheated, stolen and killed when it was necessary. He had made many enemies, few friends, but all – friends and foe alike – respected him. And they all knew that one thing held true: Don's word was law.

'Tell me,' the woman demanded as the screaming started again.

'I'll see you in hell first,' he mumbled.

She struck him hard across the face, snapping his head against the stone wall, the iron collar biting deeply into his skin, and then she laughed. 'You'll tell me first . . . and then we'll see about hell.'

CHAPTER FIFTY-TWO

The enormous Imperial Hotel in the heart of Piccadilly was suitably anonymous. Forty pounds had got them a tiny single room at bed and breakfast rates for the night. The room contained a rock-hard narrow bed, a bare wardrobe and a sink. There was no television and the bathroom was at the end of the corridor. Because of its central location the hotel was used to handling hundreds of foreigners a day, mostly tourists, and the girl behind the metal grille didn't even look up as she filled in the registration form for Miss Powers who spoke in a broad Welsh accent.

Greg, who was waiting at the newsagent just inside the hotel's double doors, watched Elaine pick up her plastic key and walk towards the lifts, and then he fell into step beside her. Not looking at one another, they travelled in the crammed and noisy lift to the sixth floor. When the doors opened, they both stepped out, one turning left, the other right, and walked down the corridor until the lift doors had closed, then turned back to room 602.

'We should have taken a room in a boarding house,' Greg muttered, glancing nervously up and down the corridor, watching as Elaine slid the electronic key into the lock.

'So when the police broadcast our descriptions on the news, the landlady can phone in?' Elaine said, stepping into the room and looking around disdainfully. 'Here, we're safe.'

Greg crossed to the window and pushed back curtains that were badly in need of a wash. He was looking across a flat roof studded with air vents towards another wing of the hotel.

Springs protested as Elaine sat carefully on the bed. 'I wonder if they check to see if the single rooms are being used by one person.'

'We're backing on to Soho,' Greg said, 'I'm sure some of the guests must bring women back to the rooms.'

'Well, if we're challenged, I'll claim I brought you back.'

'I'm sure that'll make a change – a woman bringing a man back.'

'I'm sure there's nothing you could tell the porters here that could shock them,' Elaine smiled.

Greg sank on to the bed beside her, placing the bag with the sword on the ground between his feet. Digging in his back pocket, he pulled out a leaflet advertising the Festival of Arts and Culture. 'I picked this up in the newsagent.'

Elaine leaned against his shoulder to read it. 'It doesn't tell us anything new,' she said. 'I've never heard of any of these bands,' she added, looking at the names of the groups. 'Most of them seem to have been named after Irish or Scottish islands, Aran, Skellig, Rockall, Orkney . . . and what's this writing here?'

He was pointing to script that bordered the page. 'Looks like Scots Gaelic. Welsh?'

'Not Welsh,' Elaine said. 'My father's people are from Wales. He sometimes got letters written in Welsh.' She turned the sheet of paper, trying to make out the words. 'Maybe it's some sort of greeting. See

. . . the festival is being held on the Festival of Lughna-sadh . . . the evening of the thirty-first of July, the first of August. Saturday and Sunday.' She nodded, strands of red hair curling over her eyes. 'I'll bet it's some sort of Celtic greeting.'

'You know what Alice would have said?' Greg asked.

Elaine looked at him blankly. 'Alice who?'

'Alice in Wonderland. She would have said . . .'

'. . . curiouser and curiouser,' Elaine finished.

'Yes,' Greg said lamely. 'Lots of coincidences here, you'll notice.'

'Maybe they're not coincidences.'

'That's what I was afraid of. But what about free will?'

Elaine nodded towards the bag on the ground. 'And what about the sword and everything that it represents. What has that got to do with free will?'

'Absolutely nothing,' Greg whispered.

OK, so it was stupid, but he still felt safer carrying the sword than leaving it in the bag. Stuck in the waistband of his trousers, metal cold against his leg, it felt so right, the only danger that it would slip down the leg of his trousers, or snap the waistband, leaving him with his trousers around his ankles.

Greg was smiling as he turned into the bathroom, the smile broadening as he read the sign taped to the wall over the bath. 'Residents are reminded that sleep-ing in the bath is not permitted.' Leaning over the cracked and stained sink, he stared into the spotted mirror. His appearance no longer shocked him, though he was still amazed that he could deteriorate so quickly.

There were a lot more grey and silver hairs now and the shadows beneath his eyes seemed permanent. His cheeks had assumed that uneasy stage between stubble and beard; right now it just looked untidy. Opening the paper bag, he pulled out the few toiletries he had purchased, snapping them out of their plastic and paper wrappings; a comb, razor and shaving foam, toothbrush and toothpaste. He could have done with a change of clothes, but they simply hadn't got the money and were reluctant to use credit cards in case the police had put a trace on the numbers.

Greg rubbed a circle in the mirror with the palm of his hand – suddenly realizing he hadn't brought a towel – then splashed his face with water and squirted some foam into his hand.

He had left Elaine in the room. She had already used the bathroom and was now undressing for bed. She would take the bed, he would sleep in the chair or on the floor, and in the morning they would set out for Madoc in Wales ... though once they got there, he wasn't entirely sure what was going to happen.

He scraped at the hair on his cheek, the overlong bristles catching in the cheap blade, the razor nicking a tiny piece of flesh. Greg hissed in pain and dabbed at the tiny wound, crimson-speckled shaving foam on his fingertips. Droplets of blood spattered the sink.

Blood spattered the white sand.

The boy Yeshu'a watched impassively as the Fomor gnawed on the right hand of one of the merchants it had slain. With every bite, the merchant's fat fingers wriggled, giving it an appearance of ghastly life. There were at least a hundred of the creatures on the beach.

Most of them were feasting off the fallen, though some were simply standing at the water's edge staring intently at the boat. Waiting. And, although he had made a deliberate effort to blank their thoughts, wave upon black wave of emotion washed over him, until their thoughts became his thoughts. They wanted the boat and crew, but not exclusively for food. They wanted transport and a crew to bring them south, to the fabulous centre of the known world, lands of teeming peoples, warm lands, rich lands, not like these cold, northern isles. The boy shuddered, imagining the creatures free in the cities of Italy or Egypt. All that was chaining them to the island was the barrier of salt water.

'Legend has it that they came from the dark north, the Lands of Ice.' Josea stood behind his nephew, watching him intently, aware that a cold energy was shimmering in the air above the boy's dark skin. The salt air tasted metallic and bitter.

'They are not of this world,' the boy said firmly. 'They belong to a place beyond the ken of most of humankind, the Demon Realms, the abode of spirits and raw elemental forces, where they exist as mere words of evil. But a doorway was opened – blood sacrifices and wicker burnings, the energy channelled into circles of evil stones – and these abominations have walked through, the word has been made flesh.' Yeshu'a suddenly turned his head, dark eyes flashing dangerously. 'You knew about these creatures, didn't you. That's why you brought me here.' It was a statement, not a question.

Josea resisted the temptation to step away from the boy's anger. 'These creatures have always been in this land. Once they inhabited the northern portion of this isle, barren highlands of raw stone, where the natives knew them by a score of different names. Lately however they have been moving southwards, and some have crossed into the Isle at the Edge of the World, the place known as Banba.'

Yeshu'a continued staring at him, saying nothing.

Josea raised his head and stared towards the beach. 'Your mother told me that you cast out demons,' he said lowering his voice. 'She says you have the power to command the Demonkind.'

'Why would I have that power?' Yeshu'a asked very softly, and for an instant, Josea saw something else behind the eyes, something ancient and deadly, a creature of awesome power.

'Your mother claims that you are not the son of your father.'

'And who does she say I am?'

'She says you are the son of God.'

'There are many gods.'

'But only one true God.'

'And who do you think I am?' the boy asked.

'I think you are the son of Miriam and Joseph. But your mother has told me that you have cast out demons, and I believe her.' He gestured towards the beach. 'Can you cast these out?'

'No,' the boy said simply, turning away. 'For they are not within anyone . . . they are of the land and are part of it.'

'Could you not scourge them from the land?'

Yeshu'a leaned on the wooden rails and stared towards the shore. And one by one the Demonkind straightened and looked towards him, serpents' tails hissing on the sand and stones, forked tongues flickering. One, younger than the rest, suddenly darted into the shallows, talons raised. The boy watched impassively as the salt water washed over its hooves, the white foam frothing bloody, sending it screeching back on to the beach where it lay twitching, white bone showing through the smoking skin. Several of the Fomor fell upon it, ripping it apart with teeth and claws.

'The natives claim that they mate with human women, and there are tales of half-breed abominations,' Josea said quietly. He was watching the boy intently, saw the way his knuckles whitened around the rail, the set of his shoulders. Abruptly he realized that there was such anger in him, such a terrible rage, kept tightly in control, but there, bubbling beneath the surface.

'I could send them back to their own realm,' Yeshu'a said suddenly, 'but I would need to remain here, to keep the gates closed. And I cannot stay here, for my work lies elsewhere.' He dipped his head and Josea got the impression that the boy was talking to someone. And when he raised his head, his dark eyes were sparkling. 'But I could banish them and create keys to keep the door to their world shut.' He turned quickly, eyes falling on the bundle of trade objects under the leather tarpaulin. 'I will create thirteen keys, hallowed with a power older than this planet . . .'

Pain in his leg brought Greg awake with a yelp. Where the sword touched the bare flesh of his leg the skin was burning. He jerked the broken sword free, aware of the heat radiating from the blade, the gentle thrumming in the metal.

The sound of a hunting horn, loud, insistent, metallic, the sound cut short.

'Elaine!'

Greg pulled the bathroom door open and darted out into the corridor ... and the demon reared in front of him, claws raised. Greg caught a glimpse of leather skin, bulging slit-pupilled eyes and a gaping, tooth-filled maw, in the instant before the creature launched itself on to him. The sword moved, twitched in his hand, rising to impale the creature between leathery pendulous breasts. Steam hissed, the sound shrill, screaming, and then the creature dissolved and flowed into the sword, sparkling rainbow-hued oils curling across the broken metal, scouring off the last flakes of rust, leaving the sword gleaming and elegant. He was racing down the corridor when the second creature appeared, coalescing out of the air directly in front of him. Overlong curled sabre-like talons slashed at him, the creature's arm twisting at an unnatural angle. Greg parried the blow, the sword shifting in his hand of its own volition, sparks screaming. The Fomor drew back its arm for another slashing blow, but Greg stepped forward, the metal sword screeching its way along the length of the talons, biting deep into the wrist, exiting through the other side and continuing into the creature's throat. It winked out of existence, tendrils of blue-green fire dancing along the length of the broken sword.

Greg kicked the door to room 602, the flimsy lock disintegrating under his foot. The sword was thrumming madly in his hand, making him grip it in both hands.

Elaine was missing. When he'd left her moments ago, she'd been sitting on the bed, but now a naked female sat on the edge of the bed. Against her stone-white flesh, the red hair on her head and at the base of her belly was startling. She leaned back, arching her spine, thrusting her breasts upwards; the nipples were pink, he noticed. 'Elaine,' he tried to say, but his tongue stuck to the roof of his mouth, and the sound came out as a muffled grunt. And then the woman raised her head and opened her eyes. The whites were a sulphurous yellow and the pupil was slit, like a cat's, and when the woman opened her mouth, he saw the teeth, ragged, needle-sharp spikes. Gripping the sword tightly in both hands, he brought it back over his head.

Elaine jerked back with a squeal of surprise when the door shattered inwards, the lock breaking out of the flimsy wood, sliding across the floor. She dropped the metal horn she had been examining on to the bed. The look on Greg's face was terrifying. His skin was completely without colour, a dull stone grey, his lips blood-less purple lines, drawn back from teeth exposed in a savage snarl. His eyes were wide, staring, the pupils little more than dots, surrounded by the bloodshot whites. He advanced on her, white frothy spittle drib-bling from the corner of his mouth, then he reared up and, clutching the sword in both hands, brought it back over his head.

'Greg . . . Greg . . . Greg!' Elaine threw herself back-wards off the bed as the sword descended, slicing through the thin sheets, digging deep into the mattress, springs squealing. He slashed again, ripping another slice out of the mattress, as he lunged across the bed.

'Greg!' Elaine tumbled on to the floor, and the descending sword bit deeply into the wall above her head, showering her with plaster and grit. She attempted to crawl away, but his fingers caught in her head, twisting savagely, pulling her head back, arching her spine, exposing the line of her throat.

Demonkind.

Spawn of the Night Hag and the Shining One, the Fallen Spirit.

The first inhabitants of this land called them Fomor, and originally thought them the remnants of an elder race, for there was magic in the world at that time and wonders were not unknown. But these were no eldritch inhabitants of the woods and high mountain caves, these were savage flesh eaters, who despoiled women and made them bring forth monsters. And many were their forms. Most wore the serpent form, but some were hideous beyond all reckoning, having too few – or too many limbs. And some were beautiful. Women – and men – sent to entice and ensnare the humankind. But the Demonkind could only ape the shape of men and never fully adopt it, and even the most beautiful of the creatures were never perfect.

And this one hadn't even been close, Greg realized. Perhaps the red hair was meant to make him think of Elaine – *Elaine, what had happened to Elaine, what had they done to her* – but the eyes and the teeth were those of a monster. Now he would draw the broken sword across its taut throat and feed its foul soul to the sword.

Her spine was breaking. Greg had slid off the bed and was sitting atop her, his weight a solid bar of iron across the pit of her stomach. He still had one hand wrapped in her hair, her throat stretched so far that she was finding it almost impossible to breathe, the pain in her neck incredible, black spots dancing before her eyes, the roaring in her ears louder now than Greg's grunting shouts.

The sword appeared before her face, and Elaine realized that she was going to die.

And then her flailing hands touched metal, curved and smooth. With the last of her strength, she brought it to her lips, and blew.

The sound of the horn.

'I will hallow these objects,' Yeshu'a said, 'and make of them keys and symbols that will bind the Demonkind, barring them entry to this world.' He looked over the scattered trade goods on the ship's deck. Stooping, he lifted a curved hunting horn and blew gently into both ends. 'This horn will warn of the Demonkind's approach, and its tongue will scatter them, for is it not written that my father's voice is the sound of the horn, the voice of the trumpet.' Bringing it to his thin lips, he blew hard.

And the Fomor on the beach scattered.

Greg threw himself backwards with a horrified scream. Huddling in the corner, he drew up his knees and wrapped his arms tightly around them, terrified to look, his last image – sitting astride Elaine, the sword pressed to her throat, a thin line of blood trickling from the wound – seared into his mind.

'Greg?'

The young man moaned.

'Greg?'

He was going mad – maybe he was already mad. The sights and scenes of the last few days had driven him over the edge. Now it had got that he couldn't distinguish between the hallucinations, the waking dreams and reality. There hadn't been two demons in the corridor outside, there were no such things as demons, nor had there been anything in the room when he'd burst in. But his waking dream had made him attack Elaine, hack at her with the cursed sword, made him . . .

'Greg!' A stinging blow rocked his head from side to side. 'Greg! Snap out of it.'

Greg opened his eyes. Elaine was kneeling on the floor before him, wild eyed, pale faced and terrified. There was a horizontal scratch on her throat, beads of blood edging it, but she was alive. Alive! Throwing his arms around her shoulders he hugged her close, and then the tears came, great heaving sobs that wracked his body. 'I thought . . . I thought . . . I saw a demon . . . and then I thought I'd killed you.'

Elaine felt tears on her own cheeks, and angrily blinked them away. 'I'm fine. Really I am.' She pulled back and attempted a smile. 'I blew the horn, and that helped.'

'I was fighting a naked female demon until that moment, I'd killed two more outside.'

Elaine came to her feet, and hauled Greg upwards. 'Maybe I should be insulted.'

Greg looked at her blankly.

'You can't tell the difference between me and a female demon.'

Wiping his sleeve across his eyes, he leaned forward and kissed her quickly on the forehead. 'All I needed was a little help.' He nodded to the horn. 'Don't let it out of your hands.'

CHAPTER FIFTY-THREE

Vyvienne sat bolt upright in the bed, the single sheet sliding away from her naked breasts. Staring blindly ahead, images of the astral still buzzing in her head, she pressed her hands against her breasts feeling the skin trembling with her pounding heartbeat.

Saurin sat in the ornately-carved wooden chair at the foot of the bed, fingers steepled before his face, watching the woman intently. He had seen her come awake from her astral travels in this fashion on a couple of other occasions, and knew that the news was always bad. But surely that couldn't be the case this time. Vyvienne had unleashed three simple dream-elementals on to Matthews. In his weakened state, he was particularly vulnerable to the primitive intelligences that fed off the shadows of dreams and wishes that percolated to the astral world. Vyvienne had designed the dream intelligences along with images she had plucked from Matthews' subconscious; they were designed to terrify the boy, send him back to the room in a highly agitated state. The female on the bed had been designed from Matthews' images of the perfect woman which had been added to similar features from the first woman he had dated, with the red hair to symbolize Elaine. The plan was to let him get close . . . and then she could reveal that she was Demonkind also. If Matthews reacted true to form, he would hack the demon to pieces . . . and when he awoke from his waking dream, he would discover that he had just stabbed Elaine Powys.

'I failed,' Vyvienne said. She drew breath, then threw back the single sheet to swing her legs out of the bed. Pouring a glass of water from the jug on the bedside table, she swallowed it quickly, wishing that she still drank, because right now she needed a stiff drink. 'He's strong, Saurin. He doesn't know how strong, he doesn't even understand the nature of the power, but it is coming to him, in fragments and broken pieces.'

'Is he of the Line?'

'He is . . . but I'm not sure where. I cannot follow his lineage.'

Saurin gripped the arms of the chair hard enough to make them creak. 'What happened?' he asked eventually.

'They're staying in a hotel somewhere in central London. I'm not exactly sure where, the dreamscape is terribly confused. But the dream shapes found him. He absorbed them both with the sword. He attacked the girl as we planned. He saw her as a demon, and he very nearly slew her, except that she blew the horn, and that shattered the spell. It also sent ripples through the astral that spun me away.'

'They lead a charmed life, that pair,' Saurin muttered.

'More than charmed.'

The Dark Man looked up sharply. 'You think they are protected?'

'I would not be at all surprised.'

'There are no Protectors these days,' Saurin muttered. 'The last one passed on over fifty years ago when he had distributed the Hallows to the present Keepers.'

'Well someone is watching over them.'

Saurin spun away. Crossing to a wardrobe he tugged it open and pulled out a long-bladed knife and a nickel-plated revolver. 'Can you pinpoint their location for me in London? I'll do it myself, my way.' Opening the cylinder on the revolver, he fed in five rounds and then eased the hammer down on the empty chamber.

'I could . . .' Vyvienne said, and then added with a smile, 'but there's no need to.'

Saurin looked up.

'I saw a leaflet on the bed just before Matthews attacked. It was advertising the festival.' The woman's smile was brilliant. 'They're on their way here. They are coming to you.'

Marcus Saurin allowed himself a rare smile of pleasure. He had always known that his cause was just, and that the gods – the old gods, the true gods – were on his side. And just to prove it, they were sending the two outstanding Hallows to him.

Tony Fowler and Victoria Heath stood in the middle of the devastated bedroom. The manager hovered nervously in the doorway, watching the two police officers intently, terrified that they might suggest closing down the entire hotel. He hadn't wanted to phone the police, but too many of the guests had seen the wild man with the sword in the corridor and the screams from the room had been audible across the entire floor. And now the young woman who'd registered for the room had vanished.

Sergeant Heath consulted her notebook. 'Several of

the guests report seeing a man who answers to Matthews' general description in the hallway. The witnesses say they thought the man was holding a short sword . . . but the evening papers reported that he had a sword, so I would not put too much credence on that. We also have a report of the couple being seen together in the lift. They got out on this floor and walked in different directions.' Closing the notebook with a snap, she shrugged. 'Hardly the actions of someone who is a prisoner. Maybe it wasn't them,' she added.

'It was.' Tony Fowler traced the line in the torn sheet with his pen and then looked at the long straight gouge in the walls. Metal had struck the wall above head height and scored a deep groove to about chest height. The mark was recent; plaster dust and a long curl of wallpaper lay on the floor beneath it. A tiny tracery of delicate beads of blood was speckled with the white plaster dust. Closing his hands around an imaginary sword hilt, he raised his arms above his head and simulated slashing downwards. If he had been standing too close to the wall, the blade would have struck it . . . which meant that someone was cowering on the floor. But who: Elaine or someone else? Matthews had been in this room, he was convinced of that, but what had happened, and why had they ended up here in the first place? Records had shown that a Miss Powers had registered for the room – Elaine Powys under threat from Matthews? – but once he'd got her here in this room, what had he done with her? The only blood in the room was the few droplets on the floor; there was no blood on the sheets, no traces of semen, but the room still stank like so many murder sites he'd attended over the years – a peculiar copper mixture of adrenaline and sweaty fear. No one had died in this room ... so what had happened?

'Well, Sergeant, what do you make of it?'

Victoria Heath shook her head. 'I'm not sure. Assuming Matthews was here, was Elaine Powys with him? Or was it another woman?'

'Powys,' Tony Fowler said shortly.

'Did he take her here to rape her?'

'Why?' Fowler asked. 'He could have done that in her flat or the friend's. Sex isn't his thing; Matthews likes pain. I'm not sure he's ever had a proper relationship with a woman; he's twenty-four, but as far as we can determine there have only been two casual relationships with girls since his late teens. We know his mother dominated the family. I think he's a pain freak working out his frustrations on women.' He looked around the room again. What happened in this room? It must have been terrifying. Guests in the neighbouring rooms had reported hearing terrible grunts and shouts and then the sound of tearing sheets, a metallic ringing, followed by a solid scraping sound, no doubt the sound of the sword off the wall. He was beginning to suspect that the girl had made a bid for freedom and there had been a struggle. But if so, then how had they got out of the hotel without being seen?

Sergeant Heath suddenly crouched and lifted the end of a sheet to reveal a printed piece of paper. Not touching it, tilting her head, she read, 'First International Celtic Festival of Arts and Culture'. Glancing up, she added, 'Some sort of music festival, I think.

Buses departing from Victoria,' she read. 'It's being held in Madoc in Wales, starts tomorrow night. Maybe it's significant.'

'Leaflet could have been there for days,' he said shortly.

Still not touching the paper with her fingers, the sergeant ran the end of her pen through a perfectly circular spot of blood. The blood smeared. 'What do you say it's the girl's blood?' she asked. 'I'll lay money we find his fingerprints on it.'

'Could be nothing . . . on the other hand . . .'

'It's another straw,' she smiled.

'And I'll clutch at them all . . . because that's all I've got.'

CHAPTER FIFTY-FOUR

Thirty feet from the iron-studded wooden door the Dark Man could feel the first trickles of power, like insects crawling in his hair, beads of icy sweat curling down his spine. Fifteen feet from the door and he was aware of the power as a tangible presence in the air, swirling and shifting around him, and the air itself brackish and tainted with the electric copper of what the uninformed called magic. But it was only when he stepped into the tiny windowless cell that the power washed over him, laving his naked skin like warm oils, or a lover's touch, prickling against his eyes, the power bitter and tart on his tongue.

He found it awe-inspiring to think that this was only a fragment of the power, a tiny percentage, merely leakage from the lead-lined sealed caskets.

Thirteen lead boxes were placed around the room, as far apart from each other as possible. Each box sat in the centre of a perfectly regular protective penta-gram, inscribed with the symbols of the archangels and the thirteen names of God. Ten of the boxes were locked and secured with wax and lead seals incised with the ancient talisman known as the Seal of Solo-mon. Saurin refrained from looking at the three empty boxes; their gaping emptiness mocked him and he unconsciously looked up to the shadowy ceiling, where Vyvienne was even now mocking Don Close, the Keeper of the relic known as the Knife of the Horse-man. She was taunting him with her naked body, using her flesh to drive the man wild, promising him what he would never have in return for the location of the artefact.

Three relics – Dyrnwyn the Sword that is Broken, the Knife of the Horseman, and the Horn of Bran – and he would have done what magicians and sorcerers through the ages had failed to do: collect the Hallows. The infamous twelfth-century Scots wizard, Michael Scot, had managed to collect three of them before his mysterious and untimely death; Francis Bacon had disposed of his, believing that it had brought him nothing but ill luck; the notorious Francis Dashwood, founder of the Hellfire Club, acquired two in his long life, both through gambling; and in the late nineteenth century, Samuel Liddell Mathers, one of the founding members of the Golden Dawn, also acquired two of the Hallows, although they mysteriously disappeared when he left London to set up his group in Paris. Mathers had always suspected, incorrectly, that Crowley had stolen the Hallows.

Sitting on the cold stone floor, altering his metabolism to ignore the chill that seeped up through his buttocks, he looked with pride at the ten ancient artefacts, each at least two thousand years old, though some of them were obviously older and had been ancient before they were consecrated as Hallowed objects. Reaching out he ran his long thin fingers across the nearest box which held the Cauldron of the Giant, a tiny three-legged copper bowl. Blue-white sparks leapt off the box which stung and nipped at his blackened fingertips. Easing up the wax seal, he pushed back the lid, allowing a little of the pent-up energy to spit from the box in a yellow-green light and spiral upwards towards the ceiling. It hovered just below the black-ened stones, a thin thread, coiling and uncoiling, then abruptly dissipated in a crackling explosion that sent hair-thin electrical discharges down on to the boxes holding the Hallows. The green threads buzzed around the lead boxes, outlining them in emerald before they fizzled out, unable to penetrate the combination of ancient lead and even older magical seals.

Ten Hallows.

Three to go.

How long had it taken him to reach this point, he wondered? Ten years, twenty . . . more? He was thirty-five now, and he had first learned of the Hallows when he'd been fifteen, five more years before he had even begun to comprehend their extraordinary history and their incredible power. Twenty years: a lifetime spent pursuing a dream. Those years had taught him much, taken him across the world more than once, usually into the wilder, less hospitable portions of the globe, and his search had given him glimpses of other worlds which humankind – petty, blind humankind – could never comprehend.

He replaced the tiny copper bowl, sealed the box and opened a second box, lifting out the small leather satchel known as the Hamper of Gwyddno. The first Hallow.

Acquiring the first had been the easiest. He had taken it from his aunt, having first tortured her to fire her blood and emotions, and then bathed the satchel in the gaping wound that had been her stomach.

Turning the leather purse in his hands, feeling it tremble with energy, he remembered the first time he had seen it. He had been fifteen, his Aunt Julia would have been close to fifty.

Marcus Saurin always loved staying with his Aunt Julia in Madoc. The tiny village on the borders of Wales, though it had no cinema, few shops and no amusements, held a deep fascination for the city-born and bred Saurin. He loved the silence, the cleanliness of the air, the gentle lyrical accents of the people, their open friendliness. He was also fond of his wild, eccentric Aunt Julia, his mother's older sister, and the differences between them were shocking and startling. Saurin's mother, Stephanie, was short and stout, prim, easily shocked, would not allow television on a Sunday, and controlled as much of her son's life as possible. She actively discouraged him from forming friendships with girls, and friendships with boys were also frowned upon. She censored his reading, did not allow him to go to the cinema and geared his entire life towards a college education and the academic degree which she had never had. His aunt was completely different: wild, impetuous, a free spirit who had scandalized her family with almost monotonous regularity, culminating with a much-publicized affair with a Member of Parliament that had almost brought down the government of the day.

Marcus had discovered most of this later; all he knew was that the times he spent with Aunt Julia were amongst the happiest of his childhood. But that last year, the year he turned fifteen, had determined his future . . .

Saurin pulled open the purse strings and peered inside. A hard crust of old bread lay in the bottom of the purse. Legend had it that if he were to break the crust in two and take out half, and then reach in again and break the remainder of the crust in half again, and again and again, he would be able to feed a multitude. It was a simple spell, common to most of the ancient cultures, though the Christians made much of it, hailing it as a miracle, ignoring the countless times it appeared in the histories of many nations.

So many things had happened that year, his sixteenth year. His father had died, quickly, peacefully, without fuss, the way he had lived his entire life. He had simply gone to sleep one night and never woken up. His parents weren't sleeping together – hadn't for many years – and because it was a Saturday, the one morning in the week when his father lay on, his corpse wasn't discovered until noon. Saurin found that he could barely remember his father's face now, and his mother's was a shadowy mask, but his aunt's face was vividly clear. But then, he supposed, you never forgot the woman who took your virginity.

He had known that summer was going to be different almost from the beginning. He was *aware* of his aunt in a way that he had never been before, abruptly conscious of the revealing clothing she wore, the skin-tight sweaters, the muslin and cotton blouses that were almost transparent, nipples dark against the material.

The memory of the morning he had awoken early and gone to the window to stare out over the orchard and seen his aunt standing naked amongst the trees was still vivid. Wisps of early morning fog twisted and coiled around her deeply tanned flesh, dew beading on her skin, plastering her silver-grey hair close to her skull. She was standing facing the east, arms raised above her head, a black-handled knife and short club in either hand. Around her neck she wore a leather bag on a thong. He was turning away from the window conscious of his own arousal, when Julia had turned and looked directly at him, eyes bright, expression almost mocking. And he knew then that his actions in the next few minutes would determine the course of his entire life. He could turn away, return to bed, pull the blankets up over his head, forget everything he'd seen or he could . . .

Even today, twenty years later, walking with bare feet through dew-damp grass could arouse him.

He had walked out into the orchard in his paisley-patterned pyjamas, the ends flapping against his ankles, sticking to his skin, before he had walked a dozen steps. Half way across the orchard he pulled off the clothes and approached the woman naked, stepping into the circle traced in the dew on the grass. Julia had opened her arms and drawn him to her heavy breasts, pressing his face against her dark nipples, then pulled him down on to the grass, and they had made love as the first rays of the August summer sun had appeared over the horizon, re-creating the role of the goddess giving herself to Lugh the god of light, the union of human and god, storing up life for the coming winter months.

And later, she told him what she was, a follower of the Old Ways, later still she spoke to him about the Hallow, the leather bag she wore around her neck.

In the months that followed, at weekends, school holidays, mid-term break, Marcus Saurin returned to Madoc and Julia initiated the boy body and spirit into the ways of a religion that had been ancient before the White Christ had been sacrificed on a wooden cross.

Suddenly his studies had direction and purpose, and he had left school with a scholarship for Oxford. He had devoted himself to the study of folklore and mythology, religion and metaphysics, and his PhD on Frazer's *Golden Bough* had established his reputation. However, while the public face of Marcus Saurin was of a brilliant young academic, privately his studies were leading him along darker, wilder paths as he researched the artefacts known as the Hallows.

And ten years to the day he had first learned about the Hallow that hung around his aunt's neck, he had returned to the village of Madoc and coldly, brutally butchered her, using her heightened emotions to feed energy into the Hallow. He had then set about collecting the thirteen Hallows of Britain ... because he needed the thirteen if he was to undo what the boy, Yeshu'a, had done almost two thousand years previously.

Three. And all he needed now was three.

From above, a raw scream echoed faintly through the stones, dying to a rasping, defeated sob. It was abruptly silenced, and then he heard Vyvienne's light footsteps pattering across the bare floor. Moments later the door opened behind him and Saurin turned his head. Vyvienne's naked flesh was spattered with blood, but the look of triumph on her face told him all he needed to know; Close had revealed the location. Replacing the leather bag in its lead box, he lifted an empty casket, drawing it closer, in readiness.

And now there were only two.

CHAPTER FIFTY-FIVE

Beyond the limited scope of human senses there exists a multitude of worlds undreamt by mankind. Creatures and beings that the humankind have come to know as myth or legend inhabit many of these realms, as do the creatures known as demons.

Perhaps they were once of the human race, though the legends suggest that they were the offspring of the Fallen Angel, Lucifer the Beautiful One, and a daughter of Eve. Condemned by an unforgiving god to suffer for the sins of their father, they were forever banished to a realm bordering the human kingdom, and further tormented by being able to see into the World of Men, though their own realm was hidden from the humankind. And the World of Men had everything that the Demon Realm lacked; the water was pure and clean, the air sweet and clear, and there was an abundance of fruits and foods of every description. But the greatest torment for the Demonkind was the abundance of the humans, with their soft meaty flesh and salt blood, delicate inner organs and that tastiest of morsels, the myriad human emotions and higher consciousness commonly known as souls.

The Demonkind have managed to gain access to the World of Men on numerous occasions, though usually it is but a single creature who steps through from the demon landscape and occupies a weak-minded human. Their life expectancy is usually short, for the raw emotions of the humankind are like a drug to the

Demonkind, and soon the demons are forcing the humans into greater and greater excesses in order to feed their addiction to the drug of emotion. The last time they managed to come in force however had been almost two thousand years ago.

At that time the astral Dreamscape was common to both races and humans – the foolhardy or the brave – ventured across the Abyss, many never to return. Similarly, the Fomor could come into the human dreams, plant seeds, perhaps even encourage a soul to destroy itself.

For an entire Dark Season, when there was little to do in the Northern Climes but dream, the Fomor had worked upon a tribe of savage northern shaman, instilling them with dreams of power and limitless wealth, and the ultimate prize for those questors driven to search for answers: knowledge, dark, exhilarating knowledge. With sacrifices of blood and fire and flesh and innocence, the shaman had created a rent between the worlds of men and demons and allowed the creatures to walk through. None of the shaman had survived their first encounter with the creatures, though their bodies lived on in a semblance of life, rotting on the bone, until the Demonkind chose a new fleshy host. Without the power of the shaman to fuel the gateway, it had collapsed, but not before it had allowed six hundred and sixty-six of the creatures into this realm, forever confirming the folklore of the number of the beasts in human consciousness.

In less than thirty days the beasts had ravaged the countryside, laying waste all before them. Thousands of humans died to assuage their terrible hunger, and those they did not kill immediately, they herded together in huge feeding pens. Some of the women they took and bred with, and the resultant abominations that crawled and slithered forth created the seeds of the legends that would become the vampire and werewolf.

When the Demonkind, which the humans had come to call the Fomor, had devastated the land of Britain, they had sailed west on a captured Irish pirate ship and established a reign of terror on that island that would only end when the De Danann warriors, who were not entirely human themselves, destroyed them in two great pitched battles.

But the remainder of the Fomor never left Britain's shore . . . because they were blocked by an icy-hearted bitter man-boy who controlled a power even he was not fully aware of. Using an elemental magic that was older than the human race, he had destroyed the last of the Fomor and sealed the gate between the worlds, locking it around with thirteen Hallowed words of power, and thirteen Hallowed objects. Only those thirteen words of power, and the thirteen Hallows could unlock the gate.

The Demonkind gathered behind the gate and waited in great serried ranks, and plotted their escape.

Many times they had come close to breaching the defences, and occasionally one or more of the keys had been turned in the lock, allowing a glimpse of unseen wonders – on both sides – but the Hallows had held.

So the demons formulated a plan. It was centuries in preparation, and another century had passed while they waited for the most suitable candidate to carry it out. They were patient, for they did not measure time in human spans and the prize was great indeed. The plan was simple: to bring the Hallows together, to unlock the gate between the worlds. All they needed was the right agent: a human with a desire for absolute knowledge, and prepared to do anything to achieve that end.

The demons were gathered now. They could feel the presence of the eleven Hallows and knew that the keys would soon be turned.

And this time they would not be turned back. Yeshu'a and his kind were long gone. There was no one to stand in their way.

CHAPTER FIFTY-SIX

Saturday 31 July

Elaine whimpered in her sleep, jerking Greg awake. There was a moment of terrifying disorientation, images from his disturbed sleep settling and shifting around him . . . until he remembered he was sitting with his face pressed against the cold moist window of a stale-smelling coach. Elaine was sitting in the aisle seat, her head resting on his shoulder, twitching and shifting, eyeballs dancing behind her lids.

Greg straightened carefully, wincing as stiffened neck and shoulder muscles protested, but reluctant to move too much in case he woke Elaine. The bag containing the sword was on the ground between his feet; he could actually feel the warmth of the artefact through the plastic. Rubbing a hand down the misted window, he squinted out into the night, trying to make out where they were. The coach was moving down a featureless length of motorway, sodium lamps turning the night orange and metallic. There were few cars on the road; a Volvo estate cruised slowly past, and Greg caught a glimpse of a woman dozing in the passenger seat, her face green in the light reflected from the dashboard, two sleeping children in the back seat. He found himself smiling at the scene of normalcy; ordinary people in an ordinary world, unperturbed by swords and demons . . . just like his world, a week ago. Almost unconsciously, he reached into the bag and touched the sword, taking solace from the warm metal. Now everything was up to question, for if he accepted the existence of the Hallows and the demons – which he surely must – then what else was also real? He shook his head, unwilling to pursue that thought; down that road lay madness.

'Are we there yet?' Elaine looked at him through sleep-dulled eyes.

'Not yet. I'm sorry, I didn't mean to wake you.'

Elaine returned her head to his shoulder and it seemed like the most natural thing in the world to place his arm around her shoulders and hold her close. 'Where are we?' she mumbled, her voice buzzing against his chest.

'I'm not sure.' Tilting his left arm to the light, he read the time. 'It's a little after two-thirty, so we've been on the road for two and a half hours. We must be more than half way there.'

Elaine mumbled a question, but before he could ask her to repeat it, he felt her shoulders slip into the gentle rhythm of sleep.

They had boarded the coach outside Victoria Station. It was one of a line of independent tour buses parked outside the station, with 'First International Celtic Festival of Arts and Culture' stickers in the front window. The first two buses were full, but the third was still taking on passengers, mostly students, the pavement littered with sleeping bags and rucksacks which were in the process of being loaded into the bus's dark interior. No one paid any attention to Elaine and Greg as they climbed aboard, paid the driver and took seats three-quarters of the way down the bus on the driver's side. There had been a ragged cheer when the bus pulled away from the station at exactly midnight, following the first two buses, and followed, in turn, by two more. In the first hour there had been a half-hearted sing-song, a dreary Gaelic whine that set Greg's teeth on edge, and someone near the top of the bus had played a hauntingly beautiful tune on a tin whistle, but the bus quickly fell quiet as the passengers drifted off to sleep, determined to conserve their energy for the following day.

Reaching into the bag, Greg had pulled out Judith Walker's notes, and tried to read them in the flickering street lights, looking for clues, for answers, but trying to concentrate on the spidery handwriting in the amber light made him feel slightly nauseous, and he closed the book and pushed it back into the bag. There were so many questions; so few answers. The old lady had been a Hallow Keeper. From the little he knew, he understood the Hallows to be thirteen ancient objects that did ... what? He shook his head slightly and Elaine mumbled. Most, if not all, of the Hallow Keepers had been killed, butchered in a horrific and obviously ritualistic manner by someone collecting the Hallows. It therefore stood to reason that the same person was now after Elaine and himself, and they could expect to die equally terrible deaths. Or at least Elaine would, since she was a Keeper; he was not. But if he wasn't a Keeper ... then what was he? Was his role in this more than just an innocent bystander caught up in something he had no control over? And what about the dreams, the strange bizarre dreams of the boy Yeshu'a. Sometimes it seemed as if the boy was speaking directly to him, those dark eyes boring right into his soul. And the metallic horn that warned of hunting beasts? And the demons, were they real or was he, in truth, simply losing his mind? Was he even now lying in a hospital bed and was this nothing more than a drug-induced stupor? He prayed it was, because if it wasn't then the consequences were almost too terrible to contemplate.

Vyvienne allowed her consciousness to slip out of her body. Twisting, she allowed herself to look down at her sleeping body, white flesh startling and vivid against the black sheets Saurin favoured. Her hands lay crossed over full breasts, right hand to left shoulder, left palm resting against her right. Her ankles were crossed. Even though she had travelled the astral plane since she was a child, she still found it eerie to be looking down on her own body, knowing that only the faintest of threads – gossamer and golden – connected her body to her spirit. This was one of the few images the majority of humans carried with them from the astral world: that of floating above one's own body. Few humans realized that their spirits roamed free in the astral whilst they slept, their dreams but fragments of their adventures in the grey Otherworld.

Spinning away from her sleeping body, Vyvienne allowed herself to drift higher. This, the lowest level of the astral, was crowded with the spirits of sleeping humans, insubstantial wraith-like figures moving aimlessly across the sere landscape. Most were naked, their bodies copies of their human forms, complete with imperfections. Only when they had advanced in learning would they realize that on the astral plane, form was mutable and they could adopt any shape or image they desired. Once they had achieved this understanding, they would delight in assuming a score of forms a night, human, animals and those in between. Later still, when the novelty had paled they would resort to their human forms, those usually enhancing their physical appearances slightly. Vyvienne rose higher and immediately the number of forms diminished, higher still and the figures became even rarer, though now there were hints of other presences, non-human presences in the astral, the *kas*. Vyvienne had long since learned to ignore them, realizing that many were simply the shades of the long dead, flickers of powerful consciousness that had left echoes in the fabric of the astral; others however, were truly alien presences and completely incomprehensible.

By tuning out the commonplace presences, most of the lights and presences in the astral disappeared. Vyvienne then concentrated on the Hallows' tell-tale signatures of power, shimmering spirals of intricate knot-work. Even though the Hallows were shielded and locked with lead and ancient magic, there was enough seepage to mark their presence and directly below her the astral plane blossomed with the ghostly images of eleven of the Hallows. And across the undulating grey landscape, two more approached.

Vyvienne raced towards the source of the two Hallows, falling through the layers of the astral until she was able to see into the physical world – the Incarnate World – below.

Greg Matthews and Elaine Powys in a crowded bus. Travelling to Madoc.

As Vyvienne drew back, she realized that the air about her was full of the presences of the *kas*. She glimpsed images of men and women in the costumes of a decade of centuries, of mail-clad warriors and fur-wrapped women. They were gathered in the astral, watching the couple intently . . . and then as one, they turned and looked at Vyvienne, and the wave of loathing that washed over her sent her spinning back into her own body. As she jerked awake she wondered whom they hated: Greg and Elaine . . . or herself.

'Well?' Saurin demanded. He was sitting in a high-backed chair set against the wall. With the first threads of dawn silver and mercury in the east, he was a shadowed, sinister shape.

'They're coming on a bus bringing people for the festival. They'll be here within the hour.'

'We'll be waiting for them.'

'I had the strangest dream,' Elaine mumbled, her voice sticky with sleep.

Greg squeezed her shoulders in response. He was staring into the east, watching the dawn break. He couldn't remember the last time he had seen the dawn. It looked as if it was going to be a glorious day.

'I dreamt I was standing on a platform or stage of some sort. I was naked, and all around me . . .'

'. . . were men and women wearing the costumes and dress of a score of different ages.'

Elaine shook herself out of Greg's arm to stare at him. 'You too?'

'And I dreamt that a demon tried to break through the circle of bodies, but they drove it back.'

Elaine nodded quickly. She drove the heels of her hands into her eyes, rubbing furiously. 'They were the previous Hallow Keepers,' she said decisively.

'How do you know?'

'I know,' she said firmly. Suddenly she leaned across

Greg and pointed to a road sign. 'Madoc twenty miles,' she smiled. 'Nearly there.'

The old man in the last coach didn't look too much out of place amongst the shabbily-dressed youths. His army surplus coat and trousers and ragged sneakers were identical to many of theirs, though his was in the filthy state which they could only aspire to. However, while they wore the clothing through choice, his was by necessity. Amongst the smells of unwashed flesh, beer and the sweeter stink of hash, his own stale odour went unnoticed.

Ambrose had watched the gathering of the *kas* in the astral above the bus ahead of him, drawn by the interlocking spirals of power that emanated from the two Hallows. He had seen the bright point of blue-black light approach, falling from the rarefied heights of the upper astral, the ghostly image of a black-haired woman almost visible behind the bruise-coloured light. He had watched it warily circle the *kas*, seen it assume its beast form, then its female shape, watched as the *kas* had turned on the creature, recognizing it for what it was, driving it away. He longed to use a tiny percentage of his power to blast the creature, but knew that he had to remain shielded, nor could he use his power to trace the woman to her lair. But he would find her; all he had to do was to follow the stench of evil.

And now they were returning to Madoc. He was unsurprised. It would end where it began, not fifty years, not five hundred years, but nearly two thousand years ago in a tiny village at the edge of the mountains.

CHAPTER FIFTY-SEVEN

Madoc was a community of twenty-five hundred people, nestling on the borders of England and Wales. The village was ancient, and was featured in the Doomsday Book, and had appeared in some of the Arthurian legends. The local museum contained artefacts from the distant Neolithic age, and the meagre coal seams of the nearby mountains had yielded fossils from the Jurassic and Triassic periods. When the mines had begun to close in the seventies and eighties, many of the young men had left Madoc, seeking work in Cardiff, Liverpool, Manchester and London. Having sampled the city life, few ever returned to the quiet, backward village.

In the early eighties, Madoc had followed the examples set by some of the French villages in northern Brittany, the crofts in the Scottish Highlands and some of the small towns in the west of Ireland, and made a deliberate effort to revitalize their Celtic heritage. A modest interpretative centre re-creating Bronze age village life had proven to be surprisingly successful. Reproductions of Celtic crafts – leatherwork, wood carving, jewellery making – had established the foundations of a series of increasingly successful cottage industries, and now Madoc Celtic silver and leather work was exported all over the world.

And when the local school teacher, who had been instrumental in creating the Celtic revival that had saved the village from the fate of so many others in rural Wales, had suggested the all-embracing Celtic theme festival to the village council, it had been unanimously accepted. It seemed only natural that it should take place on Lughnasadh, the ancient Celtic autumn festival at the end of July.

Although it was not yet eight in the morning, the small village was crowded, and most of the shops were open and the main street, which had been designed for horse-drawn carriages and never widened, was jammed solid with cars, mini-buses and coaches. Their destination was a series of fields at the end of the village known as the Mere, where a small town of assorted multicoloured tents had been erected. In an adjoining field, a dozen marquees had been set up, and at the end of the Mere a long stage, piled high with sound equipment, was still under construction. A BBC mobile outside broadcast unit was setting up two cameras on platforms facing the stage.

Greg and Elaine walked slowly along the crowded streets, early-morning sun warm on their faces, but the moist country air was already spoiled with the odours of burning food and a myriad of perfumes. From the far end of the town high-pitched static howled, setting the crows wheeling into the air.

'What do we do now?' Greg asked. He had managed barely two hours of uncomfortable and troubled sleep on the coach and he was exhausted, his eyelids gritty and leaden, a sour taste in his mouth and there was a constant buzzing in his ears. More than once he had twisted around, eyes wide, thinking he'd heard the sound of a hunting horn.

'We eat,' Elaine said firmly, feeling her stomach rumble. She stopped outside a cake shop and stared at the bread and confectionery. A short, stout red-faced woman stood in the doorway, arms folded across her massive bosom. She smiled at the young couple and Elaine nodded in return. 'Excuse me?'

'Yes, dear?' The woman's accent was light and lyrical, a little girl's voice in an old woman's body.

'We're here for the festival,' Elaine said, pitching her voice low, drawing the woman closer to her. It was a trick she often used with older patients, to encourage them to trust her. 'We are looking for some place to stay; have you any recommendations?'

'If you haven't booked, then it's unlikely you'll find anyplace. The hotel is full and the guest houses all booked out. You might find something in Dunton . . .' she added.

'Well, thank you very much anyway,' Elaine said. 'Perhaps you would sell us some bread?'

'Delighted to.'

The woman turned away and Elaine followed her into the shop, blinking in the gloom. She breathed deeply, savouring the odours of warm bread. 'Smells like my aunt's kitchen.'

'Your aunt likes to bake?'

Elaine nodded, abruptly unable to speak, her throat closing, tears welling up in her eyes.

'It's the flour dust,' the woman said kindly.

'Aunt Judith loved to bake,' Greg said quickly. 'In fact . . .' he stopped and looked around. 'Would this shop have been here fifty years ago, during the war?'

'My grandfather opened in 1918 when he came back from the war. The first war,' she added. 'Why do you ask?'

'Our Aunt Judith was evacuated to this village

during the war; she used to speak about a wonderful bread shop . . . I wonder if it was this one?'

'This is the only one in the village,' the old woman beamed. 'It must have been here. My mother and aunts ran it then.' She leaned her forearms across the glass-topped counter, pushing aside the 'do not lean on glass' sign. 'I played with the evacuees. What was your aunt's name?'

'Judith Walker,' Elaine said softly.

The baker frowned, looking at Elaine's hair. 'I don't remember any red-headed girls . . .'

'My aunt had jet-black hair; I get this colour from my father's side of the family. He's Welsh,' she added.

'Welsh. From where?'

'Cardiff. I'm Elaine Powys. This is my . . . brother, Greg.'

'I can see the resemblance,' the woman said. She turned her head to look out the door at the crowds streaming past. 'How long would you be staying?' she asked suddenly.

'A night. Two at the most,' Greg said quickly.

'I have a room, a single room. It's my son's room, but he's in London, working in the theatre. You're welcome to use it.'

'We're most grateful,' Elaine said immediately. 'We'll pay of course . . .'

'No you won't,' the woman said simply. 'Now you wanted some bread.'

'We were expecting ten thousand people . . . so far we've got about thirty,' Sergeant Hamilton said quietly, his Welsh accent lending the words a musical cadence. He looked from Victoria Heath to Tony

305

Fowler. 'I've got twenty additional officers on loan, and I've put in a request for another forty. If I'm lucky, I'll get ten,' he added without a trace of bitterness.

Tony Fowler stood and pulled the phone across the desk. 'I have every reason to believe Gregory Matthews, whom we want to interview in connection with half a dozen murders and the kidnapping of a young nurse, is here in this village. I'll get you all the men you need.'

Victoria Heath turned to look through the diamond-paned windows of the police station into the crowded street below. 'If he's here, he could be anywhere.'

'If he's here, we'll find him,' Sergeant Hamilton said confidently.

Tony Fowler slammed down the phone. 'Let's hope we find him before he kills again.'

Greg stood with his back to the room, a blush on his cheeks, staring out of the window while Elaine changed into a denim shirt and jeans. He had walked in on her moments earlier while she had been undressing, pulling her sweat-stained shirt over her head. He knew his eyes had lingered fractionally too long on her breasts.

'What do we do now?' Elaine asked, stepping alongside him, rolling up the sleeves of her shirt.

Greg avoided eye contact, feeling his cheeks start to burn again. He turned away from the window. 'I don't know,' he admitted.

'Brigid wanted us to come here. This was where it started, this was where they were given the Hallows.'

Greg perched on the edge of the hard bed, lifted the bag on to his lap and pulled out Judith's diary and notes. 'They were given the Hallows by an old man named . . .' He turned the pages quickly, damp thumb leaving grimy patches on the stained paper. '. . . Ambrose,' he said eventually. 'They were given the Hallows by an old man called Ambrose.'

'Didn't Brigid mention something about a cave in the woods at the edge of the village, complete with shelves, a wooden bed . . .' Elaine perched on the windowledge, looking down into the busy street below.

Greg flipped through the pages, lips moving as he deciphered handwriting. 'Yes, here it is. You're right. Listen to this. *Ambrose brought us to his cave today. It is at the end of the village, over the bridge and then left along a narrow, almost invisible path. The cave is in the middle of a thick copse, set back into a low mound, almost invisible unless you were looking for it. Ambrose had fitted its stone walls with shelves made from the branches of trees . . .*'

'We should be able to find that,' Elaine said slowly. There was something about the name of the shop opposite that rang a faint bell. Wood's Haberdashery. 'Pass me Aunt Judith's address book.' Opening it at the back of the book, she ran her chipped finger-nail down the list of names. 'Julia Wood,' she said triumphantly. 'With an address here in Madoc,' she added quietly.

'I thought you phoned all of the names in the books.'

'I did . . .' she frowned, trying to remember the fragments of conversation. Was this the woman who had gone into the nursing home, or had Elaine spoken to her nephew. Nephew, she nodded. The woman had died ten years previously, she remembered. She closed the book with a snap. 'Well, we've got two leads now: Ambrose's cave and Julia Wood's last known address.'

CHAPTER FIFTY-EIGHT

There was something moving in the woods.

Greg could feel the creature's eyes on him, actually feel the short hairs on the back of his neck rising. He saw Elaine glance over her shoulder more than once, and knew that she felt it too. Reaching into the bag he pulled out the broken sword and held it flat against his leg. 'We're being tracked,' he muttered, falling into step beside her.

'I know.'

'Any idea what it is?'

'Too many. And I hope and pray it's none of them.'

Greg resisted the temptation to turn around. 'Maybe we've missed the turning,' he suggested.

Elaine squinted through the trees. 'I don't think so. This is the only path to the left of the bridge and the track is nearly invisible,' she reminded him. 'I can make out a mound ahead. Maybe that's the mound my aunt mentions in her diary.'

A pigeon whirred through the trees, bringing two magpies into the still air, wings snapping. They both jumped.

'This has to be the mound,' Elaine said, leaving the track to cut across through the trees towards the grassy mound, covered with hawthorn and holly.

Greg followed more cautiously, ducking beneath a low-lying branch, using the opportunity to glance quickly behind him. He caught a glimpse of an indistinct shape slipping through the trees.

They had actually walked past the cave mouth before Elaine realized that the shadows were darker behind a particular curtain of leaves and twisted vines. Greg, who was walking behind her, holding the sword openly now, was horrified when she abruptly disappeared.

'Elaine!' His voice was a hoarse, rasping whisper. A hand appeared through the matted leaves, a crooked finger drawing him in. Ducking his head, he pushed through the curtain of leaves and stepped into a large natural cave. With the leaves covering the opening, the light was green tinged, shifting and dappling the walls with an underwater effect.

The cave was almost exactly as Judith Walker and Brigid Davis had described. Semicircular, with carved wooden shelving set into the walls and an ornate box-bed tucked away in one corner. The cave obviously hadn't been used in many years. A thick layer of dust, liberally speckled and scattered with animal tracks covered the floor, and the cobwebs were a thick silver gauze across most of the empty shelves. One of the shelves at the very back of the cave was piled high with cans of meat, most with labels of firms that had gone out of business decades ago. The flaking yellowed remains of a candle were still stuck to a grease-spattered rock alongside the bed.

'I feel as if I've been in this place before,' Elaine whispered. 'Everything is so familiar.'

Greg nodded; he was thinking exactly the same thought.

Elaine spun around to look at Greg. 'You realize what this means of course.'

He stared at her blankly.

'If the cave is real, and the Hallows are real then we

are forced to accept that everything else that my aunt says in her diary is also real. Ambrose was real.'

'Ambrose *is* real.'

Greg whirled round bringing the sword up, the broken blade sparkling and crackling with green fire.

'I am Ambrose.' The wild-haired one-eyed old man who stepped into the cave was shorter than Elaine and dressed in ragged army surplus clothing, oversized sneakers and carrying a tattered knapsack. Reaching out with his left hand, he touched the sword with his index finger, tendrils of emerald light curling and twisting around his hand and snaking up his arm. 'Still powerful, still strong, eh Dyrnwyn,' he murmured. 'The last time I stood in this place,' the old man continued, conversationally, moving around the cave, gnarled fingers touching the shelves, hands caressing the smooth stones, 'I was giving the Hallows to thirteen young men and women. I thought I had seen an end of them then. But now here I am, back in this place again, and you have two of the Hallows with you, and the other eleven are perilously close.' He brushed twigs and rat droppings from a smooth depression in a large boulder and sat into it. He looked up to see Greg and Elaine still standing open-mouthed before him and laughed gently. 'Happy are thy men, happy are these thy servants, which stand continually before thee, and that hear thy wisdom,' he intoned. 'From the Book of Kings,' he added. 'You should make yourselves comfortable. There is much to tell you, and little time to do it in.'

'I've lost them.' Vyvienne's eyes snapped open.

Saurin, outlined against the window, turned quickly, morning sunlight washing his face in bronze, picking up the flecks of silver in his slightly shabby suit. 'What do you mean, lost them?'

Vyvienne propped herself up on her elbows, sweat gleaming in tiny golden puddles on her naked body. 'They're here, in the village. It was difficult to follow them, because the leakage of power from the other Hallows is making it difficult to distinguish the trace in the astral. And the astral is confused with scores of curious presences, drawn to the power. Some are the spirits of other humans, some are the *kas* of the long dead, but there are others even I have never encountered before.'

Marcus Saurin nodded slowly. This had always been one of the great dangers in gathering the Hallows together: no one knew what they would attract. Crowley had briefly owned one of the Hallows and it had attracted the creature known as Pan. Crowley had spent six months in a mental asylum recovering from the experience.

Vyvienne sat up and folded her arms beneath her breasts. 'The astral is flooded with cold light, making it impossible to see from that place into this world, but I managed to isolate the signature of the sword and the horn. They were at the southern end of the village, close to the river – I could feel the current as a cool place in the astral – then they moved into the wood, and it was as if they simply winked out of existence.'

'Something is shielding them,' Saurin said quickly.

'Or someone,' Vyvienne suggested softly.

'No one has that sort of power any more,' Saurin said confidently. He looked at his watch. 'Not for another few hours anyway,' he added with a grin.

★

'Some of this you may know,' Ambrose began, looking at them. He sat back into the stone chair, his head in shadow, only his shock of white hair and single eye visible in the green light, 'but much of what I will be telling you will be strange indeed. I ask you to consider the events of the last few days and keep an open mind. I am asking for your faith.'

'You said you were the same Ambrose who gave the Hallows to the children fifty years ago. But that Ambrose was an old man . . .' Elaine interrupted.

'Am I not an old man?' He smiled quickly. 'I am older than you think. Much older.'

'But . . .' Elaine began, but Greg reached out and squeezed her arm, silencing her.

'Let's hear what he has to say,' he suggested.

Ambrose nodded. 'Thank you Gregory. Yes,' he continued, 'I know your name, Gregory Matthews, and yours too, Elaine Powys, and much else besides. Now listen to me. You have in your possession two of the most powerful Hallowed artefacts in the known world. Imbued with an ancient magic, they were created for but a single purpose: to seal the doors to the Demon Realm . . .'

Yeshu'a watched impassively as a female demon with the face and breasts of a woman, but the skin of a serpent, was hacked down by four men. They dismembered her quickly, striking off the head and driving a stake through the centre of the chest to pin the body to the ground. The Demonkind were able to absorb terrible punishment, fighting on in spite of appalling wounds.

Another demon appeared, a howling monster who

stood twice the height of a normal man, and was covered in short matted grey fur. He had the head of a wolf, but the eyes of a man. Scything claws struck down one of the terrified crewmen, slashing through wood and leather armour, cleaving through the rectangular Roman shields the men carried. A barbed spear took the beast high in the chest, a raven-haired Greek warrior pushing the spear in before wrenching it out, ripping out the beast's lungs with the hooked barbs. Two naked woad-striped women fell on the stricken beast, hacking at it with small stone axes, howling delightedly as the beast's thin green blood spattered them.

Yeshu'a stepped forward and the quartet of Irish warriors who stood guarding him locked shields and moved forward with him, swords and spears ready. But few of the Demonkind had survived the attack, and there was little left for the humans to do but mop up.

Thirty days previously, Yeshu'a had called down a fire from the heavens and washed the Demonkind from the beach in a wall of ivory-coloured flames that had fused the sand to white glass. Josea had led his mariners ashore and the surviving Demonkind had been butchered. Few of the mariners had wanted to leave the safety of the boats, but promises of rewards for the free and freedom for the slaves had spurred them on . . . though their fear of the boy had been a greater incentive.

Moving inland, they first freed a handful of tin miners who had been trapped in their mines for days by the creatures. Yeshu'a had called down tongues of fire on to the beasts who occupied the village and while they had howled in fear and pain, the humans had attacked. Those early victories lent the humans courage, and showed them that the creatures could be slain. In the days that followed, more and more humans had flocked to them, drawn by stories of the boy known as the Demonkiller. With the boy's powers, the humans were inevitably victorious, though many fell to the beasts' slashing claws and teeth.

On the tenth day of the campaign, Yeshu'a performed his greatest feat of old magic when he resurrected Josea, who had been struck dead by a creature that was neither wolf nor bear. As the human warriors watched, the boy knelt in the bloody ruins of a village the Fomor had occupied, laid his hands on the gaping wounds in his uncle's chest, closed his eyes and turned his face to heaven. Those nearest him saw his lips move, and when he spoke his words were indistinguishable. Moments later, Josea opened his eyes and sat up, hands pressed flat to the livid white scars that bisected his chest. In the days that followed many begged Yeshu'a to raise their sons or brothers or loved ones back to life, but he had always refused and once, when an enormous battle-scarred warrior had threatened him with a dagger, the boy had reached out and touched the weapon, melting the iron blade, fusing it into the man's hand. The ship's cook had taken the hand off at the wrist, but the wound had putrefied and the warrior had fallen on his own knife ten days later to escape the agony. Since then most people had left the boy alone, although Josea had insisted that the bodyguards – savage Irish mercenaries – who had come when they had learned of a fight, remain with him at all times. If the boy was killed, then the battle would end prematurely and ultimately the demons would win.

Josea staggered up. There was a long cut across his forehead, lines of blood running on either side of his sharp nose. 'Was all this necessary?' he asked bitterly, spitting the taste of blood and burnt meat from his mouth.

Yeshu'a looked around. There were bodies everywhere, human and Fomor ... and many were children.

This was the last great encampment of the beasts, tucked away in a valley at the edge of a marsh in the shadow of a ragged mountain range. The original human village had been fortified with stakes and a head-high wall. Here the Demonkind had made their last stand, protecting a tiny tear in the fabric between the worlds, which allowed a single demon to slip through, one at a time. The Fomor had brought their prisoners to this place with them – twenty-five hundred men and women, though there were more women than men, and most were young. The Demonkind knew the inherent power of virginal flesh and souls. They never had a chance to make the sacrifice. Standing atop a nearby hill, Yeshu'a had rained liquid fire and ragged brimstone down on to the village. The screams of the children still echoed in the still air.

'It was necessary,' Yeshu'a said softly. 'This is where the Demonkind come through to our world. On this night, the night of the shortest day, when the walls between this and the Otherworld grow thin, the Fomor intended to wrap the humans in wicker baskets and sacrifice them in the old way. The incredible eruption of energy would have ripped apart the opening between the worlds and allowed the Demonkind through in force. Even I would not have been able to contain them.'

'There is something you should see,' Josea said, turning away before the boy could see the hatred in his eyes.

Josea led Yeshu'a and his bodyguard through the smouldering remains of the village, stepping across charred lumps of meat that had once been human. One of the bodyguards noticed that one of the terribly burnt figures still moved, pink mouth opening and closing in a blackened crust of a face. He drove his spear through it, not caring if it was human or demon; nothing deserved to suffer like that.

There was a well in the centre of the village, a round opening in the ground, the edges of which had been raised with rough-hewn mud and straw bricks. Some of the bloodiest fighting had taken place around here, and the ground was slick with the beasts' blood. Josea walked to the edge of the well and pointed down. Leaning over the edge of the opening, the boy peered down, then quickly drew back his head, eyes watering with the stench. 'What happened here?' he coughed.

Josea shook his head. 'As far as we can tell, the well was stuffed with the bodies of children wrapped tightly in straw. God knows how many were in the well. Maybe the beasts fired the well, maybe some of the fire from heaven brought it alight.'

Taking a deep breath, Yeshu'a leaned over the well again and peered down. A greasy layer of fat bubbled atop the water and charred remains of straw were stuck to the sides of the well, along with dangling strips of what looked like burnt leather, but which Yeshu'a knew was human flesh. 'This is the place,' he whispered, 'there is an opening here, a tiny crack, but enough.' He staggered back from the well, rubbing the heel of his hand over his eyes. 'The well would have been filled with the virginal children, the rest would have been piled up alongside, and then the whole lot set aflame tonight. The pyre would have burned in this world and the next, the released energy would have torn the fabric of the worlds and allowed the creatures through . . .' the boy's voice faded away. 'We got here just in time.'

'Can we seal the opening?' Josea asked.

'Perhaps,' Yeshu'a said slowly. He padded to the edge of the well and looked down again.

And a clawed hand shot up, wrapping itself around his throat.

While two of the bodyguards jabbed at the oily water, the others attacked the arm, hacking it off at the elbow, leaving the fingers wrapped around the boy's neck. He staggered back and flung the limb from him; its fingers scrabbled and twitched on the ground until one of the guards stamped on it, breaking the bones.

'I can sense their frustration,' Yeshu'a said grimly, gingerly fingering his throat. 'They are close . . . so close, an army the like of which you have never seen. It will wipe mankind off this world for ever.'

Two Fomor erupted from the water, lank hair matted to their bodies. They were both hideously and grotesquely female. The bodyguards cut them down before they climbed out of the well.

'I cannot mend the rent,' Yeshu'a said softly, 'but I

318

can seal it.' He turned to look at his uncle. 'But someone must remain behind to ensure that the seals are never broken.'

'The well was covered over and the earth blessed with the old magic,' Ambrose continued quietly. The morning had moved on into early afternoon while he spoke, and the light coming in through the leafy covering over the mouth of the cave painted the interior in emerald. 'Then Yeshu'a used thirteen everyday objects his uncle had brought aboard his ship to trade to the Britons for tin: a knife, a cup, a whetstone, a beautiful feathered cloak, a horn . . . a sword,' he added with a smile. 'He imbued a little of the binding spell into the earth around the well, and the remainder into the objects which he blessed and hallowed. These were the keys; only the thirteen keys could open the thirteen seals he placed over the well. Then he chose thirteen men and women at random and gave each of them a Hallow and sent them on their way. So long as they kept the Hallow and believed in it, it would bring them great fortune; it had to be passed from father to son, mother to daughter in an unbroken line . . . but they must never sell it, nor move out of the country. And he made his Uncle Josea the Guardian of the Hallows, charged him to watch over the Keepers . . . but doomed him to remain alive for ever to ensure the demons never again gained access to this world.' Ambrose laughed softly. 'In the beginning of course, Josea was sceptical, but later, much later, when Yeshu'a had been killed by the Romans, Josea returned to the land of the Britons and accepted the role of the Guardian. He wrote down the first of the Hallow lore. How much of it is true of course, no one knows. But much of it makes sense. Through the centuries, the Hallows have been at the heart of British folklore, the sword . . .'

'Excalibur,' Greg said quickly.

Ambrose shook his head. 'Excalibur, the Caliburn blade, was cursed by Wayland the Smith from the moment of its first forging. It had been bathed in the blood of babes. It brought only doom and destruction to those who wielded it. Arthur could have been great, but when he lost his innocence and faith, the Sword from the Stone shattered. He replaced it with the gift from the Lady of the Lake, and she and her kind had no love for the Once King.'

'I thought Excalibur was the sword from the stone,' Elaine said.

Ambrose shook his head. 'Two entirely different weapons; one of light, the other of darkness.' Stretching out his hand, he pointed at the broken sword in Greg's hands. 'Though it has had many names, once this was the sword from the stone.' The sword shimmered briefly, like oil running down the length of the blade.

Ambrose sat back into the stone chair and when it became obvious that he wasn't going to say any more, Greg spoke. 'This is . . . unbelievable.'

'An understatement,' the old man smiled. 'How much proof do you want? You are holding the proof in your hands. You have slain those touched by demons, you have seen their true selves.'

'And now . . . what's happening now?'

'Eleven of the Hallows have been gathered together here in this village. Their ancient power has been heightened by being bathed in the flesh and blood of the Hallow Keepers.' He closed his single eye and threw back his head, breathing deeply. 'I can smell the power even now. The man who has sought them out wishes to use them to reopen the door between the worlds and allow the Demonkind through. He will do it tonight, on the eve of the Festival of Lughnasadh, one of the four times in the year when the fabric between the worlds grows thin. This is the night sometimes known as Confusion: the night is dedicated to Lugh . . . and Lugh was one of the Tuatha De Danann, the magical People of the Goddess, who defeated the Fomor demons in Ireland. But Lugh is also Bel, and Bel is the Lord of Light and Fire, and fire is the Demonkind's element. I believe that the Dark Man plans to sacrifice the people gathered for the festival by fire to achieve his ends and once through into this world, the Demonkind will feed on all mankind.'

Elaine, who had been holding the Horn of Bran in her lap while Ambrose spoke, looked up sharply. 'You're him, aren't you?'

'Who?'

'Yeshu'a. You're Yeshu'a!'

Ambrose laughed gently. 'No, I'm not Yeshu'a. I'm Josea,' he added.

'I've never heard of Yeshu'a,' Greg said quietly.

'Yes you have,' Ambrose said, 'though you would know him better by the Greek form of his Hebrew name: Jesus.'

'Jesus! You're saying Jesus came to Britain . . .' Elaine whispered.

'Legend has it that Jesus visited the country while

still a child, brought here by his uncle.' Greg stopped suddenly. 'That means that you were . . .'

'I have had many names down through the years, but yes, I was Joseph of Arimathea.'

CHAPTER FIFTY-NINE

'Mr Saurin sir, how may I help you?' Sergeant Hamilton was smiling as he approached the desk, although he disliked the tall, powerfully built Marcus Saurin, and he had his own suspicions about Saurin's involvement in the death of his aunt, Julia Woods. However, Saurin was the local school teacher, and the man responsible for bringing the Celtic Festival to the village and speaking out against him would only make him enemies.

Saurin looked over Hamilton's shoulder, dark eyes taking in Fowler, lingering on Heath. He suppressed a smile as the woman visibly squirmed in her seat. 'I've come to report a burglary,' he said smoothly. 'One of the youths down for the festival, I'm afraid. Broke into the house and stole a sword and a hunting horn from my collection of antiques.'

Tony Fowler appeared at Hamilton's side. 'My name's Detective Fowler from London. I heard you mention something about a sword.'

Saurin fixed him with a brilliant smile. 'Yes, a young man stole one of my antique swords and an ornate hunting horn.'

'Could you give us a description?'

'Yes. A double-handed claymore, a cliamh mhor . . .' Saurin said, deliberately misunderstanding the question.

'Of the suspect,' Fowler said patiently.

'Oh,' Saurin laughed easily. 'Yes, I see what you

323

mean. I got a very good look at him, as it happens. Mid-twenties, tall, dark hair cut short, skinny . . .'

Tony Fowler slid a photograph of Greg Matthews across the desk. 'Was this the man?'

'My word, but this is remarkable, officer. This is the young man.'

'Was there anyone else with him?'

'Not that I could see.' He paused, then shook his head. 'No, when he was going into the woods, he was definitely alone.'

'You saw him going into the woods?'

'Yes, just over the bridge.'

Tony Fowler grinned savagely. 'When was this?'

'Fifteen, twenty minutes ago. I would have got down here sooner, but the traffic . . .' he explained.

Fowler turned to Heath, but she was already on the radio.

'If you do get him,' Marcus Saurin asked quickly, 'could I ask you to return the two artefacts . . .'

'They are evidence . . .'

'I just need them for a couple of hours, just to mount an exhibition. You can have them back then.'

'I'm sure we can come to some arrangement, Mr Saurin,' Tony said, stretching out his hand. Marcus Saurin shook it warmly, taking care not to crush the fingers.

CHAPTER SIXTY

Greg and Elaine stood at the edge of the wood and followed Ambrose's pointing finger towards the solid nineteenth-century farmhouse. 'The Hallows are there.'

Elaine shivered and rubbed her hands against her arms and across the back of her neck; she could actually feel the small hairs rising off her flesh. Greg found he was clutching the sword in sweat-damp hands, and he kept glancing over his shoulder, almost as if he expected something to come charging out of the trees.

'You're feeling a tiny trickle of the power of the Hallows,' Ambrose explained. 'The Dark Man who collected them sealed them in lead boxes warded with words of power . . . but they are still more powerful. If he does not use them soon, then the Hallows will break their bonds of lead and magic.'

'And then?' Greg asked.

Ambrose shrugged. 'Who knows? They are powerful enough to rip through the fabric of the myriad worlds, opening doorways into unguessed-realms.'

'You never told us how you managed to have all the Hallows with you back in the forties,' Elaine said.

'This is not the first time the Hallows and their Keepers have been threatened. During the Black Death, we lost seven of the thirteen; during the Great Fire, three died; the Witch Hunts decimated the Keepers and Cromwell's reign almost destroyed us entirely. But the Great War nearly proved our undoing. Twelve of the thirteen Keepers went to fight for their King and country and gave me the Hallows as their custodian. The thirteenth was a playboy and a fool; it was only a matter of time before he gambled away the Hallow, so I took it back. Two of the Keepers returned from the killing fields of Europe; one was without his legs, the other, a nurse, had been poisoned by the gasses. So, I kept the Hallows and set about finding a new generation of Keepers.' He smiled grimly. 'I little realized that it might be the very last.'

'What do you want us to do?' Greg asked tiredly.

'You must stop the Dark Man,' Ambrose said simply.

'How?' Elaine asked.

'Only I can contain all the Hallows,' the old man said. 'We have to get into the house – which is guarded by more than human wards – and then remove the Hallows. The Dark Man and his companion must be slain.'

'You make it sound so simple,' Greg said.

'It won't be,' Ambrose promised.

Marcus Saurin was smiling as he walked back along the lane to the house. On the face of it the plan had seemed absurdly simple: why should he expend energy searching for the couple when the police had the resources to do it for him. Discovering that the police had tracked Matthews to the village was an added bonus. The gods – his lips twisted bitterly – were smiling on him.

He paused at the top of the hill, and leaned on the listing stone wall to look down across the Mere. The fields were ablaze with tents and stalls. Flags were fluttering everywhere and incongruously maypoles had been set up in small clearings. Wrong festival, he smiled. In the distance, sounding faint, and not unpleasant, bagpipe music skirled on the balmy July air. There were thirty thousand people from all across the Celtic lands – Welsh, Scots, Irish, Manx, Breton – in the fields below, with more arriving every day. The festival organizers estimated that there would be at least forty thousand before the huge bonfires were lit at sunset. The thirteen enormous pyres were scattered seemingly at random through the fields; only Saurin knew that eleven of them contained straw-wrapped portions of the bodies of the Hallow Keepers and that the fires had been arranged in a particular order. And when the fires blazed forth into the night sky and consumed the flesh, then he would bring the Hallows together, and ritually shatter them, breaking the seals between the worlds, allowing the Demonkind through. Saurin looked over the fields again; he wondered if forty thousand would be enough to dull the Demonkind's appetite.

'I cannot see any alternative, can you?' Ambrose asked reasonably.

'But hundreds could be killed, thousands injured,' Greg protested.

Ambrose shrugged. 'If they remain and the Dark Man activates the Hallows, then they will all die.'

'And can you do this?' Elaine asked.

'Oh, I can do this . . . and more, much more,' the old man promised.

'If you're so powerful, why can't you get the Hallows

yourself,' Greg demanded. 'Surely you could march in there and take them?'

'The wards of power that the Dark Man has ringed around the Hallows also weaken my own special powers. I would be helpless before the Hallows.' He shook his head quickly. 'My place is here. I will return to the cave and wait one hour, then I will begin. When you hear my signal, you will make your way into the house, secure the Hallows and kill the Dark Man and his creature.'

'How will we get the Hallows out to you?' Greg asked.

'Carry them,' Ambrose suggested.

'I didn't think we could,' Elaine said doubtfully.

'*Anyone* can carry them, but you need to be of the blood line of the original Keepers to *use* them properly.'

'But I'm not related to Judith Walker – at least I don't think so – and yet I used the sword,' Greg said.

'You are not a Hallow Keeper,' Ambrose said simply, his face impassive. 'But you fed the sword and so bonded it to you. And yes you used it, but only to kill. The great magic of the sword, Greg, is that it can also heal and create.' The old man turned to Elaine. 'You have the horn Elaine, but can you control what comes when you call? Brigid Davis could. You can do nothing with the horn, but you could work wonders with the sword, for you are of the blood of Judith Walker and she was from the line of the original Hallow Keepers. And let me tell you this, Elaine Powys, if you go up against the Dark Man in the house, it is you who must face him with your Hallow, the sword, that is the only chance you will have, for he is a Hallow Keeper too.'

'But what about Greg?'

'It would be better if Greg did not face the Dark Man,' Ambrose said softly. He glanced at the young man. 'It would be better if you gave Elaine the sword.'

Greg looked at the sword in his hands. Even the thought of handing it over to Elaine made him break out in a cold sweat.

Ambrose shook his head in amusement, then suddenly reached out and snatched the sword from Greg's grasp. Blue-green flames danced along the length of the blade, hissing and spitting like an angry cat. He thrust the sword into Elaine's hands. 'If circumstances were different, I would tell you its history and powers . . .'

Greg felt as if he'd just lost someone very close to him. He felt chilled and shaken, weak as a kitten, but the constant pressure that had sat behind his temples for the past few days was suddenly gone, leaving him light headed and dizzy.

In contrast Elaine felt herself shivering with the raw power that trickled through the sword, tingling along the length of her arms, settling into her chest, buzzing in her nipples and down into her belly. It seemed almost natural to hold the sword aloft in both hands, broken blade pointing through the green canopy towards the sun. Her red hair rose and blossomed around her in a mantle, sparkling and crackling softly.

Ambrose picked up the horn where she'd dropped it. White light coiled around the rim of the mouth of the horn. 'I'll take this with me. It will help.'

Elaine lowered the sword and when she looked at

Ambrose, her green eyes were hard and unforgiving. 'I cannot agree with what you want to do.'

'Give me an alternative,' Ambrose suggested.

Elaine chose to ignore the question. 'Tell me how you intend to panic the people into leaving.'

'No,' Ambrose said simply.

'People will die,' Greg muttered.

'Sooner or later we all die.'

Saurin was unlocking the front door when Vyvienne pulled it open and almost dragged him inside. He was disappointed to see that she was still wearing her loose robe and hadn't bothered getting dressed.

'They're close,' she whispered, face ashen with excitement.

'Who?' he asked.

'Matthews and the girl. They're close, so close. I've felt them three times this morning – flashes, vague impressions, nothing more – but each time they were closer to the house. I think they're coming here.'

Saurin rubbed his hands together briskly as he followed the woman up the stairs to the bedroom. Usually, he would have admired the sway of her buttocks beneath the thin cloth, fondled her, but not today. Today, he needed all his energy for the ritual.

'Do you want me to contact the police?' Vyvienne asked.

Saurin shook his head. 'No I had hoped they would capture Matthews but this is even better, driving them out of the wood in this direction.'

Vyvienne stood in the doorway and watched Saurin pull off his clothing, buttons popping in his eagerness.

'I think there's a third person with them,' she said quietly.

'A third person?'

'I'm not sure. It's just the way they wink in and out of the astral, and the way the astral itself is grey and twisted, making it impossible to travel through, impossible to see anything in it.'

Saurin sat on the bed as he pulled off his trousers. There couldn't be anyone with them; they knew no one. There was no one to help them. 'They are both carrying Hallows; maybe the combination of artefacts is shielding them from us.'

'Maybe,' Vyvienne said doubtfully.

Naked, Saurin stood and spread his arms wide, muscles creaking as he stretched, then he smiled at Vyvienne and allowed her to step into his arms. He kissed the top of her head, in a rare gesture of affection. 'Do you know what day this is?' he murmured.

'July thirty-first, eve of Lughnasadh.'

Saurin shook his head. 'This is the last day of the human race.'

CHAPTER SIXTY-ONE

The clouds rolled in quickly, boiling up from the south and west, flowing over the mountains in a tumbling sheet. Shadows raced across the ground, chilling everything they touched, huge drops of icy rain spattering on to the dry earth, popping off the leather tents and the cloth awnings of the stalls and stands. Almost as one, the festival-goers groaned aloud; it had looked like it was going to be such a nice day.

In the green-tinged cave, the man known as Ambrose looked at the Horn of Bran as he turned it in his hands. Once it had had another name, but he couldn't remember what it was. He'd bought it from an Egyptian ... or Greek ... no, he'd bought it from the Nubian trader who specialized in carved bones. Ambrose smiled as he remembered: that would have been two thousand years ago, and the memory of that day was still as fresh as if it had just happened. He could still smell the sweat from the man, the peculiar odour of exotic spices that clung to his skin and tightly curled hair, the distinctive stink of camel that clung to his ornate robe. He had simply admired the hunting horn for itself then, a strange and beautiful piece of work, unusual enough for him to be able to ask a good price for it. There was a Greek merchant in Tyre who had a passion for bone carvings and ivory; he would buy it, especially when Josea had spun him a suitably exotic yarn. He had intended introducing Yeshu'a to him on the return voyage from the Tin Lands, though he would have to watch the merchant, for he preferred the company of boys ... though on reflection, he remembered that the Greek preferred his boys beautiful, and Yeshu'a could never be called that.

But Yeshu'a had taken the horn – and all his other trade goods – and made them into what they were not: hallowed objects imbued with an ancient magic.

And now Yeshu'a was worshipped as a god, or the Son of God. Josea wasn't sure if Yeshu'a was a god, certainly he was more than a man, but there was a magic in the world at that time, elder magic, powerful magic. Creatures that were now little more than myth roamed free; that had been a time of wonder. There was little wonder left in the world in these modern times. Maybe that was a good thing.

Lifting the horn to his lips, Ambrose drew a deep breath and blew.

Greg's head shot up, eyes wide.

The sound of the horn.

It had echoed and re-echoed in his dreams, but this was no dream. Again and again, the low ululating sound pulsed through the wood, the sound ancient, primeval.

And in the long silence that followed, the howling began.

Padraig O'Mealoid of the Irish folk group Dandelion was climbing on stage when the sun vanished behind tumbling grey-black cloud. He swore silently; this was just his luck: his first big break – he knew there were at least two record scouts in the crowd, and the BBC were recording it – and right now the concert was going to be a washout. He glanced at Shea Mason, the drummer, and raised his eyebrows in a silent question; do we go on?

Mason nodded and grinned. He was sitting at the back of the stage under the awning. If it rained, Padraig and Maura McHugh, the lead singer, would be soaked.

The crowd were shifting impatiently, turning to watch the gathering storm clouds as Padraig picked up the guitar. Static howled, drowning out Maura's greeting in Irish. The guitarist stepped up to the mike and repeated the greeting in carefully rehearsed Welsh. There were whistles and cheers and in the distance someone blew a horn and a dog howled. 'We'd like to welcome . . .' he began, and the lightning bolt struck him through the top of the head. The incredible surge of power shredded his body, boiling flesh exploding, spraying slivers of cooked meat on to the front row, the guitar bursting into molten metal. The electrical charge rippled through the power lines, and the speakers erupted in balls of flames, red hot cinders spinning out into the audience. All over the stage, power cables began to burn.

Those nearest the stage started to scream, but their cries were misinterpreted by those at the back, unable to see clearly, who began to shout and roar.

A second lightning strike danced over the drummer's metal kit and arced on to Mason's studded leather jacket, fusing it to his body. He tumbled backwards into the heavy black curtain decorated with the Celtic Festival logo. It wrapped itself around his body and immediately started to burn. Mason was still alive, but

334

his screams were lost as a series of rattling lightning detonations rippled across the field destroying people at random, blue-white balls of light dancing from metal chairs and tables, arcing from metal studs and jewellery. In the sudden gloom, the lightning flashes were incredibly white and intense, blinding everyone in the vicinity. The crowd panicked and ran. Then the heavens opened, a solid deluge of rain – some of it electrically charged – immediately turning the field into a muddy quagmire.

A three-hundred-year-old oak was split down the middle, burying twenty people beneath its branches. A jewellery stall exploded, shards of red-hot metal hissing out into the crowd. A food stall took a direct hit, the gas cylinder detonating in a solid ball of flame, spraying long streamers of gas and grease and hot fat in every direction. Those who fell were crushed underfoot.

And above the screams of pain and terror, the lightning cracks and the rolling continuous thunder, no one heard the sound of a hunting horn and the triumphant howling of savage beasts.

Vyvienne jerked and twitched with every peal of thunder, every lightning flash. The room was in almost total darkness, but every lightning flash silhouetted Saurin against the window, naked flesh white and stark. In the distance they could hear screams and explosions, and the fields below the house were speckled with fires.

'What time is it?' Saurin asked numbly.

'Close to midday, I think.' She was standing near enough to feel the chill radiating from his body.

'Looks like twilight,' he said absently. 'It can't be natural.'

'I don't know. I can feel the Hallows buzzing below us, flooding the astral with light. I'm blind there.'

Saurin watched as one of the carefully prepared pyres burst into flame, long streamers of light flowing up off the oil-soaked wood. Burning figures whirled away from it. Saurin ignored them as he concentrated on the location of the bonfire; he didn't think it was one of those holding the wrapped piece of Hallow Keeper's flesh. Spinning away from the window, he caught Vyvienne by the arm. 'We can't wait any longer. We've got to use the Hallows now.'

'But the missing two . . .'

'We don't have a choice,' he said savagely. 'We have eleven of the thirteen. If we break enough of the locks, then the Demonkind may be able to break their way through.'

'It's too risky,' Vyvienne said. 'The storm isn't natural. Someone – someone powerful – has called it. And that sort of magic, elemental magic, is one of the oldest in the world. Something's out there, something old.'

'I've waited too long for this.' Lightning washed his face bone white and shadow. 'The bonfires will burn, taking the last of the Hallow Keepers, the people are fleeing: we will never have this chance again. I'm using the Hallows now!'

Tony Fowler watched lightning dance down Madoc's main street, skipping from metal to metal, reducing cars to blackened ruin, wrapping metal lamp-posts in writhing fiery worms. A manhole was reduced to smouldering slag and Fowler turned away as a young man ran straight into the seething mess.

'Everything's dead,' Victoria Heath said numbly. 'Phones, radio, power.'

The detective turned back to the window. 'Dear God, what's happening?' he whispered. The street was jammed with tourists. He saw two kick open the door of a house opposite and push their way past the old woman who appeared in the hallway. A score of people ran into the hall, trampling the woman underfoot in a desperate attempt to escape the lightning. Thunder boomed directly overhead shaking the entire building, lead tiles sliding off the roof to shatter in the street. A young woman went down, a rectangular tile protruding from her throat; the youth who tried to help her collapsed as another dozen tiles rained down atop him.

In his long career in the police force, Tony Fowler had known fear on many occasions: his first night on the beat, the first time he had faced an armed assailant, the first time he had stood at a murder scene, the first time he had stared into the pitiless eyes of a killer, but time had dulled that emotion and lately he had only been feeling the terrible anger of the victims. That anger had driven him to hunt down evil people like Matthews who could kill and maim without hesitation. In the last few years Fowler had found he had been able to strike back at these people without compunction, treating them as they had treated their victims.

But Tony Fowler felt fear now, the cold empty fear the rational mind experiences when it is faced with the unnatural. He was turning away from the window when light blossomed directly outside and it exploded inwards. He caught a brief glimpse of the tiny red pattern on Victoria Heath's white blouse . . . funny he couldn't remember a pattern . . .

Ambrose lowered the horn from his lips.

He knew all the Hallows by heart – their names had changed through the years – but he had handled them all . . . indeed he supposed he had chosen them all. Innocent objects, but imbued with a terrible power. They had been created to do good, but through the ages they had always ended up touched and tainted by evil. The Sword of Dyrnwyn had been used to kill, the Knife of the Horseman used to wound, the Spear of the Dolorous Blow used to maim, the Red Coat used by butchers and torturers, the Mantle of Arthur used to terrify. It was not that the objects themselves were evil: they were merely powerful, and the powerful attracted the curious, and so many of those who set out on this path of discovery were seduced by the attractions of evil. He turned the horn over in his gnarled hands. He had used the Horn of Bran to call the elements. Once it would have been used in ceremonies to welcome the coming of spring, or to drive off a particularly harsh winter. He had used it to kill. Many lives had already been lost, he knew, and more would die in the next few minutes. He could rationalize it by pretending that they had given their lives to save so many others. But that didn't help. He looked at the horn again, ran his thumb across the smooth ivory. Sometimes he wondered about these gifts Yeshu'a had given the world. Sometimes he wondered about Yeshu'a. He had never believed he was a god . . . but sometimes he wondered if he was not worse than the Demonkind.

The old man bent his head. If he had tears he would have wept them, but he'd long ago forgotten how to weep.

CHAPTER SIXTY-TWO

'What the fuck does he think he's doing.' Greg's voice was high and shrill. 'It sounds like a war zone.'

Elaine ignored him. Her eyes were fixed on the farmhouse directly in front of them. With the sword clutched in both hands, she felt so confident, so assured. She was aware of the thunder and lightning booming and crashing over the village – and only over the village. The fields below were awash beneath a torrential downpour, yet the effect was particularly localized, and although they were less than two hundred yards from the village, there was no rain here.

Moving stealthily forward, Elaine could actually feel the presences of the Hallows buzzing in the air around her. There were whispers that were almost words, snatches of what might have been song, though faint, indistinct, ethereal. But she could tell that they were calling, calling, calling. They were trapped and in pain.

'They're here,' she said simply. 'Below ground.'

Greg didn't ask how she knew; he was feeling the loss of the sword like a missing limb. While he'd held it, he'd felt confident, assured . . . but now . . . now he wasn't sure what he felt any more.

The farmhouse was in darkness, no lights showing within. The couple padded across a cobbled courtyard, keeping to the shadows, looking for an open window, but the house was locked up tight, and heavy drapes covered the lower windows. They completed a circuit of the house and returned to the kitchen door.

The thunder and lightning had stopped booming and crashing over the village and now the screams of the injured drifted clearly up on the still air. Car and house alarms were ringing everywhere, and the stench of bitter smoke was replacing the ozone in the air.

Elaine reached out and touched the door handle. Green fire spat and she snatched her hand back with a hiss of pain. In the gloom, they could see the blisters forming on her fingertips.

'Ambrose said that the place would be guarded by more than human wards,' Greg reminded her. 'Some sort of magical protection.'

Shifting the sword to her left hand, Elaine stretched out and pressed the broken end against the door. Green fire danced over the blade which came alive with cold white light. Then the light flowed out of the sword and raced across the door, outlining it in a tracery of white. Glass exploded inwards, then the handle started bubbling, the metal running liquid down the scarred wood. Greg caught Elaine's arm and dragged her away as the door went crashing inwards, liquid metal from the hinges puddling on the tiled kitchen floor.

'I think they know we're here,' Greg muttered.

Vyvienne looked up sharply. 'What was that?'

Saurin ignored her. Sitting naked in the centre of the perfect circle, he gradually opened himself up to the power of the Hallows, first absorbing the trickle of energy, allowing it to seep into his flesh, settle into his bones. Images flickered and twisted behind his closed eyes. Power from the burning bonfires flowed into him, the last tendrils of power of the original Hallow Keepers touching him.

Vyvienne stood up. She was sitting with her back to Saurin, facing the door to the underground chamber, and although she couldn't see what he was doing, she could feel the power gathering in his body, feel the solid darkness radiating out from him into the astral, blanketing the white light of the Hallows.

'There's someone upstairs,' she said, her voice sounding numb and distant. She caught a flash of a red-haired young woman holding a broken sword – that was wrong, Matthews had been carrying the sword – but she knew that they were upstairs. Saurin had warded the doors and windows with spells that had been ancient in Babylonian times, designed to keep were-creatures at bay, but obviously they hadn't held. Vyvienne turned to look down at Saurin. The man was completely unaware of her, conscious only of the ritual he had practised every day for five years, only this time he was doing it for real.

Saurin's hands worked on the floor, brushing back the light dusting of earth revealing a metal door set into the ground. The door was circular, of old metal, studded with great square-headed rivets set into a frame of massive rough stone blocks. The rust and verdigris stained doorway was inset with thirteen huge keyholes. Shapes flickered behind the keyholes. Two thousand years previously Yeshu'a had banished the Demonkind and sealed their doorway. Yeshu'a and his world were long gone, but the demons remained.

Saurin reached for the first lead box.

Vyvienne tried to see into the astral, but the Hallow light and Saurin's blackness were blanketing everything else. She got the fleeting impression of the other astral presences fleeing like fish when a shark enters their waters.

Saurin opened the box. A solid beam of cold white light lanced upwards, blinding them, flooding the room with the scents of a thousand stale-plumaged birds. Reaching in, Saurin lifted out the Red Coat, allowing it to fall open, the birds' feathers from which it was woven hissing and whispering softly.

This was the signal Vyvienne had been waiting for. Kneeling behind Saurin, she wrapped her arms around his chest, pressing her breasts against his back and poured her strength into him.

The Dark Man picked up the first Hallow – in the astral the darkness folded over the light – and began to pluck out the tiny red feathers.

A key appeared in the topmost lock – and turned with a rasping click.

In his green cave, Ambrose staggered, pressing his hand to the centre of his chest. He felt as if he'd just been stabbed. One of the Hallows had been destroyed. But there was nothing he could do, except wait . . . and listen to the screams of the dying and injured.

Greg stood at the bottom of the stairs and looked up into the gloom. He was cold; the building radiated a greasy chill, and he wanted to turn and run, and knew that he could not. The house was silent and empty. Above all the doors arcane symbols had been carved into the wood, and the windowsills were also incised with the curious designs. He had felt an almost over-powering desire to stretch out and trace one of the twisting patterns, and had actually been reaching for it, when Elaine had touched the flesh of his hand with the flat of the sword. The snap of cold metal brought him alert again, and he realized that he'd been following the twisting Celtic spiral, tracing it to a nonexistent centre. 'More of the Dark Man's wards,' Elaine said, 'designed to ensnare.' She had changed since she'd taken the sword, subtle, almost imperceptible changes in posture and attitude. She looked taller, the skin on her cheeks tighter, emphasizing the bones and she acted with absolute confidence. Remembering how he had felt, Greg found himself envying her, envying her the sword. 'Down here,' she said, reaching out to touch the handle of the cellar door with the tip of the broken sword. The frame came alive with tracery of fire which scorched the wood, searing away the symbols.

'I don't think we should . . .' Greg began.

'They're down there,' Elaine said simply. The sword was trembling in her hands, vibrating softly as she pushed at the door. It fell off its hinges and clattered down the steps.

She could feel them.

In an instant of calm when the astral had been washed clean of colour by the destruction of the Hallow, Vyvienne had seen the couple standing at the head of the stairs, looking down into the cellar.

She wanted to tell Saurin, but he was deep in the ritual now, transferring the energy from the Hallows, now augmented by the burning flesh of the Hallow Keepers, into the locks of the metal door. She watched his hands reach blindly for a second box, pull it over

344

and open it. Again the white light flowed up, but was almost immediately extinguished as Saurin's large hands closed over it. The Bowl of Rhygenydd, perpetually filled with dark blood, crumpled beneath his powerful grip, spraying his naked flesh with crimson. He folded its companion piece, the Plate of Rhygenydd over and over in his fingers, finally snapping it into four quarters.

Another key turned in a lock. Something hit the metal door a single blow from below, the sound deep and booming, echoing around the small chamber.

The smell at the bottom of the stairs was indescribable. Old and long dead, the ripe foulness hung in the air in a solid miasma. Greg and Elaine knew it was a body – or bodies – and were both glad that the light didn't work. With Greg's hand on her shoulder, Elaine walked confidently forward. She felt as if she was leaning into an unfelt breeze; she could feel the Hallows power washing over her, insects crawling and slithering under her skin, her clothes heavy and irritating where they rested against her body. The air itself had become thick, soupy, making every breath an effort, drying the moisture of her eyes, her mouth and throat, until she felt as if she was breathing sand.

And then Dyrnwyn flashed alight, burning away the stale air, blue-white light bathing the corridor in harsh shadows, illuminating the iron-studded wooden door directly ahead.

Elaine darted forward, her grin feral.

Six locks were broken now.

Saurin concentrated on opening the seventh seal, but the pounding of the demons on the far side was incredible, the noise deafening as they hammered on the metal, howling and screeching, rocking the door on its hinges, disturbing his concentration. Claws and taloned hands kept appearing in the openings and the door was visibly straining upwards, metal bulging where the locks had been turned.

The Dark Man was tiring. The incredible effort of will was draining him, leaching the energy from his body, and the arcane occult formulae which he needed to keep crisp and clear were beginning to shift and blur in his head. He could now feel Vyvienne's energy flowing into his body, seeping out of her skin, melding into his; he was aware that the Demonkind was frantically trying to push open the door and that the ancient metal was shivering in its stone frame . . . but he knew that he should be aware of nothing. Any lapse of concentration would be worse than fatal, for Saurin knew that death was not the end, and this close to the Demon Realm, there was every possibility that his *ka* would be sucked into that place, to suffer an eternity of damnation.

Holding the seventh Hallow – the Whetstone – in his hands, he squeezed it. The ancient granite stone should have snapped and burst, but nothing happened. Leaning forward, he pressed his left hand, palm down on the shivering metal door. 'Give me strength,' he prayed. 'Give me strength.'

Noise and movement on the other side of the door ceased and then the answer flowed up his arm.

Ambrose was dying, he knew that now. With every

Hallow the Dark Man destroyed he killed a little more of the one-eyed old man. There was blood on his lips, a tracery of veins visible in his eye. He had felt the destruction of the six Hallows as physical blows, had seen the shadows swallow the light, and for the first time in two thousand years felt the terrible despair of the truly lost. So, it had all been for nothing, all those deaths he had caused, and now Greg and Elaine were probably dead too.

Now it ended.

They had waited so long for this.

The legends of their own kind spoke of the time they had walked in the World of Men and feasted off the delicacy known as flesh. There were stories too of those who had escaped through other hidden or temporary doors.

But now the time of waiting was over. Six of the burning locks that sealed the door between the planes of existence had been turned. Odours, rich and meat and salt and full of possibilities and opportunities, flooded through the tiny cracks, driving those nearest the opening into a frenzy.

The key turned in the seventh lock.

Standing before the iron-studded wooden door, Elaine gripped the broken sword in both hands and squared her shoulders. Their plan was simple: they had no plan.

Elaine reached forward and touched the end of the sword against the door. The metal studs hissed and bubbled and then the wood dissolved in fine dust.

As Greg followed Elaine through the opening, he

could have sworn that her skin shimmered with metal-lic highlights.

The tiny room was an abattoir. A naked man crouched in the centre of the room, straddling the butchered body that wasn't immediately recognizable as female. Much of the face was missing, and the teeth marks on the chin and edges of the jaw, where flesh remained, looked like human bites. The man's face, neck and chest were covered in thick blood. Her torso had been opened from throat to crotch, the skin pulled back to reveal the curve of ribs and palpitating internal organs. The remaining Hallows were lying on the woman's body, thick with gore.

Saurin twisted his head to look at the young woman in the doorway. His smile was bloody. 'Good of you to bring me the sword,' he hissed, and plunged the Hallow – a tiny intricate carving of the Chariot of Morgan – into the gaping wound in the body below him, bathing it in blood and fluids. Lifting it out, he crumpled it in his hands to a shapeless mass.

Elaine and Greg both heard the click and snap of a lock, and then the butchered body shifted upwards slightly. They saw now that she had been laid across a metal manhole that was black with blood. The manhole jerked, straining upwards, and a gnarled black tongue slithered in the opening, lapping at the blood.

'Too late,' Saurin hissed.

Elaine felt the sword move, twist of its own accord, and suddenly she was moving forward, the weapon gripped in both hands, keeping the sword low and to the left, bringing it up . . .

Saurin jerked up the closest Hallow and shook it out. Elaine caught a glimpse of fur, a stag's head complete with antlers, in the instant before the sword struck it, sparks flying in the air. 'Behold the Mantle of Arthur.' The Dark Man straightened and spun the cloak about his shoulders, settling the antlered hood on to his head.

The knight stood in the forest and turned to face the horned hunter and his red-eyed hell hounds.

The sudden image caught Elaine off guard and in that instant Saurin's left hand shot out and caught the sword blade in an explosion of green-white fire. She pulled it back, but it was caught fast.

The hammering beneath the round metal cover was deafening, demanding.

'My subjects hunger,' Saurin whispered. He tugged at the sword, and Elaine felt it slide from her grasp. 'The sword is the most powerful of all the keys. If I open its lock, I won't need to use the others.' He tugged at the sword again, almost wrenching it from her hands. 'You should be honoured: the beasts will feast on you first.'

Greg threw himself at Elaine, hitting her high on the shoulders, pushing her forward, driving her *into* Saurin's arms. Still clutching the sword, the sudden blow sent it slamming forward, the metal blade scoring down Saurin's hands, the broken point of the weapon taking him high in the chest, sliding off ribs with a soft grating, rupturing lungs and heart. Saurin looked at the sword, and then his eyes widened as the sword began to glow and burn, and Elaine stepped forward and turned the blade full circle before jerking it out of his chest. Elaine and Greg were both thrown by the sudden explosion of light back into the hall, out of the circular room, which now throbbed with fire. The lead boxes melted, flames spitting and hissing off the stone floor as the Hallows came to brief, incandescent life. For a moment the two magics – dark and light – warred. It lasted less than a heartbeat, and then the room plunged into total darkness.

In the long silence that followed, the crack and snap of the settling foundations was deafening. Stones grated, earth rumbled, and then a shaft of sunlight appeared in the blackened room. Elaine and Greg crawled to the doorway and peered inside, blinking in the light, the sky now visible in a V-shaped crack high in the wall. The bodies of Saurin and Vyvienne had completely vanished, nothing remained to mark their presence. The broken sword, its blade now shining silver and complete, lay on the floor atop the Mantle of Arthur.

The ancient door in the floor had been fused into the stone, the keyholes sealed with white glass.

CHAPTER SIXTY-THREE

It took them a moment to realize that the tiny wizened creature lying slumped in the stone chair was Ambrose. Greg and Elaine knelt before him and spread out the six remaining Hallows.

'These were all we could save.' Elaine brushed strands of hair off the old man's forehead. His skin was so fragile and translucent, the bones and ridges of wasted muscle could clearly be seen beneath it.

Ambrose straightened with an effort and touched each in turn with trembling fingers, seeing them for what they were, remembering what they had once been. 'It is enough,' he whispered.

'We've won,' Greg said encouragingly.

'For now.'

'What about the Hallows?' Elaine asked. 'What do we do with them?'

'You must find new Keepers.'

'Me?' she asked.

'No.' Ambrose's lips curled back from his yellowed teeth in a parody of a smile. 'You,' he said, looking at Greg. 'You are of the line of Joseph of Arimathea.' Brittle dry fingers touched his flesh. 'You are my descendant, you will take up my mantle . . .'

'I cannot.'

'I uttered the same words. You have no choice. Take the remaining Hallows, and return them to their rightful owners. You will know them when you find them.'

'But I don't know what to do!' he protested.

'There are only two rules: the Hallows must never be brought together, and they must never leave Britain. Everything else will come in time . . .'

It was several moments before they realized that the old man was dead.

CHAPTER SIXTY-FOUR

Sunday 1 August.

FREAK STORM KILLS HUNDREDS

The freak storm which struck this island yesterday has now claimed three hundred lives. Most of the victims were visitors to the First International Festival of Celtic Arts and Culture which was being held in Madoc, in Wales. Meteorologists are still puzzled why the massive depression didn't appear on their radars. The nine thousand injured are being cared for in a number of hospitals, including . . .

SUSPECT BELIEVED KILLED

Police believe a man they wanted to interview in connection with a series of murders in the capital was one of the victims of the Madoc disaster. Although the body in question is too badly burnt to make a proper examination, it is hoped that forensics will provide the answers.

POLICE MOURN OFFICER

Two of the victims of the Madoc disaster, Detective Anthony Fowler and Sergeant Victoria Heath, were laid to rest today. The Chief Constable, Sir . . .

AUTHOR'S NOTE

Most of the Hallows mentioned in this novel still exist, as do the group of people known as the Keepers.

The last changeover of the ancient artefacts took place on Friday 16 October 1987 during the night of one of the worst storms ever to hit Britain.

Legend has it that this will be the last generation of Keepers.

SIGNET

Published or forthcoming

THIS PERFECT DAY

Ira Levin

Chip is a good, obedient citizen of the brave new world. A world where sex is programmed and regular treatments keep people docile. A world where everyone is scheduled to die at the age of sixty-two, for efficiency.

But Chip encounters a group of subversives who tempt him with ideas of freedom, original thought and love. The dilemma that ensues is both horrific and irresistible.

'A futuristic nightmare' – *The New York Times*

SIGNET

Published or forthcoming

ROSEMARY'S BABY

Ira Levin

When the truth is more sinister than imagination ...

Rosemary and Guy Woodhouse's new apartment in the Bramford was everything the young couple wanted. Yet as soon as they'd signed the lease Rosemary began to have doubts.

The neighbours were quaint but friendly. Too friendly. Especially after Mr and Mrs Castavet learned that Rosemary was planning to have a baby.

'A darkly brilliant tale of modern devilry that induces the reader to believe the unbelievable. I believed it and was altogether enthralled' – Truman Capote

'This horror story will grip you and chill you' – *Daily Express*

'Diabolically good ... the pay-off is so fiendish it made me sweat' – *Sun*

'A terrifying book ... I can think of no other in which fear of an unknown evil strikes with greater chill' – *Daily Telegraph*

SIGNET

Published or forthcoming

BORN IN FIRE

Sarah Hardesty

A child of the wild, unspoilt Clare country-side, Margaret Mary Concannon is as tough, beautiful – and vulnerable – as the exquisite glass sculptures she creates from sand and flame.

Rogan Sweeney, a wealthy and sophisticated Dubliner, is the owner of the Worldwide top international art gallery, who can bring fame and fortune to Maggie: if she will submit to his terms.

But Maggie is not given to submission. Wilful, solitary and determined to be beholden to no one, she is drawn into a tempestuous battle with Rogan over which of them has control of her work, her money, her life – and her heart.

SIGNET

Published or forthcoming

Prophecy

Peter James

They met by chance but archaeologist Franni
Monsanto was soon deeply involved with hand
some Oliver Halkin and Edward, his youn
son. Yet, unknown to them, their paths hav
crossed and recrossed over the years.

As their relationship develops – and slides int
a bizarre nightmare – Frannie realizes that i
she is to survive, she must prevent her own ter
rifying fate. Too late she discovers the rea
meaning of the Halkin family motto, *Non Omni
Moriar – I shall not altogether die* ...